LEGEND OF THE GALACTIC HEROES

VOLUME 9
UPHEAVAL

WRITTEN BY
YOSHIKI TANAKA

Translated by Matt Treyvaud

T0308986

Legend of the Galactic Heroes, Volume 9: Upheaval
GINGA EIYU DENSETSU Vol. 9
© 1987 by Yoshiki TANAKA
Cover Illustration © 2008 Yukinobu Hoshino.
All rights reserved.

English translation © 2019 VIZ Media, LLC
Cover and interior design by Fawn Lau and Alice Lewis

No portion of this book may be reproduced or transmitted in any form or
by any means without written permission from the copyright holders.

HAIKASORU
Published by VIZ Media, LLC
P.O. Box 77010
San Francisco, CA 94107

www.haikasoru.com

Library of Congress Cataloging-in-Publication Data

Names: Tanaka, Yoshiki, 1952- author. | Huddleston, Daniel, translator.
Title: Legend of the galactic heroes / written by Yoshiki Tanaka ; translated
  by Daniel Huddleston and Tyran Grillo and Matt Treyvaud
Other titles: Ginga eiyu densetsu
Description: San Francisco : Haikasoru, [2016]
Identifiers: LCCN 2015044444| ISBN 9781421584942 (v. 1: paperback) | ISBN
  9781421584959 (v. 2: paperback) | ISBN 9781421584966 (v. 3: paperback) | ISBN
  9781421584973 (v. 4: paperback) | ISBN 9781421584980 (v. 5: paperback) | ISBN
  9781421584997 (v. 6: paperback) | ISBN 9781421585291 (v. 7: paperback) | ISBN
  9781421585017 (v. 8: paperback) | ISBN 9781421585024 (v. 9: paperback)
  v. 1. Dawn -- v. 2. Ambition -- v. 3. Endurance -- v. 4. Stratagem -- v. 5. Mobilization --
  v. 6. Flight -- v.7. Tempest -- v. 8. Desolation -- v. 9. Upheaval
Subjects: LCSH: Science fiction. | War stories. | BISAC: FICTION / Science
  Fiction / Space Opera. | FICTION / Science Fiction / Military. | FICTION /
  Science Fiction / Adventure.
Classification: LCC PL862.A5343 G5513 2016 | DDC 895.63/5--dc23
LC record available at http://lccn.loc.gov/2015044444

Printed in the U.S.A.
First printing, July 2019

LEGEND OF THE GALACTIC HEROES

VOLUME 9
UPHEAVAL

YOSHIKI TANAKA

HAIKA
SORU

SAN FRANCISCO

MAJOR CHARACTERS

GALACTIC EMPIRE

REINHARD VON LOHENGRAMM
Kaiser.

PAUL VON OBERSTEIN
Minister of military affairs. Marshal.

WOLFGANG MITTERMEIER
Commander in chief of the Imperial Space Armada. Marshal. Known as the "Gale Wolf."

OSKAR VON REUENTAHL
Governor-general of the Neue Land. Marshal. Has heterochromatic eyes.

FRITZ JOSEF WITTENFELD
Commander of the Schwarz Lanzenreiter fleet. Senior admiral.

ERNEST MECKLINGER
Rear supreme commander. Senior admiral. Known as the "Artist-Admiral."

ULRICH KESSLER
Commissioner of military police and commander of imperial capital defenses. Senior admiral.

AUGUST SAMUEL WAHLEN
Fleet commander. Senior admiral.

KORNELIAS LUTZ
Fleet commander for Phezzan region. Senior admiral.

NEIDHART MÜLLER
Fleet commander. Senior admiral. Known as "Iron Wall Müller."

ARTHUR VON STREIT
Senior imperial aide. Vice admiral.

HILDEGARD VON MARIENDORF
Chief advisor to imperial headquarters. Vice admiral. Often called "Hilda."

FRANZ VON MARIENDORF
Secretary of state. Hilda's father.

GÜNTER KISSLING
Head of the Imperial Guard. Commodore.

HEIDRICH LANG
Junior minister of the interior and chief of the Domestic Safety Security Bureau.

ANNEROSE VON GRÜNEWALD
Reinhard's elder sister. Archduchess.

JOB TRÜNICHT
High counselor to the Neue Land governorate. Former head of the Alliance.

RUDOLF VON GOLDENBAUM
Founder of the Galactic Empire's Goldenbaum Dynasty.

DECEASED

SIEGFRIED KIRCHEIS
Sacrificed himself to save Reinhard, his closest friend (vol. 2).

KARL GUSTAV KEMPF
Killed in base-versus-base defensive battle (vol. 3).

HELMUT LENNENKAMP
Committed suicide after failing in an attempt to assassinate Yang (vol. 6).

ADALBERT FAHRENHEIT
Marshal (posthumous). Died in the Battle of the Corridor (vol. 8).

KARL ROBERT STEINMETZ
Marshal (posthumous). Died in the Battle of the Corridor (vol. 8).

ISERLOHN REPUBLIC

JULIAN MINTZ
Commander of the Revolutionary
Reserves. Sublieutenant.

FREDERICA GREENHILL YANG
Leader of the Iserlohn Republic.

ALEX CASELNES
Vice admiral.

WALTER VON SCHÖNKOPF
Vice admiral.

DUSTY ATTENBOROUGH
Yang's underclassman. Vice admiral.

OLIVIER POPLIN
Captain of the First Spaceborne Division at
Iserlohn Fortress. Commander.

LOUIS MACHUNGO
Ensign.

KATEROSE VON KREUTZER
Corporal. Often called "Karin."

WILIABARD JOACHIM MERKATZ
Veteran general.

BERNARD VON SCHNEIDER
Merkatz's aide. Commander.

MURAI
Chief of staff. Vice admiral.

DECEASED

YANG WEN-LI
Legendary military talent. Never defeated
in battle. Assassinated by Church of Terra
(vol. 8).

JESSICA EDWARDS
Antiwar representative in the National
Assembly. Casualty of coup d'état (vol. 2).

DWIGHT GREENHILL
Frederica's father. Chief conspirator behind
coup d'état, killed when it failed (vol. 2).

IVAN KONEV
Cool and calculating ace pilot. Died during
Vermillion War (vol. 5).

ALEXANDOR BUCOCK
Commander in chief of the Alliance Armed
Forces Space Armada. Died in battle
defending the alliance (vol. 7).

CHUNG WU-CHENG
General chief of staff. Died alongside Bucock
(vol. 7).

EDWIN FISCHER
Master of fleet operations. Died in the
Battle of the Corridor (vol. 8).

FYODOR PATRICHEV
Deputy chief of staff in Yang Fleet. Died
protecting his superior officer (vol. 8).

FORMER PHEZZAN DOMINION

ADRIAN RUBINSKY
The fifth landesherr. Known as the "Black
Fox of Phezzan."

DOMINIQUE SAINT-PIERRE
Rubinsky's mistress.

BORIS KONEV
Independent merchant. Old acquaintance
of Yang's.

CHURCH OF TERRA

DE VILLIERS
Secretary-general of the Church of Terra.
Archbishop.

*Titles and ranks correspond to each
character's status at the end of *Desolation*
or their first appearance in *Upheaval*.

TABLE OF CONTENTS

CHAPTER ONE:

I

THE BENCH TUCKED AWAY in a corner of the wooded park
had been one of Yang Wen-li's favorite places. Since Yang's sudden passing,
Julian Mintz, his adopted son and apprentice in the arts of war, had come
here in his place. Julian did not believe in communication with the dead
any more than Yang had, but taking the time to sit quietly beneath the
trees had become a kind of daily ritual that gave his restless heart something concrete to hold on to.

Julian had not mentioned this habit to anyone, but word must have
gotten around. Today he saw a boy with curly black hair lurking nearby.
After some hesitation, the boy stepped closer to speak.

"Excuse me, sir, but aren't you Lieutenant Julian Mintz?"

Julian nodded.

The boy's eyes shone. Color filled his cheeks; even his breathing quick-
ened. He became the very image of adoration.

"I've been following you for ages, sir—I mean, following your career. It's
an honor to meet you. You're only a few years older than me, but you've
done such amazing things, and, well…I really admire you!"

"How old are you?" Julian asked.

"Thirteen, sir."

The sands of the hourglass rose upward before Julian's eyes. The film of his memory rewound through the projector; Julian felt himself shrink, and the curly-haired boy's eyes were replaced by another pair that gazed down at him, mild, warm, and intelligent.

"Can you guess what I'm thinking, Captain Yang?"

"You've stumped me, Julian. What is it?"

"I really admire you! See—I knew you wouldn't be able to guess."

Julian ran a hand through his flaxen hair. Just a few years ago, he had been in the boy's shoes himself, no doubt looking at Yang in exactly the same way. The galaxy's greatest magician, now gone forever. Julian had respected him, admired him, wanted to be just like him—or at least to follow in his footsteps somehow. Now he was the object of another boy's starstruck adulation.

"I'm not the great man you think I am," Julian said gently. "I just found my place beside Yang, and that always put me on the winning side. It was luck, pure and simple."

"Oh, no, sir, luck alone can't take someone at the head of Iserlohn's armed forces at the age of just eighteen. I really respect you, lieutenant—I mean, commander. Really!"

"Thank you. I'll try not to disappoint."

Julian held out his hand. He knew from his own experience that this was what the boy was hoping for. After their handshake, the boy ran off crimson with excitement. Julian settled back down on the bench and closed his eyes.

Was this how his own ideas would be passed on? It was certainly how he had inherited Yang's. Not all, of course—only a fraction—but they had come to him, a handing of the torch from one generation to the next. From trailblazer to follower. Anyone who valued that flame had a responsibility to pass it on to the next runner before it went out.

It was August, SE 800, three days after the proclamation of the Iserlohn Republic. Julian was eighteen years old. He could be a boy no longer, neither in years, nor in experience, nor in his responsibilities.

In later ages, historians would deride the Iserlohn Republic as "joint rule by widow and orphan." The republic's early stages, at least, justified that derision. When Yang died, undefeated in battle, his grieving widow Frederica became the political leader of the republic, while Julian, as his admirer in the park had noted, took command of its military.

All this had been decided by the leaders of Iserlohn, but it had not been seen as the best choice so much as the only one. If outsiders had their criticisms, these could not be shrugged off completely. But without a core, Iserlohn could not hold, and the afterimage of Yang Wen-li was the only core they had.

Alex Caselnes's head for administration, Walter von Schönkopf's bravery, Dusty Attenborough's leadership and willingness to act, Olivier Poplin's prowess in the cockpit, Wiliabard Joachim von Merkatz's reputation—all of these helped stabilize the core, but none could have taken its place. To their credit, all of these men were aware of this.

"The greatest miracle in the story of Yang Wen-li is not his string of victories in the face of superior numbers but the fact that, even after his own death, there was no struggle for power among his followers"—thus wrote one historian of the period. There had been a significant exodus of Iserlohn's population after Yang's passing, true, but no one had had sought to usurp Frederica's or Julian's position.

Of course, interpretations being more multitudinous than facts, for other historians this very stability became an object not of admiration but ridicule. "Who, after all, would actively pursue the kingship of some barren backwater? In the end, Yang Wen-li's officers crowned his wife and ward with thorns. They were nothing but exiles on the outer frontier…"

Confronted with ungenerous assessments of this sort, Julian was forced to concede one thing: they were indeed on the frontier. Not of the galaxy or the Free Planets Alliance, but of the human race itself. Alone in all of known space, Iserlohn refused to bend the knee to Kaiser Reinhard von Lohengramm. The base was a holy place, populated by heretics who refused to rejoin the overwhelming majority of humanity. Only on the frontier could such a place exist, and for this reason Julian wore the word with pride. *The frontier is closest to the horizon*, he told himself, *and the horizon is where the new age dawns.*

Walking back from the park to his office, Julian ran into an acquaintance stepping off the elevator. She was dressed in a pilot suit, and her hair was the color of weakly brewed tea. "Corporal von Kreutzer," he said with a nod.

"Good day, Lieutenant Mintz."

They were still awkward around each other. Still? Perhaps they would be forever. What lay between Katerose "Karin" von Kreutzer and Julian was not so much a stable alliance or entente as the word "neutrality" inscribed on thin ice.

But in a group as small as theirs they could not afford to be at each other's throats—and, after all, both Julian and Karin had chosen to remain in Iserlohn. Some part of their hearts overlapped—a part that was determined to see an important ideal made reality. Perhaps, at least for the time being, that was enough.

They exchanged a few more pleasantries before Karin turned their conversation to the topic of the departed.

"Marshal Yang never really seemed that impressive when you met him in person. But he was supporting half the galaxy—politically, militarily, even philosophically."

Julian said nothing. She knew that he agreed.

"I still can't believe that I stood alongside him," Karin continued. "Even if it was only briefly. It's strange to think of yourself as a witness to history."

"Did you ever speak to him?"

"Once or twice, but never anything important. Funny, though—things I forgot immediately after they happened come back to me now clear as day." Karin put her finger lightly to her lips. "To tell you the truth, I didn't think of the marshal as such a great man while he was alive. But now that he's gone, I'm finally beginning to understand. Here in Iserlohn, we feel his spirit directly, but as time goes on it will grow and grow until it streams through all of history."

With that, Karin raised a hand in farewell and walked away. Her expression might have suggested embarrassment at having said too much, but her stride overflowed with life and rhythm. Julian watched her go, adjusting his black beret for no particular reason, then turned back toward his office.

Three centuries ago, when Ahle Heinessen had died during the Longest March, those left behind wept and lamented their loss, but none tried to halt their collective journey into the unknown. Those who remained in Iserlohn, too, had cried their fill, and were beginning to face the present once more—and the future.

Heinessen had fallen, Yang was lost, but history marched on. Lives went on. Power molded those who held it; ideals were conveyed from one bearer to the next. As long as the human race survived, the deeds of those who had come before would be recorded and passed on to the generations that followed.

History, Yang had once told Julian, was the common chronicle of all humanity. Painful as some memories were, they could not be banished or ignored.

Julian sighed. It hurt to remember how Yang's life had ended. But to forget would be more painful yet.

II

When people of later ages were quizzed on Yang Wen-li's final rank in the Free Planets Alliance, most answered, without hesitation, if not quite accurately, "Supreme commander of the Alliance Armed Forces" or "Alliance Navy high commander." Some were more precise: "Director of the alliance's joint operational headquarters and commander in chief of its Space Armada, known by the term 'supreme commander.'" Of course, all of these were wrong: from the year 796 to his death in 799, Yang Wen-li was officially "Commander of Iserlohn Fortress and commander of Iserlohn Patrol Fleet."

In April of SE 799, when the Vermillion War began, Yang Wen-li did command essentially all of the alliance's armed forces. Certainly, virtually every alliance ship capable of interplanetary travel was gathered together under his command. All this was of course with the blessing of Alexandor Bucock, actual commander in chief of the space armada.

As a result, while none criticized Yang's actions as illegitimate or insubordinate, it was impossible for him to satisfy everybody. There were even those who called him timid, incapable of action without proper legal grounds.

But Yang was too busy to bother himself with every quibble and slander directed at his person. His own tendency toward introspection aside, action and creation had to take priority over criticism.

Which meant that the same was true for Julian. Even as he took action, Yang had always asked himself, *Am I in the right? Is there no other way?* Julian did the same. He formulated the question somewhat differently, however: *What would Marshal Yang do? If he were still alive, would he agree with me?*

A meteor swarm left behind by a planet's disintegration—such was the Iserlohn Republic after Yang's death. It was only natural that so many of its residents should have felt that the festival was over and abandoned the base.

"Personally, I'm impressed that more than six hundred thousand stayed," said Dusty Attenborough, steam from his paper cup of coffee rising up around his chin. "Takes all types, I suppose."

Attenborough was working frantically to shore up Julian's leadership abilities. Today, too, he had "politely" kicked out an influential civilian leader who had sighed that they'd have been happy to stay if only Marshal Yang were alive.

"We don't need fair-weather friends like that anyway. If this were some cheap solivision series, enough complaints from the audience might bring a dead protagonist back to life. But we don't live in that world. We live in a world where a life lost is gone forever, which is what makes life itself so priceless."

"Hear, hear!" Olivier Poplin applauded from across the table. "In a kinder age, Admiral Attenborough, you could have been the next Job Trünicht. What a waste to put you in military duds."

"Thank you, thank you. When I make chairman, you'll be first in line for the Job Trünicht Memorial Prize."

Julian laughed at their banter, partly with relief.

He remembered their first meeting with Poplin after Yang's death, finding the commander shut up in his quarters in a fog of alcohol, more than a dozen liquor bottles on the table.

Olivier Poplin's personality was made up of three elements—fearlessness, cheer, and refinement—but all three had now evaporated, exposing the skeleton of his psyche. Once known for his unapologetic and inveterate dandyism, Poplin had stopped bathing, abandoned shaving, and certainly given up on inviting women to his bed, preferring instead to brood at the center of a self-woven web of rage, intoxication, and despair. Even the sight of his two visitors did not inspire the unhappy human spider to rise from his seat at the table.

"Looks like the booze has finally poisoned my brain," said Poplin. "I'm hallucinating things I don't even want to. Why the long faces?"

"Commander Poplin, you have to stop drinking. It's not good for you." No reply.

"Please, commander."

"Shut up! What does a kid like you know?!"

Poplin's voice was loud and sharp, but lacked its usual vigor and luster.

"Why do I have to take orders from anyone except Yang Wen-li? I have the right to decide who orders me around. Isn't that democracy? Huh?"

His hand shook as it reached for his tumbler, and succeeded only in knocking it over, along with the whiskey. He took this in with green eyes that brimmed with intoxication, then reached for a new bottle—his last. Julian caught Poplin's arm in both hands, but could not find the right words to say. Three and a half seconds later, Attenborough broke the silence.

"Commander Poplin, consider this your formal notification. Following the death of Marshal Yang, Julian will be our leader."

The ace pilot's electric gaze pierced Julian and Attenborough through, but he listened.

"Allow me to be blunt, commander Poplin," continued Attenborough. "I will not permit any questioning of Julian's right to lead, or any word or deed that undermines the authority of our leadership. Julian may permit these things, but I will not."

No reply.

"Got a problem with that? Then get out. If you can't make yourself useful to Julian, Iserlohn doesn't need you."

After a few seconds of silence, Poplin said, "No. There's no problem." He seized the edges of the table with both hands and, somehow, forced himself up on unsteady feet.

I'm sorry, Julian. I know you must be suffering much more than I am… But this was something that Olivier Poplin could never say aloud. He vanished into the shower room for twenty minutes, then reappeared perfectly groomed and dressed, if still in poor complexion, and offered Julian a respectful salute.

"Commander! By your leave, as of today I am a new man. Please don't give up on me."

From that moment, Poplin never lost his reason in front of others again, nor forgot his responsibilities as captain of the First Spaceborne Division.

"You're not the only one whose mettle is being tested, Julian. History poses the same question to us all. We've already lost Yang Wen-li; can we avoid losing hope, unity, and direction?"

Attenborough's musings perfectly described how the younger generation who had remained in Iserlohn felt. Yang Wen-li had been their rock, but they had lost him forever. All of them, Julian included, had to ask themselves once more what they were fighting for. Even if Attenborough's answer was his famous "foppery and whim," he could not ignore the results his actions would have.

Julian had once brought a certain idea to Attenborough for discussion.

"What's that? Force the empire to adopt a constitution?" Attenborough boggled at the idea, but after a moment's thought it did seem the best of the options available to them. Even an undemocratic constitution could still serve as a milestone on the road from autocracy to democracy.

"Yes," said Julian. "There's no need for radicalism, if constitutionalism gives us the opening we need to slowly infiltrate the Galactic Empire itself."

An easy thing to say, Julian thought with a rueful smile. But he had no interest in making a last stand in Iserlohn and becoming tragic martyrs to the empire's overwhelming force. He felt this way partly due to Yang Wen-li's influence, but the entire Yang Fleet shared this psychic territory. Only in the successful transmission of democratic republican governance to later generations would their "foppery and whim" complete itself.

To change the Galactic Empire from an autocracy to a constitutional state—if this were possible at all, it could perhaps be realized most effectively at the moment when all humanity was united in the same state.

Rudolf von Goldenbaum had seized a single democracy and turned it into an autocracy. Would it be impossible to do the same in reverse?

A tiny thorn at the back of Julian's mind nagged at his ruminations. He remained unable to identify it for several seconds before Attenborough changed the subject.

"So, Julian—I mean, Commander Mintz. You don't think it's likely that the kaiser will lead a fleet to attack the Iserlohn Corridor?"

"No, I don't. Not right now. For the time being, the kaiser will be concentrating his efforts on reorganizing the galactic order around the Phezzan Corridor."

"But it's in the kaiser's nature to love war. Won't he eventually tire of peace, and reopen hostilities under the pretext of completing galactic unification?"

"I can't imagine him doing so. If Marshal Yang were still alive, the prospect might intrigue him. But…"

But with Julian Mintz as his opponent, he simply won't be interested, Julian thought. This was not self-deprecation but an objective assessment. Julian was a nobody; his name had no ring of authority or influence, just as Yang's hadn't before the Rescue of El Facil. Although Julian's situation was slightly different in that he could at least call on the name of his deceased father and teacher, which had not been an option for Yang. Julian understood that he would never be Yang's equal, and perhaps that understanding was what granted direction and stability to his stride as he walked toward the future.

Frederica Greenhill Yang was resting in her quarters, hazel eyes turned to the photo of her late husband that sat on her nightstand.

Yang Wen-li smiled bashfully back at her from within the frame. They had met when Yang was a newly minted officer with little apparent prospect for promotion or decoration. He had left her for the last time looking exactly the same. How many facts had accumulated in the twelve years between first meeting and final parting? And yet those facts paled by comparison with the volume of memory and the depth of feeling.

A washed-up lieutenant from the El Facil Patrol Fleet, sandwich in hand, looking stunned by the vastness of the responsibility placed upon him. When they had slipped through the fingers of the Galactic Empire to arrive safely at the planet Heinessen, Frederica had left her parents to their embrace at the spaceport while she searched for the man who had saved her. She finally found him in the crowd, but he had become a hero overnight and was surrounded by the media, frozen. She could not even get close to him. Finally her parents remembered their daughter and called for her to return. She was fourteen, and at the end of her beginning.

Yang would probably not find his family's current situation entirely to his liking. His wife had become the leader of a revolutionary government, his ward the commander of a revolutionary army, and he himself a kind of patron saint of democracy, drafted into service even after death to provide spiritual succor and ensure Frederica and Julian's legitimacy.

" 'Can't I even rest when I'm dead?' I know that's what you want to say. But if you were still alive, we wouldn't have to bear this burden in the first place."

Even as she spoke, Frederica realized that she had learned this logic from Yang.

"It's your fault, Yang Wen-li, everything's all your fault. Me becoming a soldier. This imperial base somehow becoming the last redoubt of democracy. Everyone remaining here, chasing the dream of the festival. If you had any understanding of your responsibilities, you'd come back to life right now."

But, of course, the dead could not come back to life. Nor could the living stay unchanged. Time, once lost, could never be restored.

Which was exactly why time was more precious than a billion gemstones, and life must not be lost in vain. Yang had always maintained these truths. His characteristic retort to religions that insisted on the eternal soul or reincarnation, making light of physical death, was, *If death is so great, why not die? I won't stop you. Why is it always those who say such things who cling to life the longest?*

"Come back to me, Yang," Frederica whispered. "It's against the laws of nature, but I'll overlook it just this once. And this time I won't let you die before me."

Frederica could see him so clearly, mumbling, "Well, that really puts me on the spot" into his beloved black beret.

"It's terrifying to think about how many people I've sent to their deaths," Yang had once said. "Me dying once myself is hardly enough to atone for that. The world can be a pretty unbalanced place."

There was no end to the egoism humans could fall into. Frederica had not wanted Yang to atone for his sins. She had wanted him to live, even if it meant draining the life from others. To live a life so long his pension was a burden on public resources.

"It's true that I lost you. But compared to never having you at all, I was truly blessed. You might have killed millions, but you made me, at least, very happy."

Frederica had not heard Yang's final words. But this was one point on which she felt no regret. She knew that those words had been either "I'm sorry" or "Thank you"—and most likely the former. It did not matter if nobody believed her. She knew what she knew, and that was enough.

III

After Admiral Murai led the dissatisfied and restless elements away from Iserlohn Fortress, the unity between those who remained should have been unshakable. But nobody was perfect, and alcohol in particular was prone to awaken dozing uncertainties. One day, a half-drunk officer buttonholed Julian by the door to the central command center and began harassing him. Karin happened to witness the confrontation, and to hear something she could not let pass:

"You need to learn your place, kid. You couldn't even save Marshal Yang's life, and now you call yourself commander?"

Even during her own opposition to Julian, Karin had never gone that far. She knew that those words must never be spoken. Julian's pain and self-recrimination over Yang's death were greater than anyone's. It was not right to add to his suffering. Karin, as a member of Iserlohn Fortress, bore part of the responsibility for failing to save Yang too. The man's heartless attack on Julian proved nothing but his own poverty of spirit.

Above all, I can't imagine Marshal Yang blaming Julian for what happened. He'd be more likely to apologize for not managing to hold on until Julian came running.

On reflection, Yang had been a mysterious man. Karin's words to Julian a few days earlier had been the truth: when Yang was alive, he really had not seemed such a great man to her. But hour by hour, day by day, Karin was coming to understand. Understand that all of them—Julian, Commander Poplin, the man who had been her mother's lover for a brief moment, everyone—had been dancing with sublime rhythm and footwork on Yang Wen-li's open palm.

Marshal Yang, Karin mused, was both home port and alma mater to the Iserlohn Spirit. Even if graduation had been inevitable one day, she wished that they could have enjoyed their time together just a little longer.

For now, though, rather than sinking into the abyss of her thoughts, she chose to take surface action. If nothing else, she could not bear to watch Julian quietly enduring the man's abuse and responding with nothing but a rueful smile. She tossed her hair and approached the two in an orderly stride. When they turned their gaze on her, naturally she did not flinch or hesitate.

"Lieutenant Mintz, why aren't you saying anything?" Karin said, directing her indignation at Julian rather than the drunk. "This man's criticisms are completely unfair. If it were me, I'd give him a good two dozen slaps. Isn't it your responsibility to defend your rightful authority, for the sake of those who depend on you?"

Julian and the drunk turned and looked at the pilot. Neither said a word, although they bore different expressions.

"I…I know it's none of my business. But—"

Karin's voice was drowned out by another, several times louder. The drunken man had shrugged off her interruption and returned to his tirade.

"And don't think I'm letting Marshal Yang off the hook, either!" he slurred. "Assassinated by the Church of Terra? What kind of ridiculous way to die is that? If he'd fallen in the heat of battle, staring down Kaiser Reinhard, he could have died a hero—but no! Talk about embarrassing."

"Say that one more time," Julian snarled, his expression utterly transformed. Criticism of Yang had switched his emotional channel in an instant. "You're saying people who are assassinated don't measure up to those who die in battle?"

The other man's expression changed too. Julian's voice was crystallized rage. It had struck genuine fear into him.

Just then a hand came down on Julian's shoulder from behind. The gesture was casual, but it sent a kind of wave rippling from the palm that soothed Julian's fury.

"Come on, Julian—uh, commander, that is. You can't strike a subordinate. Not even a worthless one."

Julian looked from hand to arm, arm to shoulder, and finally met a pair of familiar green eyes that seemed to dance with sunlight.

"Commander Poplin…"

The drunk opened his mouth to speak again. Poplin smiled at him. The smile was not friendly.

"All right," he said. "This is the point at which you exercise your imagination a little. Here's your topic: what people might think of a man who's abusing someone not just much younger than him but also burdened with far greater responsibility."

The man said nothing.

"Back off while you still can," Poplin continued. "If Julian gets really mad, you'll be turned into meatballs. I'm putting myself on the line for your well-being here."

The man walked off, muttering to himself. Poplin flashed a generous smile at Julian and Karin, both standing stock-still.

"Looks like you youngsters are at a loss for something to do," he said. "Why don't you keep me company while I have my coffee?"

Eventually news of this minor dust-up reached the ears of Walter von Schönkopf and Alex Caselnes.

"Julian knew he didn't have the experience to be head of Iserlohn's military," von Schönkopf said. "He let us put him in that position anyway because he saw it as a way to make amends for failing to protect Marshal Yang. He's determined to take up the mantle of Yang's philosophy and see it realized in practice. If that drunk was too dim to grasp such an obvious fact, he's useless to Iserlohn anyway. We'd be better off if he just left."

"Personally, I feel the same way," said Caselnes, "but I'm not sure that purging ourselves of dissident elements is compatible with the fundamental principles of democratic governance."

"You're saying democracy is a system for legally codifying self-restraint on the part of the powerful?" said von Schönkopf, a wry grin twitching at the corners of his mouth. " 'The powerful' in this case being our Julian, of course. Well, Marshal Yang didn't look the slightest bit heroic, so I suppose it makes sense that his beloved pupil wouldn't look the part either."

The two men lapsed into silence. Currents from the air conditioning cycled lazily through the space between them.

Both had rebuilt their shattered psyches after the shock of losing Yang forever. But the memory of winter survives the coming of spring. Their psychic landscapes were as rugged, as dauntless as ever, but the glaciers within them had permanently advanced.

The three and a half years between Yang's appointment as commander of Iserlohn Fortress at the end of SE 796 and his assassination had been an age of vitality and unity. Despite the interruption of their temporary abandonment of the fortress itself, those years had been filled with a light and heat that were now difficult to believe. The younger members of the republic had probably believed those times would last forever. Even their elders—although neither Caselnes nor von Schönkopf had yet reached forty—had not expected festival season to end so soon.

As if to banish the silence, Caselnes said, "Julian feels no envy for his predecessor. This is a rare quality among those who inherit their power. Here's hoping he only grows from here."

Von Schönkopf put his beret back on and nodded. "As Yang himself might have put it, the question now is whether history will speak of 'Julian Mintz, disciple of Yang Wen-li' or 'Yang Wen-li, teacher of Julian Mintz.' As for me, I have no idea."

"All we know for sure is this: Not one of us on Iserlohn knows how to quit while we're ahead. Do I have your agreement, Admiral von Schönkopf?"

"Much as it pains me to admit it, you do," said von Schönkopf with a smile. He raised his arm in farewell and left the office. Iserlohn was at a severe numerical disadvantage; if their military was not elite, there was no point in fighting at all, and the responsibility of training their forces into that elite fell to him.

Caselnes turned back to his own work. He had his own responsibility: to keep the minority who had remained on Iserlohn fed.

IV

However unlikely an early attack by the empire might be, Iserlohn could not be lax in preparing for a military response. Julian, of course, but also Merkatz, Attenborough, and Poplin found their days entirely consumed with the demands of formations, supply, human resources, and facilities management.

The younger generation showed particularly striking diligence, partly because of their sense of duty, but also, undeniably, in an attempt to remain busy enough to keep the memory of Yang's death at bay.

"When Marshal Yang was alive, we were busy preparing for the festival," Attenborough would later recall. "After he died, we found that he'd left us homework, and we worked our fingers to the bone getting it done."

Julian was inspecting some port facilities one day when Attenborough called him into the command center. He arrived to find the vice admiral wearing an uncharacteristically grim expression.

"What is it, Admiral Attenborough? I didn't think anything could faze you."

Attenborough jerked his chin toward a screen. Julian's gaze shifted as directed and was immediately transfixed. His reason sought to deny the information his vision supplied. Could the imagery of a personnel announcement from the empire really be true?

The screen showed a familiar smiling face. A face that had charmed hundreds of millions of citizens, electors, and supporters within the Free Planets Alliance as its onetime leader.

"Job Trünicht," Julian said, voice no louder than a whisper. He seemed to be having trouble even breathing, as if the function of his lungs had been suddenly degraded. *High counselor to the Neue Land governorate, Job Trünicht*—the words were a waking nightmare.

"Don't get me started on the kaiser's judgment here," Attenborough said, "but this man is a wonder. I don't know what's inside his head, but I'm astonished that he can smile like that, even if it's only superficial. It seems that Trünicht was more monstrous than we imagined."

Attenborough's observations prodded at Julian's memory. Even as Yang had despised Trünicht's fondness for mob rule, hadn't he actually feared the other sides of him?

"How can you take this news so calmly?" Julian asked Frederica, who was staring at the screen in silence.

"Oh, I'm far from calm," said Frederica. "But we have to think about it. About what this appointment means."

Frederica was right. No appointment was entirely unwanted. At the very least, either the appointer or the appointee desired it. Who, then, had sought Trünicht's appointment as high counselor to the Neue Land governorate, and for what purpose? If it was simply a manifestation of Trünicht's brazen lust for power, Julian could rest easy. But that only explained the flower that had bloomed. The problem was the root—and the soil. Julian did not yet have the vision to discern their true nature. Above all, he lacked information. Yang had always been wary of the foolish practice of reaching convenient conclusions from poor information, and Julian hoped to follow his example there if nowhere else.

Yang's death had forced Julian to quietly revise his dreams for the future. He had never revealed this to anyone, but he had come to hope that once everything was over he might extricate himself from both war and politics and become a historian instead, testifying as a contemporary to the events of his age.

But there were two things he had to do first. One was to triumph over the greatest conqueror in history, Kaiser Reinhard, and sow the seeds of democratic governance in history's soil. This duty was his bequest from Yang, but a reflection of his own ideals as well.

His other duty was revenge.

Much as he blamed himself for failing to save Yang Wen-li, Julian would not allow those who had plotted and carried out the assassination to escape punishment.

If Yang had been slain at the hand of Kaiser Reinhard, be it in battle or through treachery, the only path remaining to Julian would be to loathe and defeat Reinhard. If the difference in strength between their forces made victory in battle impossible, then he would simply have to resort to the scourge of terrorism. Even if that choice was not what Yang would have wished, Julian would have been obliged to take it anyway.

The fact that Yang had been murdered by the Church of Terra spared Julian such pointless hatred of Reinhard. And it would have no small influence on the unfolding of the history that was still to come.

ᴠ

On August 10 of year 2 of the New Imperial Calendar, Job Trünicht arrived at the planet Heinessen to take up the position Reinhard had appointed him to: high counselor to the Neue Land governorate.

As was well-known to everyone involved, until just one year before Trünicht had been head of state in the very same territory. The Free Planets Alliance itself no longer existed as a state. The two men who had led the military efforts to prevent its disappearance, marshals Alexandor Bucock and Yang Wen-li, were also gone forever. Trünicht alone had survived to present himself before Marshal Oskar von Reuentahl, the Neue Land's governor-general.

How dare he even show his face here, after draining his fatherland of its very life like some parasitic vine?

So von Reuentahl thought, but he did not speak the words aloud. His heterochromiac gaze glinted coldly as it slashed across Trünicht's face.

The two of them had met before. When the Imperial Navy had descended on Heinessen and forced the alliance government to sign a humiliating peace treaty the year before, von Reuentahl had been one of the three representatives of Supreme Command Headquarters who accepted Trünicht's surrender. The other two were Wolfgang Mittermeier and Hildegard von

Mariendorf. Different as the three were in personality and thinking, they were united in their disgust for Trünicht's actions. They could barely even accept what he had done, much less find reason to praise it. The sight of Trünicht sauntering back to his old haunt, this time as an *imperial* official, added another thick brushstroke to the canvas of von Reuentahl's loathing.

Trünicht did not appear shaken in the slightest by von Reuentahl's evident ill will. He delivered a long speech of welcome, ending with the following: "Marshal von Reuentahl, you are the greatest of the Galactic Empire's retainers and its most renowned military leader. I can hardly imagine that what little wisdom I possess could be of use to you, but if I am able to serve you in any way, such would be my honor."

Just as prejudice and partiality threatened to cloud von Reuentahl's piercing mind, he detected a menacing shadow drifting beneath Trünicht's elegant verbiage. Or so, at least, it seemed to von Reuentahl.

Some chemical reaction transmuted his loathing to murderousness, but von Reuentahl remained in control. Precisely because the emotion was so fierce, in fact, it pushed against the bounds of his reason and invoked a strong suppressive reaction.

On one occasion, von Reuentahl had reprimanded Domestic Safety Security Bureau Chief Heidrich Lang strongly enough to earn his resentment. He had not viewed Lang as a threat, and the sight of his close friend Mittermeier humiliated had been enough for him to respond with pure anger. For Mittermeier, von Reuentahl often took greater risks than he otherwise would, and Mittermeier returned the favor.

But none of that would be possible this time. Von Reuentahl sensed the need to armor himself. He responded to Trünicht's continued droning with perfect courtesy, but left their meeting quickly. Immediately after this, he summoned Admiral Bergengrün, his inspector general and second in command in military affairs.

"Monitor Trünicht," von Reuentahl said. "He's sure to be planning something unpleasant."

Bergengrün furrowed his brow slightly. He would not dream of disobeying the orders of a superior, he explained, but he also saw little reason to waste any effort on a nothing like Trünicht.

"In principle I agree with you," von Reuentahl said. "But look at it from another perspective. Yang Wen-li died an unnatural death, but Trünicht is not only alive but thriving."

Bergengrün considered this caustic observation, but apprehension still filled his earnest face.

"Your Excellency, this may not be useful, but might I offer a word of warning?"

"Go ahead. Since you became my lieutenant, I don't recall you offering a single piece of advice that wasn't useful."

Bergengrün bowed, acknowledging the compliment. "Please do not allow yourself to be replaced by a cipher like Trünicht," he said with intensity. "You support the very Galactic Empire as a key retainer to the Lohengramm Dynasty, and it is my fervent wish that you recognize the importance of this role."

A smile filled both of von Reuentahl's eyes, but it was more than half artificial.

"It is precisely because I recognize this that I am having you monitor him. But your warning is accepted with thanks."

"What I find mystifying," Bergengrün said, "is why the kaiser has seen fit to place such trust in Trünicht. Perhaps His Majesty's thoughts in this matter run too deep for an ordinary man like myself to understand."

I doubt it, von Reuentahl thought. To Reinhard, simply recognizing Trünicht's existence surely felt like befouling the fertile plains of his psyche with effluent. The kaiser would surely strike his name from the list of the living if such were possible, but it would not do to kill a man simply because he disliked him. Von Reuentahl felt the same way.

The face that was drawn in von Reuentahl's mind was not the kaiser but his pale, sharp-featured secretary of defense, Marshal Paul von Oberstein. Von Oberstein devoted himself to eliminating every possible impediment to the kaiser and his empire. Could he not be hoping that von Reuentahl would slay Trünicht for them—and in so doing, give him a pretext to dispose of von Reuentahl too?

"In any case, Trünicht is the man His Majesty has chosen. Whatever his sins, it is not my place to punish him for them. Monitor him closely, never relaxing your vigilance. I doubt you will have to do so for long."

With that, von Reuentahl sent his trusted inspector-general away. Alone in his office, the handsome general ran a hand through his dark brown hair and thought in silence.

Many historians have argued that Oskar von Reuentahl was, at this point in time, the "second most powerful man in the galaxy." Considering that military authority at the center of the empire was divided between von Oberstein and Mittermeier, von Reuentahl had dictatorial authority over the mightiest single force of all the empire's retainers, if only within the confines of the Neue Land. By comparison, von Oberstein did not command any actual forces, while Mittermeier took his orders directly from the kaiser. In which direction, though, would von Reuentahl's staggering authority and power direct itself? At this stage, the answer was unclear even to von Reuentahl himself.

CHAPTER TWO:
LAST ROSES OF THE SUMMER

I

REINHARD VON LOHENGRAMM, history's greatest conqueror,
was still living in a hotel on Phezzan, the planet he had made the capital
of his new empire.

It was August in year 2 of the New Imperial Calendar, and Reinhard
was 24 years old. Four years and seven months after succeeding to the
county of Lohengramm, he had been crowned emperor, and more than
a year had passed since then. The months and years had been filled with
wars of conquest and the demands of governance, and despite his power
he still had no permanent abode.

He had used the hotel on Phezzan as the command center for Operation Ragnarok in the days before he had become kaiser. Following its
official designation as Imperial Headquarters, a few renovations had been
carried out, but from the outside it looked like any other hotel between
first and second grade.

Reinhard disliked excessive security and preferred simplicity in his sur-
roundings, leaving his retainers no choice but to station guards out of their
golden-haired kaiser's sight to protect his safety. Every time Commodore
Günter Kissling, head of the Imperial Guard, recalled young Baron von

Kümmel's attempted assassination of the newly crowned Reinhard, he broke out into a cold sweat no matter what the weather was like.

What was more, in June, Yang Wen-li, the Galactic Empire's strongest, most feared, and most respected enemy, had fallen victim to terrorism on his way to an audience with the kaiser himself. That attack had shaken even the core of the empire's leadership. Of course there were those who danced with glee at the news of the death of Yang Wen-li, official enemy of the entire empire, but Reinhard and his senior officers, like Marshal Mittermeier and Senior Admiral Müller, felt the death of their enemy painfully. For Kissling, of course, it was also a pointed reminder that he must remain vigilant in guarding the kaiser's personal safety.

Reinhard's office was on the third floor of the west wing. For living quarters, he kept a suite on the fourteenth floor. There was an elevator, but sometimes, as the mood struck him, he took the stairs, so there were soldiers stationed on every landing.

The design of the future imperial residence, tentatively named Löwen-brunn, had been left in the hands of Reinhard's secretary of works, Bruno von Silberberg, but von Silberberg's assassination had left the work stalled at the planning and site selection stage. Reinhard himself had no strong attachment to the project. Unlike the Goldenbaum Dynasty's founder, Emperor Rudolf, Reinhard was not interested in projecting imperial power and authority through buildings of staggering scale.

Von Silberberg's replacement as secretary of works, Gluck, had urged Reinhard to rethink his personal austerity. "Over-abstemious habits restrict those who serve your majesty to frugality too. For their sake if nothing else, please consider making some changes."

Reinhard had promised to take this under advisement. The problem had not occurred to him before; he was oddly ill-informed about topics other than politics and war. In this case, he had obediently heeded Gluck's counsel and decided to move his headquarters to the former state hotel on Phezzan, effective September 1. His minister of domestic affairs, Count Franz von Mariendorf, and of military affairs, Marshal Paul von Oberstein, were also instructed to establish residences on the planet, as was Marshal Wolfgang Mittermeier, commander in chief of the

Imperial Space Armada, and several mansions were purchased or leased for this purpose. Von Mariendorf moved with his daughter Hildegard into the residence Nicolas Boltec had used as acting secretary-general of Phezzan. Mittermeier was offered a palatial mansion with more than thirty rooms that had once belonged to one of Phezzan's richest retired merchants, but he found its gilded excess not to his liking, and leased an unremarkable two-story house ten minutes' walk from headquarters instead.

On August 22, Mittermeier went to Phezzan Spaceport 2 alone, with neither deputy nor orderly, to meet an arrival from a distant planet. Finally he spotted the young woman with cream-colored hair and violet eyes. He raised his hand and approached her.

"Eva!" he called.

"Wolf! How are you?"

The highest-ranking admiral in the imperial armada, and one of only three imperial marshals, pulled his wife close and kissed her for the first time in almost a year.

"How am I?" he said. "After such a long time without your cooking, not very well, I'm afraid. My taste buds' standards have slipped dramatically."

"I see the standard of your flattery has increased though."

The two exited the spaceport arm in arm. An uneducated observer might have mistaken them for a young couple at field officer or, at most, lieutenant grade. But a few of the people they passed turned to stare in astonishment. Could it really be Wolfgang Mittermeier, senior retainer to the empire that controlled most of the galaxy—if the galaxy were a human body, the empire would account for all but the last few hairs—and his wife Evangeline? An imperial marshal of the Goldenbaum Dynasty would have been driven in a luxury car, scattering the people before him with beeping and batons, and accompanied by at least a division's worth of orderlies alone. But the Mittermeiers simply boarded one of the many autonomous taxis that roamed the streets. Evangeline had an audience with the kaiser to attend.

Mittermeier had married at 24, the same age Kaiser Reinhard was now. But about the imperial person there was no suggestion even of romance, let alone marriage. For his senior retainers and aides, this inevitably became a source of mild vexation.

Had Reinhard been a philanderer like Oskar von Reuentahl, another imperial marshal, his staff would have had other headaches. For his part, Mittermeier would have preferred the kaiser to walk the middle path— call it the common one, if you prefer—of household and heir. A private citizen could remain single or even celibate until death if this pleased them, but the ruler of an autocratic state had two duties: governance, and the continuation of their line. There were no grounds for criticizing Reinhard regarding the first of these, but regarding the second he was at present a perfect failure. There were even rumors—whether true or not Mittermeier did not know—that the Ministry of the Palace Interior had, with the best of intentions, dispatched a series of elegant beauties to his bedchamber—but that every single one of them had been left solemnly waiting outside that chamber's door.

Reinhard received the Mittermeiers at Imperial Headquarters. His fever had flared again the previous night but subsided in the light of morning, leaving him full of energy to apply to the tasks of government.

"Frau Mittermeier," he said. "Thank you so much for coming. Your husband is a steadfast friend on the battlefield. It gives me immense pleasure to have him as my subordinate."

"You are too kind, Your Majesty. My husband's position under your command is his greatest joy in life."

Reinhard's bodyguard Emil von Selle brought in three cups of coffee with cream. As their rich aroma filled the room, what had begun as somewhat awkward conversation soon flowed freely. Reinhard was not a master raconteur by nature, but he appreciated the time he spent with the Mittermeiers and enjoyed their stories about how they had met and their life together.

"And what kind of flowers did Marshal Mittermeier take with him on that occasion?"

"I'm afraid I'm too embarrassed to say," Mittermeier said with a rueful grin. He knew now that in the language of flowers yellow roses were not the appropriate choice for a proposal of marriage.

Their conversation was not overlong, and the kaiser saw the Mittermeiers as far as the entrance to Imperial Headquarters when it was time to leave. Excusing themselves once more, they walked side by side back to their new residence.

Mittermeier was still thinking on their audience with the kaiser. So much about it had been somehow unusual. "If His Majesty wished it, his life could be a field of flowers," he muttered. "What a waste."

"Do you mean Countess von Mariendorf?" asked his wife.

"And many others, if he pleased. But if it were within my authority to do so, I would advise the kaiser to make her his empress."

To have a woman as insightful and quick-witted as Countess Hildegard "Hilda" von Mariendorf by his side would surely be to the kaiser's benefit. Furthermore, she was beautiful. Beautiful enough to bear comparison to Reinhard himself. Did any other woman meet the conditions for empresshood as well as her?

However, as far as Mittermeier could observe, while the kaiser recognized the countess's intellect and treated her with respect, he did not seem especially moved by her beauty. Of course, he showed no more interest in his own good looks, apparently viewing them as only what he might be expected to possess. The sources of his pride and self-confidence were wisdom, valor, and principle, not appearance. Had he been susceptible to intoxication by his own beauty, neither Mittermeier, nor his dear friend von Reuentahl, nor any of his other men would have been inclined to about entrust their fates to him, much less the future of mankind to him. Still, if he was lacking in sentiment in the common sense, that was something to consider too…

Mittermeier shook his head. He wanted to be a soldier and nothing more. He could not concern himself even with politics, let alone the kaiser's private life, or there would be no end to his worriment.

He shifted his gaze and smiled as he pointed out to his wife their new home, standing quietly in the afternoon sun.

Summer was almost over. The death of Yang Wen-li at the beginning of the season had shocked the entire galaxy, from its most powerful men to the powerless masses. The unseen force that had seeped into their breasts at the news was finally departing, leaving behind it a sense of desolation, as if an age were coming to an end.

II

"Whether revolutionary autocrat or autocratic revolutionary, Reinhard von Lohengramm dispensed with most of the wicked practices and traditions of the Goldenbaum Dynasty, but one proved resistant to any attempts at dislodgment: the habit among assassins of targeting the emperor."

The incident which historians would speak of in these terms took place on the evening of August 29.

It had rained until late afternoon, but the clouds then receded to the horizon, allowing every particle in the cleansed atmosphere to catch the light of the setting sun and tint the vision of the populace a limpid scarlet.

Reinhard's final official duty for the day was his appearance at a ceremony marking the end of construction of the new cemetery for those who fell in battle. After the ceremony, Reinhard accepted the expressions of gratitude of a few families who had lost members to the war and then began his regal walk down a passage cleared for him through a formation of 30,000 soldiers.

"*Sieg Kaiser! Sieg Reich!*"

The cheers came in waves, fervent and rhythmic, forming walls of sound on both sides. In the days of the Goldenbaum Dynasty, the cry of *Sieg Kaiser!* had been nothing but a custom preserved by the nobility. Today, it was a concrete expression of the troops' enthusiasm and loyalty.

His Majesty's condition seems to have improved, thought Commodore Kissling, a small torch of relief flickering in his topaz eyes. The brave and loyal head of the Imperial Guard deplored his powerlessness in the face of the kaiser's health issues, which were evidently grave. He was also infuriated by the bafflement of Reinhard's phalanx of doctors, not selected for their ineptitude, in the face of the kaiser's frequent fevers. Despite all their studies, despite the high salaries they drew, they had proved utterly useless.

When not in his sickbed, however, Reinhard remained the picture of youth and vitality. His vigor seemed fully intact, right down to the molecular level. There was absolutely no external indication whatsoever of weakening due to illness.

With the kaiser at this event were twenty-four officials in total, including the minister of domestic affairs, Count von Mariendorf; the minister of military affairs, Marshal von Oberstein; commissioner of military police and commander of capital defenses, Senior Admiral Kessler; fleet commander for the Phezzan region, Senior Admiral Lutz; chief advisor to Imperial Headquarters, Vice Admiral Hildegard von Mariendorf; chief aide to the kaiser Vice Admiral von Streit; secondary aide to the kaiser Lieutenant von Rücke; and Reinhard's personal bodyguard, Emil von Selle. A careful observer would also have noted two doctors in the party. They wore military uniforms, but not without awkwardness.

Marshal Mittermeier and Senior Admirals Müller, Wittenfeld, Wahlen, and von Eisenach—the highest ranks of the military's leadership—were away from Phezzan on a two-week reconnaissance mission, as part of the plan to protect the new imperial capital by building military bases at both ends of the Phezzan Corridor. As a result, those accompanying Reinhard at the ceremony were the most important military leaders currently on Phezzan. Those responsible for security were accordingly tense. The core officers of the kaiser's personal guard had been forced into close acquaintance with the abdominal pain that intense psychological pressure could called. The guard's second-in-command, Colonel Jurgens, was known as the "Iron Stomach" despite his minimal appetite simply because he had never felt this pain.

And it was the Iron Stomach himself who first noticed that something was amiss. As he explained some days later, "The others were watching the kaiser, but I was watching the ones who were staring at the kaiser."

At a whisper from the colonel, Kissling turned his eyes to a man in the crowd. The man looked to be in his midthirties and wore a soldier's uniform, but his actions lacked the discipline of the group. Kissling's orders were terse and to the point.

The would-be assassin had adopted the precise opposite of the Iron

Stomach's principle of action. His eyes, full of loathing and murderous intent, were fixed solely on Reinhard, seeing nothing else around him.

He was arrested about ten feet from his target. A ceramic canister of sprayable cyanide gas and a bamboo knife painted with nicotine poison were found on his person. The drama of his arrest was completed almost disappointingly quickly, but the true performance by this attempted regicide began afterwards. As soldiers grabbed him under his arms and dragged him away, his wrists in electromagnetic handcuffs, ability to resist sapped by a voltage gun, he turned his head toward the coolly watching Reinhard and, fiercely, shouted, "Golden brat!"

Reinhard had grown accustomed to hearing this insult before his ascension to the throne. To utter it was, of course, *lèse-majesté*, but this was just another raindrop added to the vast pond that was attempted regicide.

Seeing that the man was about to yell again, Kissling slapped him hard enough to risk damaging the muscles in his neck. At this, even the would-be assassin flinched.

"Impertinent wretch! Are you one of those fanatics from the Church of Terra, seeking only the destruction of order?"

"I am no Terraist," the man growled, split lips dripping blood and loathing. His gaze was so intense it was as if he sought to incinerate the handsome emperor where he stood.

"Have you forgotten Westerland? Have you already forgotten the atrocity you committed just three years ago?"

Westerland. The word flew like a formless crossbow bolt into Reinhard's ears to run his heart through. He repeated it in a murmur, and for a moment it robbed his face of its vital gleam. The would-be assassin, conversely, had recovered his own vigor, and began a furious impeachment of his intended target.

"You are no kaiser, no wise ruler. Your authority is founded on bloodshed and deceit, as you well know. You and Duke von Braunschweig saw to it that my wife and child were burned alive!"

Kissling's hand, raised to strike once more, suddenly hesitated. He looked at the kaiser, seeking a decision or an order, but the golden-haired conqueror only stood and stared as if in a daze.

"Come, kill me!" shouted the man. "Just like you and von Braunschweig plotted to kill two million innocent civilians! Children, infants who had never done you any harm, cremated in your thermonuclear inferno! Kill me as you killed them!"

The man's voice rose to a shriek. Reinhard made no answer. His cheeks, so recently flushed with fever, were now so pale that it seemed the ice blue of his eyes had spread to them. Emil stepped closer, placing one hand on the kaiser to support him.

"The living might have forgotten Westerland, blinded by your splendor," the man continued. "But the dead will not forget. They will remember forever why they were incinerated alive!"

Just as Emil felt the faintest of trembles transmitted from the kaiser's form, another voice was heard—a voice cold enough to freeze even the would-be assassin's cries. Its owner was Paul von Oberstein, minister of military affairs. He stepped between Reinhard and his would-be assassin as if to shield the kaiser from the force of the tirade.

"Your hatred is founded on false premises. It was I who urged His Majesty to tacitly permit the thermonuclear attack on Westerland. I should have been your target, not the kaiser. You might even have been successful. Certainly fewer people would have interceded."

Von Oberstein's voice was at the minimum possible temperature, and utterly resolute.

"Villain!" the man shouted, but nothing more. His rage and enmity seemed to lose their direction and dissolve into incoherent turbulence against an invisible wall of ice.

"After the Westerland Atrocity, Duke von Braunschweig lost popular support completely," von Oberstein continued. "With the hearts of the people turned against him, the confederated aristocratic forces crumbled from within. As a result, the rebellion was ended at least three months earlier than would have been possible otherwise."

Even as von Oberstein's words further chilled the frozen air, his famous cybernetic eyes gleamed calmly, illuminating the scene around him.

"Three more months of revolt would have added at least ten million to the death toll," von Oberstein said. "Only the revelation, at the appropriate juncture, of the true nature of the duke and the aristocratic forces ensured that those ten million deaths remained in the realm of the hypothetical."

"That's what those with power always say! 'To save the many, we must sacrifice the few'—this is how you justify yourselves. But has that 'few' ever included *your* parents, *your* brothers and sisters?" The man ground his heel into the earth. "You are a murderer, Reinhard! The golden brat's throne floats on a sea of blood! Remember this, every second of every day! Von Braunschweig's sins were repaid with defeat and death. You yet live, but the bill for your sins will come due one day. There are many in the galaxy whose reach extends farther than mine. There will come a time, and not very far in the future, when you will rue your misfortune at not being killed by me!"

"Take him to military police headquarters for now," ordered Kessler. "I will interrogate him personally later."

The seemingly inexhaustible geyser of denunciation was silenced as the would-be regicide was swarmed by enough military police to form three divisions. When they dragged him away, all that remained was the deepening evening gloom and the imperial procession. Emil felt the kaiser's white hand rest on his head, but it did not seem to be a conscious act. Reinhard's eyes did not register the boy at all.

"Kessler," he asked, "how will the law judge that man for his actions?"

"Any attempt on the kaiser's life, however unsuccessful, is punishable by death."

"That is the law of the Goldenbaum Dynasty, is it not?"

"Yes, Your Majesty. But the laws of the Lohengramm Dynasty are not yet settled in this area, leaving us no choice but to adhere to the former code…"

Kessler detected unfamiliar particles in the young, brilliant ruler's expression, and fell silent. Von Oberstein spoke instead, with his usual unsettling composure.

"If it is Your Majesty's wish to salvage the man's honor, execution is how that may be done. Have him shot at once."

"No. I will not permit his execution."

"If you offer to pardon him, he will only repay your mercy with another attack on your authority.

Despite Reinhard's image as cool and collected, the look he cast Kessler then was uncertain, even pleading. But Kessler, too, gave an answer undesirable to him.

"Your Majesty, on this matter I am in agreement with the minister. It need not be execution. The captive might be granted the right to an honorable suicide."

"No. That will not do." Reinhard shook his head, golden hair seeming to shed a melancholy pollen instead of its usual dazzling light. "There must be no more killing for Westerland. Do you understand? He is not to be killed. When I decide his punishment, I will…"

The young ruler trailed off, the indistinctness of his speech clear testament to the indecision in his heart. He turned and began the walk back his landcar. Kessler almost gasped at the sight. The glorious kaiser's shoulders were *drooping*…

III

The crimson hemisphere rose on the planet Westerland's horizon. Swelling rapidly, it transformed into an eerie mushroom-shaped cloud, howling with a burning wind that became a firestorm searing across the planet's surface at seventy meters per second. Two million people—men and women, adults and children—were cremated alive.

It had been three years ago—year 488 of the old Imperial Calendar. The atrocity had been ordered by Duke von Braunschweig, but Reinhard had let it happen in order to further his strategic aims. This act had left deep cracks in the psychological horizons he had long shared with Siegfried Kircheis.

Kircheis's first reaction to learning the truth had been grief for his friend. "Lord Reinhard, the nobles have done something they never should have done, but you…you've failed to do something you should have. I wonder whose sin is greater."

In his fourteenth-floor suite at Imperial Headquarters, Reinhard's pale hand gripped a bottle of 410-vintage red wine and tilted it over a crystal glass. It appeared that not will but emotion controlled the movement of his hand, and the wine overflowed the glass and stained the white silk tablecloth an ominous red. Reinhard's ice-blue eyes, more than half under the control of alcohol, gazed down at the sight. Even in this half-stupefied state, he was beautiful, but compared to the image of Reinhard that had spurred great armies across the sea of stars, his natural magnetism was severely curtailed.

The wine reminded him of a pool of blood. An unremarkable connection to make, but in Reinhard's case, it opened another wound. Red hair soaked in red blood. The flame-haired youth Reinhard had begun to avoid after their difference of opinion over Westerland, but who had nevertheless given his own life to save his friend's. Even at death's door, he had not uttered a word of protest or discontent. Instead, he had said this:

"Take this universe for your own."

It was an oath written in royal blood, and Reinhard had kept it. The Goldenbaum Dynasty, Phezzan, the Alliance of Free Planets—he had crushed them all and become the greatest conqueror in history. His oath had been kept, and now…and now he had been confronted once more with the sins of his past. At the end of glory, at the pinnacle of power, what had he won for himself? The fetters of a criminal, not worn in the slightest by the passage of time. The screams of children burned alive. He had thought he had forgotten. Just as the would-be assassin had declaimed, however, the dead would never forget the atrocity visited upon them.

Another presence disturbed the fog of intoxication. Reinhard's dark eyes surveyed the room, stopping where they found a head of dark-blond hair. Its owner, Hilda, had been allowed in by Emil Selle, who stood outside the door, half in tears.

Reinhard gave a low chuckle. "Fraulein von Mariendorf." Bereft of grandeur, his voice skimmed the frozen surface of the air. "It is just as the man said. I am a murderer, and a coward besides."

"Your Majesty…"

"I could have stopped the duke, but I did not. Yes, he committed that evil of his own accord. But I let it happen, and accepted all the profit. I know the truth—that I am a coward. The kaiser's throne aside, I am not worthy of the cheers my men offer me."

Hilda was silent. Like Reinhard, she was bitterly aware of her own powerlessness. She produced a handkerchief and wiped the damp table-cloth, along with Reinhard's hand and sleeve. Reinhard closed his even lips to stem the flow of self-recrimination, but Hilda heard the wounds on his psyche creak.

She had entered the room willingly, but it would not be easy to tend the kaiser's wounds. An appeal to proportion—"a mere two million"—would never do. That was precisely the logic of power that Rudolf von Goldenbaum had employed. Reinhard's life had begun in opposition to such ideas. Finding a justification for his sins would be the first step on a slippery slope to self-deification and becoming a second Kaiser Rudolf.

Like Reinhard, and indeed like Yang in life, Hilda was neither omnipotent nor omniscient. She had no confidence that she could offer the right save to his wounds. But, having dried his hand, his sleeve, and the tablecloth, she had to move on to her next action. Hesitantly, she opened her mouth to speak.

"Your Majesty, if you have sinned, I believe you have already paid the price for it. I believe, too, that this experience served as the basis for sweeping reform of both politics and society. There was sin, and that sin was paid for. The results are what remain. Please, do not judge yourself too harshly. There are those to whom your reforms came as salvation."

The price Hilda spoke of was the death of Siegfried Kircheis, as Reinhard well understood. His eyes darkened further, but the miasma of drink was abruptly dispersed. He watched as Hilda folded her handkerchief neatly, bowed, and made to leave the room. Half rising from his chair, he surprised even himself when he spoke.

"Fräulein."

"Yes, Your Majesty?"

"I would not have you leave. Stay with me."

Hilda did not reply at once. Doubt that she had heard correctly rose in her breast like a swelling tide, and when it rose higher than her heart she knew that she and the young emperor had taken their first step in a certain direction.

"I do not think I could bear to be alone," Reinhard said. "Not tonight. I beg you, do not leave me alone."

A pause.

"Yes, Your Majesty. As you wish."

Was this the correct answer? Even Hilda did not know. But she did know one thing: it had been the only one she could give. For Reinhard, the situation was different. Hilda was, she knew, but a single straw at which he was grasping in desperation on a stormy sea. But tonight, for his sake, she resolved to be the best straw she could.

IV

August 30.

Hans Stettelzer, the von Mariendorfs' butler, had been visibly unsettled and anxious since the previous evening. Fräulein Hilda, his pride and joy, had not come home that night. At six in the morning, he caught a glimpse of her short, dark-blond hair as she emerged from a landcar at the front gate, and hurried out to meet her.

"Fräulein Hilda! Where in heaven have you been?"

"Good morning, Hans. Up and about early, I see."

Her reply only sowed new seeds of anxiety in the faithful servant. Hans had known Hilda since she was a baby, and regarded her vigor and clarity of thought with both pride and admiration. The scioness of the House of Mariendorf was not like the sheltered daughters of other noble lines. She did not fritter away money on gowns and shawls; she did not play at romance with her piano tutor, or seek out the scandals of her peers to pin in a mental specimen case.

The only disappointment Hilda had ever caused Hans was in not being male. As a man, she might have become secretary of state or an imperial marshal; after all, of all the children of the aristocracy, she was the most sagacious and even of temper. So Hans had thought, only to watch Hilda rise to the position of chief advisor to Imperial Headquarters, far beyond the abilities of any male mediocrity—and then, almost as an afterthought, become secretary of state, too.

During the Goldenbaum Dynasty, the House of Mariendorf had been far from the center of aristocratic society. Today, descendants of that once plain and undistinguished line stood at the core of the system of authority that ruled the galaxy. This, too, was all Fräulein Hilda's doing.

And here she was, not only coming home at six in the morning, but looking more distracted than Hans had ever seen her.

But what Hans saw was not the truth. Hilda's apparent distraction was a pretense to hide the vague feeling of shame that prevented her from looking him in the eye. She stole up the stairs to her bedchamber, showered, dressed, and came back down for breakfast at half past seven.

Her father, Count Franz von Mariendorf, was already at the table. Hilda knew that if she did not break fast with him it would only deepen his concern, but having taken her seat she could not look him in the eye either. Mustering all her abilities as an actor, she greeted him and began forcing meal into a stomach that did not seem to be even on speaking terms with hunger.

Suddenly her father turned to her and said, "I gather you were with His Majesty last night, Hilda?"

Hilda's mind seemed to echo with his quiet, calm voice. Her spoon slipped from her right hand and into the soup with a splash that sent droplets as high as her chin.

Hilda had long known how wrong they were who sneered at her father, saying that he owed his current position entirely to her—that there was nothing to commend him personally but sincerity. The wisdom and insight that informed his sincerity might not offer much in the way of spectacle, but they ran deep. The very fact that he had never sought to curtail her intellectual development, even in that earlier age when the fetters of noble convention were crueler, made his true merits apparent to any who cared to see.

"Father, I…"

"I understand, child." There was a hint of loneliness in his face, but also gentle understanding. "At least, I think I do. You need not say it aloud. I only wished to make sure."

"I'm sorry, Father."

Hilda had done nothing wrong, but she had no other words even for her cherished father at that moment. It was as if her powers of expression had entered an epoch of drought.

Footsteps outside the dining room broke the silence between father and daughter. Hans flew in, gigantic form quivering.

"Sir! There is—the entrance hall—a visitor—" Hans gasped, chest spasming, before he was finally able to report who had arrived. "When I opened the door, I saw H-His Majesty the kaiser! His Majesty was right there! He wishes to see both of you."

The count's eyes shifted to his daughter. Hilda, gifted and beautiful chief advisor to Kaiser Reinhard, whose mind was said to be worth more to the military than an entire fleet, was gripping the edge of the tablecloth and staring down into her soup, petrified.

"Hilda?"

After a moment, she said, "Father, I cannot stand."

"It seems His Majesty has something to discuss with you."

"I'm sorry. Please, father." Hilda's words were devoid of both intelligence and spirit.

The count muttered to himself as he rose from the table and walked to the entrance hall.

There he found the greatest conqueror in human history waiting patiently and cradling an overlarge bouquet of flowers. Roses in full bloom, red, white, and pale pink. The last roses of the summer, no doubt. When Reinhard saw the master of the house, his fair visage suddenly turned as pink as the flowers.

"Your Majesty."

"Ah—ah. Count von Mariendorf."

"It is an honor to receive you in my humble dwelling. Might I ask what brings Your Majesty here this morning?"

"The honor is all mine. I apologize for the early hour."

If such an expression may be forgiven, the golden-haired king of conquest appeared to be blushing from nerves. His misty eyes met the count's. "For Fräulein von Mariendorf," he said, thrusting the bouquet at him.

"Your Majesty is too thoughtful," the count said. He accepted the flowers, and his upper body was engulfed in a cloud of perfume so intense that for a moment he could not breathe.

"Marshal Mittermeier once told me," said Reinhard, "that when he asked Mrs. Mittermeier to marry him he brought her a huge bouquet of flowers."

"Indeed, Your Majesty?" The count's vague reply belied his total discernment of why the young emperor was here. *Still*, thought the count, *he might have chosen a better mentor in the art of courtship than Marshal Mittermeier, of all people.*

"So," Reinhard continued, "I wanted to do the same—no, I realized that I *must* do the same. And so I took the liberty of choosing those. Does the fräulein care for flowers?"

"I do not imagine that she dislikes them, Your Majesty."

Reinhard nodded. For a moment he seemed lost in a maze that lay between him and his goal, but then he spoke the decisive words: "Count von Mariendorf, I wish to take your daughter as my empress. May I have your permission to marry her?"

Von Mariendorf recognized the sincerity of the man who stood before him, less emperor than unsophisticated youth. Such sincerity was not to be disdained, although the count did think it rather hasty to request Hilda's hand in marriage the very morning after whatever had happened between them.

To von Mariendorf, this visit was proof of something he had long suspected. In both the military and political spheres, Kaiser Reinhard's successes were unprecedented in scale and breathtaking in rapidity. Yet his gifts were grossly unbalanced, and in other areas, and particularly what lay between men and women, the boy genius was remarkably naive.

Reinhard spoke again, still blushing. "If Fräulein von Mariendorf had— that is, if things had turned out as they might have, and I had shirked responsibility, I should be no better than the debauched emperors of the Goldenbaum Dynasty. I—I have no intention of joining their number."

The count allowed himself a rueful sigh that was highly unsuitable for a retainer before his lord. There were many ways to feel responsibility. Reinhard's was no different from that of a punctilious and idealistic young boy.

"*Mein Kaiser*, responsibility need not be worn so heavily. I am sure that my daughter acted of her own will. She is not the sort to use the events of a single night as a weapon to ensnare Your Majesty for life."

"But…"

"For today, Your Majesty, please let her be. She does not seem to have put her own feelings in order yet, and I fear she may speak or act disrespectfully. She already enjoys a position far higher than could have been expected. I will be sure to send her to Imperial Headquarters when things have settled."

Reinhard was silent.

"Forgive my impertinence, but please leave matters here to your humble servant while Your Majesty takes his leave."

It was less a conversation between a brilliant emperor and a dull minister than counsel from a mature adult to a callow youth.

"Very well," said Reinhard. "I leave it in your—in the count's hands. I apologize not only for the early hour of my visit but also for troubling you with a request you cannot immediately grant. I shall return at a more opportune time. Please forgive my many discourtesies."

Reinhard was about to turn on his heel when he hesitated and added one final remark.

"Give my regards to Fräulein von Mariendorf…"

The comment was devoid of all grace, but von Mariendorf allowed that his young lord might have had no other way to say it. He watched Reinhard's back recede down the entry hall until Kissling, head of the kaiser's personal guard, opened the door for him and followed him out.

The count entrusted the giant bouquet to Hans and returned to the dining room still smelling of roses. In response to Hilda's gaze, which was part question and part plea, he said, "All is probably as you imagine, Hilda. His Majesty said he wants to take you as his empress."

He heard a quiet gasp from his daughter.

"I…I'm not worthy of such an honor. Marry His Majesty! That's preposterous."

"Be that as it may, *someone* will become his consort one day," said von Mariendorf, although not in the hopes of fanning the flames of his daughter's womanly ambition. He revered Reinhard as kaiser, but his standards for a son-in-law were different. "You know, Hilda," he continued, "in the seventeenth century AD, there was a king known as the Shooting Star of the North. He was crowned at fifteen and soon recognized as a military genius. Under his rule, his tiny country held its own against the vast armies of its neighbors. And reportedly he knew absolutely nothing of the physical passions, be they for the opposite sex or his own, right up until he died in his thirties."

Hilda said nothing.

"Unusual talents seem to require some kind of equivalent flaw in another area. I am reminded of this when I look at Kaiser Reinhard. Although I suppose I should just be glad that our ruler is not an outlier in the other direction."

"The kaiser does not love me," Hilda said, suddenly but firmly. "Even I know that much. He sought my hand in marriage solely out of a sense of duty and obligation, father."

"Maybe so. But what about you, Hilda?"

"Me?"

This confirmed the count's suspicion that his daughter's sagacity had developed a nick in its edge.

"I wonder if *you* do not love *him*, childish sense of duty and obligation and all."

Father has finally asked me outright, thought daughter. *I finally asked her outright,* thought father. It was the sort of question one was loath to ask— but also the sort that would, left unasked, linger forever as a seed of regret. The rage and grief of the would-be assassin whose wife and children had been senselessly killed had, in the end, forced a decisive choice on three men and women at the heart of the Galactic Empire.

Hilda shook her head, trying to escape the mists of fantasy. She was not successful.

"I don't know," she said. "I respect him. But do I, as a woman, love him as a man? I don't know."

The count exhaled a deep sigh. "I see Kaiser Reinhard is not the only one who means to vex me. Darling daughter, my pride and joy, sometimes it is better to listen to your heart than your head. Not always, but sometimes."

Instructing his daughter to take her time thinking through the confusion she had dragged behind her since the night before, the Count von Mariendorf left the dining room. He settled himself into the easy chair in a corner of his library and gazed at the unlit fireplace.

"I wonder how well the two of them *did* get on last night," he murmured with a rueful grin. He could not recall a time when such a serious proposition had been in balance with one so comical.

As far as statecraft and war went, the galaxy had never seen the likes of Reinhard and Hilda before. But there were surely many couples with far less spectacular careers who nevertheless had matured more in their private lives.

Speaking to his daughter, the count had mentioned only Reinhard's flaws, but in fact his total lack of physical desire was a characteristic Hilda shared. Her interests had always leaned more toward political and military studies and analysis than romance. Just as society contains individuals of excessive physical lust, it also includes those at the other extreme. How fortunate that Reinhard and Hilda, both at that very extreme, should have safely found each other—even if external causes had played a rather large role.

For the past three years, the fortunes of the House of Mariendorf had been seized by a violent whirlpool. They had safely ridden the waves only through Hilda's genius. This was fact, and the count recognized it as such.

You are a better daughter than I deserve, Hilda, he thought. *But—pointless as it would be to say so—if you had only fallen for a more average man, a less ambitious one you could admire from closer at hand, I could perhaps have lived a simpler life more suited to my lot…*

It was almost time for the count, too, to begin his duties as minister of domestic affairs. He returned to his bedchamber to dress with the help of his servants. *Somehow*, he thought, *I doubt I will be minister for long.*

V

Reinhard returned from the von Mariendorf residence to Imperial Headquarters, but he entered his office in no mood for statecraft.

He was ashamed. What weakness he had shown—he, the emperor of all humanity, the greatest conqueror in history! Hilda's intellect was incomparable, her will indomitable, but she was younger than him, and a woman besides. Reinhard did not look down on women, but he had never imagined that he might be dependent on one—with one exception.

As Count von Mariendorf had perceived, as Mittermeier had feared,

YOSHIKI TANAKA

49

there was indeed a certain lack within him. "Despite the kaiser's beauty and power, he maintained strict self-control, even to the point of abstinence"— such historical assessments were erroneous, or at least overgenerous. It was not that Reinhard imposed abstinence on himself. His physiological desires, although not entirely absent, were simply very weak. Beauty and power he might have, but to lust he had always been a stranger. This was, perhaps, beyond understanding for a normal person—a man of the common herd.

To those who lived for pleasures of the flesh, as well as those who believed the folk wisdom that heroes did so, Reinhard must have seemed a baffling character. We can understand those of more powerful lusts than our own, but we struggle to do so when faced with someone whose drives are weaker.

Nevertheless, however impoverished Reinhard's desires were, it is true that he did exercise self-discipline so as not to abuse his power in private life.

From around the time he had inherited the title of Count von Lohengramm, women had flocked to him. When he became supreme commander of the Imperial Military and then imperial prime minister, dictator in all but name, the surviving nobility fought over the right to present their sisters and daughters to him. There were even those who, having no daughters of their own, adopted comely girls from other families specifically to offer the kaiser. Reinhard never plucked a single bloom from this dizzying array of beauties. One man even offered his own wife to the kaiser, but this despicable display only incurred Reinhard's wrath and contempt.

Ever since losing his dear friend Siegfried Kircheis, Reinhard had remained partly in the thrall of that shock and regret. This, perhaps, was what cast a shadow over his heart and placed a seal of guilt over the desires of the flesh he did feel.

Kircheis had left the world without even marrying. To save Reinhard's life, he had given his own. He had only been twenty-one years old.

And yet, here I stand, alive solely through his sacrifice, seeking marriage myself. Can this be forgiven? Not just by the living, but also by the dead?

Reinhard was gripped by the sense that he was on the verge of committing a wrong so great it could hardly even be expressed. But if he did not take responsibility for the night he had spent with Fräulein von Mariendorf, he would be no better than the lecherous emperors of the Goldenbaum Dynasty, who had been despised, derided, and ultimately toppled. The young kaiser did not notice the change in Count von Mariendorf's eyes when he had voiced such thoughts to him. By this point his psychological blindness could only be called willful. At the very least, he was conscious solely of how others would judge his sincerity as a public figure.

He swept his golden hair back from his forehead and felt the late-summer breeze on his skin. His melancholy eyes were like crystal vessels filled with moonlight. Of their beauty there could be no question, but it was not without an unstable fragility. Until this day, he had not realized how immature he truly was. In politics, in war, he was wise and magnanimous, able to flawlessly mend the gap between subject and object. But when it came to romantic relationships, he was exactly the opposite.

It was only when he faced a great enemy that Reinhard's heart truly sang. Only he and a handful of others knew this. An enemy of sufficient power could drive the heat of Reinhard's passion. When this happened, Reinhard glowed from within. But he no longer had any such enemies…

Just after ten o'clock, Senior Admiral Kessler, his commissioner of military police, arrived with a sad and solemn expression. The kaiser's would-be assassin, he reported, had committed suicide in his cell.

"You did not force him, I hope?" Reinhard asked, voice trembling as the shock came back to him. Kessler denied this firmly. And his denial was true: he had not lifted a finger to help the man take his life. However, neither had he made any effort to prevent him from doing so. Even pardoned for his crime by the kaiser himself, Kessler knew the man would have no other choice.

For his part, Reinhard sensed what remained unsaid, but couldn't bring himself to criticize Kessler. The sin was his own failure to make a decision. He dismissed Kessler with orders to bury the man in secrecy but with all due honor. He could not feel hatred for his would-be assassin. He had never stood a chance against Reinhard's power.

If Fräulein von Mariendorf were there, she would surely offer her counsel. But her father had made clear that she would be absent from her duties for the time being. Nor was Reinhard sure what expression to wear when they did meet again. When the count had politely declined to let Reinhard see her, a fragment of his unconscious mind had twitched with something like relief.

"What Kaiser Reinhard sought from Countess Hildegard von Mariendorf," wrote one historian, "was less sexual and romantic fulfillment than wise counsel and thoughtful advice in matters both public and private. The kaiser was free of the terrible prejudice that might have led another to undervalue her genius by reason of her being a woman…" Even this assessment, however, while praising Reinhard's achievements and genius as a public figure, pointedly ignored his private immaturity.

"Regaling children with tales of 'great men' and 'heroes' is plain stupidity. It's like telling a fine, upstanding human being to take lessons from a freak."

Thus had Yang Wen-li once spoken to Julian Mintz, although of course Reinhard had no way of knowing that. If he had known, he might have nodded in agreement, albeit with an expression of unflattering bitterness. Even when it did not inconvenience anyone else in particular, he had not failed to notice how different he was from the vast majority of other people.

In any case, in his private life, Reinhard would experience major changes this year. And, for better or worse, the nature of autocratic governance means that a ruler's private life cannot but affect the state and its history. Before these private developments, however, Reinhard and the Galactic Empire would face danger of unprecedented scale and severity. Later ages would refer to year 2 of the New Imperial Calendar as "the year of trouble and strife," and its final season was yet to come.

CHAPTER THREE:

I

THE EVENTS OF THE FIRST DAY of September on the planet Heinessen would go down in history as the Nguyen Kim Hua Plaza Disturbance—or simply the September 1 Incident.

Kaiser Reinhard's immaturity in one facet of his private life may have been exposed, but his governance had lost not a whit of its justice or freshness, and as far as anyone could see he continued to tread the path from epic conqueror to great ruler, his pace unbroken. As a public figure, Reinhard was certainly making sufficient use of his talents for political construction.

Five thousand light years from the empire's new capital of Phezzan, Marshal Oskar von Reuentahl had begun his administration of the planet Heinessen, invested with the full authority of the kaiser as its governor-general.

The Neue Land Governorate could not last forever as an administrative unit. Eventually, like the rest of the former empire's territory, it would be ruled like any other region through the ministry of internal affairs, establishing a separation of powers over political and military affairs. On that day, the final unification of human society would be complete.

"The power and authority of the Neue Land Governorate were so great that they destabilized the empire's very system of governance," wrote one later historian. "Appointing von Reuentahl to this position brought his latent ambition to the surface and sowed seeds of strife in what should have been peaceful soil. It must be admitted that this was one of the kaiser's gravest errors."

At the time, however, von Reuentahl was universally seen as a capable and effective administrator. First, he was commander in chief of the 5,226,400 members of the Neue Land Security Force. This would have permitted him to impose a brutal and militaristic rule, but instead he opted for elasticity and flexibility in his policymaking.

One example of von Reuentahl's remarkable political instincts was his drastic correction of certain abuses that had gone unaddressed in the alliance's time. Excising the rot that the *ancien régime* had permitted on this holiest of planets proved a superb opportunity for von Reuentahl's administration to convince the people of its justice. Six hundred pork-barrel politicians and corrupt military contractors, who had hitherto gone unpunished by the law despite denunciation by journalists and anti-government forces, were rounded up in a single operation.

Put in the baldest terms, this treatment was intended solely to send a message. But von Reuentahl knew that what was necessary at that juncture was not slow, steady progress but swift results. The suspects had taken certain precautions against the possibility of official action— destroying evidence, arming themselves with legal defenses, and buying off witnesses—but these were all predicated on a democratic republican system, and proved useless. Von Reuentahl's administration brought the full power of the state to bear on the wrongdoers, showing not the slightest concern for democratic procedure. Every probe, every interrogation was authorized by a single order with the governor-general's signature— and, what was more, every one was successful. These criminals who had mocked democracy were judged and punished for their wicked deeds by autocracy—an ironic turn of events indeed.

Von Reuentahl sought to lay bare before the citizenry the one unavoidable flaw of democracy—its glacial pace—in order to force that citizenry to acknowledge the positive side of imperial rule. Initially, he seemed to be successful in this.

And then came September 1.

The Free Planets Alliance's government and military had long since been dissolved, but former civil servants and veterans had gathered together to organize a joint memorial service. Von Reuentahl had granted permission for the event, but neither attended nor sent a message of solidarity. Such insincere gestures were not to his taste. Unsurprisingly, Job Trünicht also chose to stay away. In the end, most of the two hundred thousand attendees on the day were everyday citizens of no special distinction. Even the speeches were given by veterans of relatively low rank.

The ceremony should have ended peacefully. If events had proceeded according to the plans of the Neue Land's director general of civil affairs, Julius Elsheimer, who had specified the venue, it would have. But not everyone shared the desire for peace.

A crowd of two hundred thousand people can, by virtue of size alone, become hostile to order and discipline. Von Reuentahl had successfully commanded military units millions of soldiers strong, but controlling a crowd was a different matter. On the governor-general's orders, Admiral Bergengrün had stationed a guard of twenty thousand armed soldiers around the plaza. Both men thought this measure excessive, but the soldiers at the plaza did not entirely agree.

We could feel the crowd growing more hostile with every passing second—more than one soldier present at the scene testified to this effect. *Our formation was widely spaced at first, but we gradually gathered into a single location.*

As the soldiers watched the ceremony with a vague sense of unease, cries began to arise from here and there within the plaza.

"Long live Marshal Yang!"

"Long live democracy!"

"Freedom forever!"

So passionate were these cheers that they would have made Yang Wen-li shrug helplessly at Julian without saying a word. But among the excited crowd, those who could maintain strict rationality in the way that Yang had were an absolute minority. The fervor of two hundred thousand individuals merged into a single, gigantic torrent of feeling that was soon expressed in song across the plaza. It was the anthem of the Free Planets Alliance.

> *My friends, someday, the oppressor we'll o'erthrow,*
> *And on liberated worlds,*
> *We'll raise freedom's flag...*

The anthem had originally been composed in protest against the despotism of the Goldenbaum Dynasty. No song could have been better suited to whipping the crowd to new heights of passion.

> *From beyond the darkness of tyranny,*
> *With our own hands, let's bring freedom's dawn...*

As the crowd's passion and intoxication swelled, the imperial soldiers around them exchanged uncertain glances. They had an intoxicating cry of their own: *Sieg Kaiser!* They knew what it was to let passion run wild, to feel tears stream down their faces as communal energy unaccompanied by reason rose up and outward toward a single focus—but they had never realized how ominous such a thing could look to those outside the group.

"Long live Yang Wen-li!"

"Long live democracy!"

"Down with oppressors!"

The cries began small, but multiplied in geometric progression until they set the very atmosphere ringing under the dome. The imperial soldiers called for order, for quiet, but they were already unsettled and glancing anxiously at each other.

According to official records, the first stone was thrown at 1406. By 1407, the imperial soldiers were being pelted by a veritable meteor shower.

"Get out of here, you imperial dogs!"

"Invaders go home!"

This was the first public expression of hostility the imperial forces had seen since the beginning of their direct rule. The citizens were supposed to have resigned themselves to their fate and accepted the rule of the powerful. But the thin ice of civility had concealed boiling waters beneath, and with that ice about to melt, the imperial soldiers who stood atop it were in danger of drowning.

"Get them under control!"

Officers gave the orders and soldiers did their best to obey, but any hope of controlling the situation was long gone. Even armed and trained soldiers struggled to hold their own against the rioters—as the soldiers now saw them—when five or six leapt on them at once. Even as one rioter fell beneath the butt of an imperial blaster, another would attack the same soldier from behind, fingers scrabbling for the soldier's eyes.

At 1420, the use of batons and incapacitating agents was authorized, but this was only ex post facto recognition of a state of affairs that already existed.

The governorate resisted authorizing the use of firearms for a few minutes longer, but at 1424 that restriction was broken too. With a single muzzle flash, two civilians were killed and a hundred hatreds ignited.

"Rioters wrenched firearms from soldiers' hands, endangering their lives. Authorizing the use of weapons was the only choice. It was a valid self-defensive measure."

This was the imperial army's official version of events. As a partial view of the situation, it was even factual. But elsewhere one found other facts. Imperial soldiers facing the raging mob, overcome by a hysterical sense of peril, had fired on unarmed civilians.

Screams rang out. They ran through the overwhelming roar like a headwind, calling up reflexive terror which, in turn, provoked rage.

The disturbance spread.

At 1519, the incident was formally brought under control, with 4,840 citizens dead. The wounded numbered over fifty thousand, and most were taken into custody. The riot had been disastrous for the imperial side, too, with 118 soldiers killed.

"What fine subordinates I have," von Reuentahl said. "Firing on unarmed civilians—what a display of courage and chivalry."

His caustic tone might have been too harsh on the subordinates in question. But with all his efforts in the sphere of governance undone, he could not hold his anger inside.

"What I want to know," he continued, "is who got the people riled up enough for this to happen."

His sharp mind had immediately recognized the possibility that the riot in the plaza was not a protest against the empire itself but an attempt to undermine von Reuentahl's authority as governor-general. It was an exceedingly distasteful idea to entertain, but it could not be ignored. Not von Reuentahl himself would deny that his personality was the type to make enemies.

Even if there had been an agitator, however, riots or unrest could not break out where there was no dissatisfaction or anger to begin with. To the former citizens of the Free Planets Alliance, Reinhard's greatness and von Reuentahl's abilities did not change the fact that they were invaders, plain and simple. The abuse hurled at the empire by the rioters might have been uncouth, but it was not unfounded.

"Good governance by an invader is nothing but hypocrisy, then? I suppose they have a point. But that leaves the question of how to take things in hand…"

Von Reuentahl was still irritably dealing with the complexities the riot had left in its wake when a message arrived for him. It seemed that one of the men arrested was an acquaintance of his.

"Sitolet?"

Von Reuentahl furrowed his brow, very slightly. In the past, Marshal Sidney Sitolet had been a high-ranking member of the Alliance Armed Forces, first as commander in chief of its space armada and then as director of Joint Operational Headquarters. Three or four years ago, however, he had resigned his post after the alliance's rout at Amritsar. Reports were that Sitolet himself had opposed the alliance's reckless adventurism in that case, but as the head of the military hierarchy, ultimate responsibility lay with him.

Von Reuentahl ordered Sitolet brought to him in his office. When the middle-aged marshal arrived, he was not at his beset. He was filthy, his clothes were torn, and there was still dried blood on his face. But his spirit was unbowed, and he drew himself up to his full six feet and met von Reuentahl's heterochromatic gaze directly.

"Marshal Sitolet," von Reuentahl said. "Am I to infer that it was under your leadership that the recent memorial ceremony ended in such tragedy?"

Sitolet was unshaken by von Reuentahl's tone. "I was just an attendee like any other," he said calmly. "If attendance was a crime, then I am guilty."

"I admire your forthrightness. In that case, let me ask you this: do you know who *was* responsible for that ugly scene?"

"I do not. But I would not be able to tell you even if I did."

Not the most original response, von Reuentahl thought, but he was not disappointed. Had Sitolet answered in the opposite way, that would have been disappointing.

"In that case, we are not able to set you free either."

"If I were set free, I would only start a movement protesting your unlawful rule—this time with myself at the head. My only regret is that I allowed myself to be swept away by the mob."

"I respect your bravery. But as the kaiser's representative, I must protect public order according to the His Majesty's laws. I am placing you under arrest once more."

"As indeed you must. This, to you, is justice. Virtue. I sense no personal animosity in you whatsoever."

There was no sense of triumph in his words. Quiet but aloof, the former leader of the alliance's military allowed himself to be led away. Von Reuentahl watched his broad shoulders recede until the door closed behind him, then turned to his trusted lieutenant.

"Bergengrün, do you think a single death could awaken hundreds of millions of people?"

Bergengrün knew without asking that the "single death" his superior meant was that of the black-haired magician Yang Wen-li. "Perhaps, sir," he said. "But I would rather not face such an awakening directly."

Von Reuentahl nodded, eyes still fixed on the door. "Just so. If they were to mount a full-scale rebellion, we would have to put it down by force of arms. Matching wits with a mighty commander is an honor for a warrior, but suppressing a popular uprising is work fit only for dogs. What a miserable prospect."

Bergengrün glanced in surprise at his superior. In profile, he saw only von Reuentahl's right eye, with its deep, limpid black.

Could it be that elements lurked within von Reuentahl's psychology, subtly different from his liege the kaiser's, that rejected the prospect of life amid peace and prosperity? Even before September 1, the success of his masterful administration had not seemed to bring him contentment.

Marshal Yang, your untimely death may have been a blessing to you. What is a warrior in times of peace but a dog on a leash? What remains for him but a life of tedium, indolence, and gradual decay?

On the other hand, on the memorial to his opponent, Yang Wen-li, was inscribed the following sentence:

The ultimate victors are those who can endure the indolence of peace.

Validity of this assertion aside, even von Reuentahl knew that the "indolence of peace" would likely prove unbearable to him. His opposite number, minister of military affairs Marshal Paul von Oberstein, had also apparently observed as much, presumably with cynicism.

"Marshal von Reuentahl is a bird of prey. He is not the kind of man who could spend his life singing songs of peace in a cage."

Thus do the minister's words come down to us, although sources differ on the second sentence.

It appears that von Reuentahl himself had been made aware of von Oberstein's assessment through some route or other. But how he would respond to it was not yet clear.

II

Among the admirals of the Imperial Navy, von Reuentahl both maintained the most extravagant lifestyle and was most suited to the same. Ernest Mecklinger might surpass him in artistic refinement, but in the naturalness with which he wore his wealth and position von Reuentahl had no rival. It was difficult to believe that he could possibly be a colleague of

Fritz Josef Wittenfeld, who still gave the impression of a young officer living in barracks and probably always would. (Of course, Wittenfeld's disinterest in living the life of the *nouveau riche* could be considered one of his virtues.)

Some criticized von Reuentahl's "aristocratic tastes," but this was not entirely fair. How he lived was not a matter of taste at all. It was the natural expression of who he was.

Scholars of Kaiser Reinhard's life seldom hid their astonishment at the simplicity and plainness of his private life in light of his breathtaking appearance, ambition, ability, and achievements. If anything, they would say, it was von Reuentahl who lived like royalty.

The foundation of von Reuentahl's lifestyle was the property he had inherited from his late father, but he did not content himself with becoming just another industrialist's son. Instead, he entered officer's school without relying on his inheritance at all. As a military man, he was able to sleep in even the worst conditions as if slumbering in a four-poster bed, and accepted plain food and hard work without complaint. As a result, the luxury of his day-to-day existence did not arouse resentment among the troops.

There is a legend. When von Reuentahl was in officer's school, studying the rise and fall of a certain empire on ancient Earth, he encountered the story of a once-trusted minister who raised the flag of rebellion against his emperor. The emperor asked: *What grievance has turned you against me?* And the rebellious minister replied: *I have no grievance. I simply wish to be emperor.* At this, the heterochromatic youth had murmured to himself, "No other reason for rebellion could be as just."

Thus the legend—although it was not in circulation before year 2 of the New Imperial Calendar. Nor is it clear whether anyone was present to hear von Reuentahl's words. Overall, it seems unwise to place too much store in it.

As for Kaiser Reinhard's view of von Reuentahl's lifestyle, he had no intention of enforcing abstinence on those under him simply because his own physical desires were so weak. Violence against women on the battlefield was strictly forbidden, with offenders punished severely and without mercy, but this was to ensure that military discipline and general trust in the armed forces was maintained. Reinhard resolutely refrained from meddling in the private affairs of his admirals, which is perhaps further proof of his magnanimity as a ruler.

And there were certainly grounds on which von Reuentahl's private affairs might be attacked. Even excluding those who bore ill will toward him, like Junior Minister of the Interior Heidrich Lang, he did not lack for critics. There were many who felt that a high-ranking admiral of the New Galactic Empire should be of good conduct and high morals.

Once, during a meeting in his office, the kaiser suddenly asked Mittermeier, "By the way, do you know the color of Marshal von Reuentahl's current lover?"

Mittermeier hesitated, turning the pages of his memory. Finally he offered the vague response, "I believe she had black hair, *mein Kaiser*."

"Wrong. Bright red. Apparently our marshal continues to monopolize the flower of the empire." The kaiser laughed merrily at Mittermeier's expression. He had gotten his information from his bodyguard Emil, who had noticed a single hair fall from von Reuentahl's shoulder as he left following a report on the repositioning of forces in the Phezzan Corridor battle zone.

Mittermeier was embarrassed on his friend's behalf, but Reinhard only meant it as a fleeting jest, not an indictment of von Reuentahl's private pursuits. The kaiser had no interest whatsoever in the romantic lives of others; furthermore, as a leader, he respected the individuality of each man he led.

"Imagine a gloomy, reticent Wittenfeld, a celibate von Reuentahl, a talkative Eisenach, a philandering Mittermeier, a boorish Mecklinger, an overbearing Müller! Everyone has their own nature. If von Reuentahl were breaking the law or deceiving others, that would be a different matter, but we can hardly put only one participant in a love affair in the dock."

The Reinhard who said such things certainly had the magnanimity necessary to control his admirals. Under a more critical ruler, who ignored individuality and judged men only according to how closely they adhered to his ideal, a man like Wittenfeld could never have flourished. When

Reinhard had first inherited the County Lohengramm, he had a tendency to link disappointment, anger, and admonishment directly together, punishing subordinates severely for their errors. After the death of Siegfried Kircheis, however, repentance for his intolerance seemed to have driven him toward self-control. And of course, as a practical matter, if every failure were punished severely, the famed upper ranks of the Galactic Imperial Navy would be empty. After all, virtually all of Reinhard's admirals had tasted defeat at the hands of Yang Wen-li, as indeed had Reinhard himself.

As the kaiser now saw it, his many tactical losses to the Magician had not been entirely without their positive side. They had served as a training ground for improving both his magnanimity as a ruler and his refinement as a general. And however miraculous Yang's string of victories had been, he had never managed to overturn the immense strategic advantage that Reinhard had secured over the alliance at the outset of their conflict. For the commander of a navy rather than a fleet, tactics meant less than strategy, and winning the battle paled beside winning the war. Reinhard had known this intellectually, of course, but his struggle with Yang had proven it in practice.

If the Free Planets Alliance had not had Yang Wen-li on their side, Reinhard's victory would have been far easier—perhaps too easy even to learn from. His awareness of this, indistinct as it was, was why he felt the death of Yang so keenly.

"And to think—when Kircheis died, I thought I had nothing left to lose," Reinhard murmured. He himself only partly realized how serious the words he spoke were, and how deeply connected to the purity of his vital energy.

Von Reuentahl was no rival to Yang Wen-li, but Reinhard rated his capacity and ability as a commander highly.

"If we judge based solely on the balance between intellect and valor, Oskar von Reuentahl was a singular presence at the time, whether among friend or foe"—this was Ernest Mecklinger's assessment of his colleague. In Mecklinger's view, Yang had leaned toward the intellectual side, while Wolfgang Mittermeier by nature preferred valor. Even the kaiser, who had surely reached the human limits of strategic thinking, was drawn to offensive tactics. His tactical defeat in the Vermillion War had partly been caused by neglect of his defenses. Von Reuentahl was at present untroubled by that particular vice.

III

After the September 1 Incident, minor riots and acts of sabotage continued to break out across the Neue Land.

Admiral Bergengrün delivered a report to his superior in his capacity as inspector general of the military. "Planned, systematic rioting accounts for half the total," he said. "The rest appears to be happenstance, or copycat incidents."

"What does our director general of civil affairs have to say about this disturbance of the peace?"

"Director Elsheimer feels that as long as travel and communications remain secure, there is nothing to fear from local unrest, and with luck it will remain at that level."

"He has pluck for a civilian officer. I suppose that we in the military should ensure that his modest request is granted. I leave the details in your hands."

"Yes, Your Excellency. By the way…"

"What?"

"A letter arrived at the governorate recently that I think you should read."

Von Reuentahl accepted the missive from Bergengrün and scanned it quickly before looking up with an ironic gleam in his mismatched eyes. "Well, well," he said. "What have we here?"

An hour later, Job Trünicht was summoned to the governor-general's office. He met von Reuentahl's unfriendly gaze with equanimity, being quite used to it by now.

Without a word, von Reuentahl tossed the letter onto his marble desk. He watched Trünicht's expression coldly as the high counselor began to read. When Trünicht remained uncharacteristically silent after finishing, von Reuentahl broke his silence.

"Quite an interesting letter, don't you think, High Counselor?"

"If I may, Your Excellency, what is interesting is, regrettably, not the same as what is true."

"Gather together a hundred items of interest and they'd surely add up to at least one truth, I'd say. And there is no need for evidence if those with power are willing to forgo it. Particularly in the autocratic system of governance you and your fellows despise—I mean, despised."

The irony in his voice was searing.

The letter was a denunciation of Trünicht. It alleged that the former head of the alliance was behind the wave of unrest that had rolled across the Neue Land since September 1, that his goal was to seize back the reins of power, and that he would eventually target the governor-general directly.

"Conversely, the democratic republicanism you put your faith in makes the will of the people concrete—or claims to, at least."

"The people are a kite on the wind. Powerless, however high they may rise."

"Surely they don't deserve such scorn from you. Weren't they the ones who made you head of the alliance, and supported you in that position? Ingratitude will not endear you to them."

In all honesty, von Reuentahl despised both Trünicht and the people who had placed him in the seat of power. He had no quarrel with those who would praise Ahle Heinessen, father of the Free Planets Alliance, or the republicans who had shared the travails of his Longest March. But the descendants of the alliance's founders had done nothing but live off their legacy for two hundred and fifty years. Finally defeated in war with the empire, some had even switched sides to preserve their comfortable lifestyles.

Trünicht was in that last category too, and had no right to criticize the people so shamelessly. And yet, as he considered this, von Reuentahl felt an unusual displeasure stir within him anew. He had detected a peculiar sincerity in Trünicht's dismissal of his supporters. Could the man truly have felt nothing but contempt for them all along?

•   •   •

Compared to Kaiser Reinhard, the "revolutionary who sat on a jeweled throne," von Reuentahl's political imagination was a few steps behind. He could carry out the tasks assigned to him with nothing overlooked, but was more noted for efficiency than creativity.

He had perfect respect for his superior and ruler as a public figure, but had not failed to notice Reinhard's private flaws and weaknesses. However immature the kaiser might be in private, however, his achievements, ability, and valor as a public figure could not be denied. Von Reuentahl, at least, was neither petty nor unjust enough to take this line of criticism.

Ernest Mecklinger's assessment of von Reuentahl after their first meeting is of interest here. "Ultimately," Mecklinger wrote, "I had the impression of a man who would never be satisfied under the authority of another." The one man who outranked him was the kaiser himself, and von Reuentahl had willingly accepted his position as Reinhard's retainer.

In turbulent times, the relationship between an ambitious lord and a capable minister is often as perilous as riding a unicycle along the blade of a sword. Reinhard and von Reuentahl's relationship conformed to this pattern, although special circumstances were also at work.

It was often suggested in later ages that if Kircheis had survived beyond IC 488, if he had remained the unambiguous "second man of the empire," the tension between Reinhard and von Reuentahl might have remained submerged. If nothing else, von Reuentahl would not have clashed so sharply with von Oberstein in the latter's capacity as minister of military affairs. All speculation, of course, but because Kircheis died young, having attracted almost no criticism as a public or private figure, the rich possibilities that may have lain in his future, and the future of the empire itself, cannot be denied.

After dismissing Trünicht, von Reuentahl summoned Bergengrün back to his office and issued a series of orders. Most concerned what remained of

Yang Wen-li's forces on Iserlohn Base. A few imperial ships had attempted an invasion of Iserlohn Corridor, despite the absence of orders to do so, and von Reuentahl made it clear once more that such ill-considered haste would not be tolerated from the military.

The governor-general was not, however, fool enough to permit free movement of people, supplies, or information in the corridor itself. Bottling up and isolating the remnants of Yang Wen-li's forces was the natural foundation of the Imperial Navy's strategy. Iserlohn Corridor might be the very definition of a hard target for offensive maneuvers, but simple isolation was easier to achieve. By cutting off the republic's access to information and supplies, the empire would increase the psychological pressure on its citizens.

As a result, for Julian Mintz and the other leaders of the Iserlohn Republic, the quality and quantity of the information they could gather would determine their very chances of survival.

IV

Julian Mintz, too, spent his days buried under the tasks and responsibilities that had been placed upon him.

Every day he put his materials in order a little more, preparing for the eventual writing of his biography of Yang Wen-li. Yang himself had not written any substantial works before his death. Had that death not come so early and after such a turbulent career, and had the length of his remaining years matched the scale of his youthful achievements, he would surely have been able to generalize his vast intellectual activities in written form. These rich possibilities, however, had been closed off by the end forced upon him.

Even so, he had left a mass of memorabilia behind, albeit fragmentary. The material covered many topics: strategy, tactics, history, contemporaries, politics and society, tea and alcohol. Julian was taking these disordered scraps of thought, speech, and action, putting them in order, and reconstituting them along with commentary of his own. In the brief moments where his responsibilities as leader of Iserlohn's military did not intrude, he sat at his desk and worked on his project of conveying the individual that Yang Wen-li had been to future generations. He did not find the work lonely. It felt like speaking to the dead.

The fragments of verbiage were also shards of the memories and moments that had made up the past six years for Julian himself. A single word could summon up rich background in his mind. And in every scene, Yang was there. He grew taller and shorter depending on the occasion— the memories were all viewed from the perspective of Julian, who had grown more than a foot taller since their first meeting, and the scenes did not come in chronological order.

"There are certainly things that can't be said in words, but you can only say that once you reach the limits of speech yourself."

"Words are like icebergs floating on the sea of our heart. Only a fraction of each is visible, but through them we perceive and feel the larger things beneath the surface."

"Use words deliberately, Julian. That lets you say more, more accurately, than you can with silence alone."

And:

"The right judgment depends on the right information and the right analysis."

All these things Yang had said to Julian.

Three years earlier, when the Alliance's military had fractured after the coup d'état by the Military Congress for the Rescue of the Republic, Yang had been forced to battle the powerful Eleventh Fleet. Because the two sides were fairly evenly matched in strength, and because Yang's defeat would have meant the end of the faction that opposed the coup, he had searched for the enemy desperately. When he received firm information that the Eleventh Fleet had divided its forces, as well as the locations of each individual division, he had thrown his reports into the air with joy, dancing clumsily and singing off-key with Julian as partner. Such was the value of accurate information.

As a result, Julian sought it through every avenue he could think of, and some more suggested by his deputies. It was only a matter of time before there was political and military upheaval at both ends of Iserlohn Corridor. Kaiser Reinhard was currently ignoring them as he built a new galactic order. But when cracks began to show in the glorious armor of his authority, the upheaval would begin.

Having made this strategic prediction, Julian's next task was to come up with countermeasures—he was not a historian of later ages, after all, but an active contemporary participant. The difficulty was that their best options in that moment would not necessarily remain optimal as their situation changed.

Who could have predicted what the galaxy would look like today just five short years ago? In SE 795, the Goldenbaum Dynasty's Galactic Empire had been locked in endless war with the Free Planets Alliance. When there were lulls in the fighting, squabbles on Phezzan filled the gaps. It had seemed as if the situation would roll sluggishly and monotonously on forever.

But even the calmest river has the occasional waterfall along its length. Might they be going over the edge of such a waterfall at that very moment? If so, the upheaval might come even earlier than expected. If only Marshal Yang had been alive, Julian could have sat back and let him captain the boat. Was it small-minded of Julian to miss Yang on one hand and hate those who had murdered him on the other?

At this thought, Yang Wen-li spoke in a whisper that came from some obscure corner of Julian's memories.

"No, Julian, I don't think so. You can't love unless you can also hate. That's how it seems to me, anyway."

He was right. Yang, the people in his orbit, the microcosm they had made—how Julian had loved and treasured them all! It was inevitable that he would hate those who had soiled and smashed what he loved.

In the same way, precisely because Julian held the principles of democratic republican governance in the highest esteem—no doubt partly due to Yang's influence—he loathed the autocratic system that stood against them. To love everything was an impossibility.

But Yang's words should not be interpreted too broadly. They were not an encouragement of hate. They simply pointed out the fundamental contradiction in platitudes like "love conquers all."

This introspective side of Julian was clearly part of his inheritance from Yang. The risk was that it might undermine his enterprising dynamism, or take him from a conservative position to a reactionary one.

This was a source of mild concern for Alex Caselnes and certain others among Julian's self-appointed "guardians." But their younger fellows mocked them for fretting.

"Don't you think it's his talent you should be worried about?" asked Poplin with a grin.

"Or he might get mixed up with some femme fatale and meet with disaster," said Attenborough.

Not everyone in their generation had reconstructed their psyches as well as these two. One example was Lieutenant Commander Soon "Soul" Soulzzcuaritter, who had fought valiantly to protect Yang from his assassins. When reunited with Julian at the hospital in Iserlohn, he could barely force his words through the pain.

"I survived. Alone…"

Devastation at having outlived two commanders, Bucock and Yang, had robbed Soul's expression and voice of their former forthrightness and good cheer.

"We're lucky you did, commander," Julian had told him. "Your survival is our only consolation."

Julian couldn't let himself sink into melancholy alone. However reluctantly, however much the outward form preceded the reality, as leader of the Iserlohn Republic's military, he had to fulfill the duties of his office. He could not lead the people in a pessimistic direction. Though cursing himself as inadequate to the task, he wished he could salve Soul's wounded heart.

He had not lied to Soul, after all. That someone had been rescued from that ship, even just one man, was an undeniable consolation to Julian, von Schönkopf, Rinz, Machungo, and the others who had tried and failed to rescue Yang.

Nor did Soul allow himself to wallow in grief forever. As soon as he could walk again, he found a new position under Attenborough.

The only topic of conversation among the leaders of the Iserlohn Republic these days was Job Trünicht.

The mere fact that Trünicht was allowing Kaiser Reinhard to order him around was enough to arouse the suspicion and distrust of Caselnes and von Schönkopf. Attenborough half-seriously considered sending Reinhard a letter warning him not to trust the former head of the alliance.

"It's Trünicht, after all," Attenborough said to Julian. "He's obviously up to no good. I don't want to see the kaiser killed by some nonentity as well." He smiled ruefully. "Although I suppose that to him we're nonentities too. Anyway, whatever that old fox Trünicht is planning, anyone taking on the famous Marshal von Oberstein has their work cut out for them."

"The Golden Age."

Julian felt that he had finally begun to understand the meaning of this term. If he did not actually speak it aloud, this was less because he feared ridicule than because applying the label at this late stage seemed unnecessary. It was only once an age had passed that its true preciousness could be appreciated—surely a cruel trap laid by the Creator in the understanding and sensibility of humanity.

Even so, it was not impossible for a Golden Age to return. Building something similar, at least, was the goal toward which Julian and his colleagues strived.

He saw Karin more often these days, although they only ever spoke over lunch tables or offices. If their shared mentor Poplin heard this, he would doubtless roar with laughter.

"Are you going to work on the *Record of Marshal Yang* after work today too?"

"I had planned to."

"You're such a shut-in!"

This was Karin's judgment. More accurately, it was her way of expressing concern, in a tone others might reserve for passing judgment. Julian understood this. More accurately, he felt as if he did. Karin was a woman rich in emotion and not skilled at keeping it under control when she spoke.

Just the other day, Karin had run into her biological father, von Schönkopf, in the walkway outside headquarters.

"How are you today, Corporal von Kreutzer?" he asked.

"Suddenly much worse."

Even this could be called progress—it *was* a reply, after all. In the past she had sometimes simply turned and walked away the moment she caught sight of him.

"Oh, dear, how unfortunate. And you must be so charming in a good mood, too, if that's how pretty you are in a bad one," was the sort of tired line von Schönkopf did not reply with.

"No need to hide how delighted you are to see me," he said instead. "We both know the truth."

And with that casual pronouncement, he walked off. Karin watched him go, at a loss for words.

As much as Karin might hate to hear it, Julian thought, she simply wasn't on von Schönkopf's level when it came to acting. Karin apparently recognized this too, and her attitude toward von Schönkopf had softened somewhat. If anything, she seemed more irritated by her own inability to remain calm and composed around him.

"I'm sure Frederica was telling the truth," Julian once heard her mutter. "But still…"

At a meeting on the topic of base defense, Julian raised the topic of Karin with von Schönkopf himself. Not to criticize, but simply to learn what von Schönkopf was thinking.

"Corporal Kreutzer's opinion of me is her problem, not mine," said von Schönkopf. "If you're asking about my opinion of her—well, that one is *my* problem."

"And what is your opinion of her, admiral?"

"I've never disliked a beautiful woman. Much less one with spirit."

"Is she like her mother in that way?"

"What's this? I see our young commander's planning to expand his horizons!"

Von Schönkopf laughed obnoxiously, but then patted Julian on the shoulder and offered a surprisingly serious comment.

"In any case, the daughter is far more impressive than the mother in this case. No doubt about that."

Frederica Greenhill Yang also spent her days amid a blizzard of work. She had done the same thing after her father's death. Concentrating on duty and responsibility is a way to put grief aside for the present moment, and presumably that psychological effect was at work in her case too.

"I wonder if it would be better if I could drink," she would say, and Julian had no reply. "It's too late now, of course, but I think if Jessica Edwards had been alive we could have been good friends."

Now that Frederica mentioned her, Julian realized that Edwards had also thrown herself into politics after the death of her lover. He shuddered at the thought of Frederica ending up as Edwards had. Shaking his head to banish the unwanted images, he asked Frederica if she had given Karin some advice.

"I only told her that Admiral von Schönkopf has never been a coward," Frederica said. "It's the truth, after all."

"It seems to have affected her deeply. Corporal von Kreutzer reveres you, you know. I've heard her say she wants to be just like you."

"Oh, my! Hopefully not as far as cooking is concerned, at least. Taking Madam Caselnes as her model would be a better choice for her future."

Frederica smiled, and Julian felt the winds of early spring rise in his heart. Warm and kind, but still containing wintry particles that were here to stay. And Julian was powerless against it.

Later that day, he received a telephone call from Mrs. Caselnes herself.

"I'm having Frederica and Admiral von Schönkopf's daughter over for dinner," she said. "You must come too, Julian. The more, the merrier."

"Thank you," said Julian, "but are you sure it wouldn't be better to invite the admiral instead of me?"

"Fathers have their own lives to lead by night. Besides, he's not the type for family time."

Inviting Karin and arranging a meeting with her father would only make things worse, Mrs. Caselnes explained.

She might be the most powerful person on Iserlohn Base, Julian thought. He gratefully accepted her invitation. Neither he nor Frederica had made any effort to cook since Yang's death. There seemed little point in making the effort when they were eating alone.

With four Caselneses and three guests, dinner was a lively affair. But the husband of Iserlohn's greatest power broker seemed less than enthused as he ate. Once the meal was over and they had retired to the living room, he said, "All right, Julian, let's leave the chattering women to their games while we men have a drink." With a final parting glance at the women, he fled into his combined library and parlor. Julian followed, and shortly afterward Mrs. Caselnes brought in a tray for the fugitive pair, loaded down with ham, cheese, ice, sardines in oil, and more.

"You boys have fun in here," she said. "I have to wonder about a host who abandons the battlefield so quickly, though."

"It was just too dazzling with the flower of Iserlohn's womanhood all gathered under one roof," Caselnes said. "We needed to take refuge somewhere cool and dark."

"Admiral von Schönkopf or Commander Poplin can get away with lines like that, but you, my dear, cannot," said Mrs. Caselnes.

"But saying one occasionally keeps things fresh. Right, Julian?"

Julian smiled and declined to weigh in.

Frederica, Karin, and the two young ladies of the Caselnes household were playing a game called Horsemania. This involved placing two tiny horse-shaped pieces in a shaker and letting them tumble onto a mat. The player's score depended on how the horses landed. If they were both on their backs, twenty points; if one was on its feet and the other on its side, five points—and so on.

The man of the house frowned at the laughter that bubbled out of the library. "I don't know what they see in that pointless game," he said, refilling Julian's glass. "Although I will grant that laughter is much better than weeping."

Julian felt exactly the same way. Whatever the reason, Iserlohn was laughing again. There was still a chance of regression, but the people had recovered from the memory of winter and were moving from spring toward summer.

VI

Did what later ages referred to as "the rootstalk of that poisonous flower men call conspiracy" truly exist at that time?

It did. But it was not in a position to publicly reveal that existence, or what it had achieved. Only once it had become the strongest and largest power, or at least close enough that it was certain of its advantage, would it show itself above ground.

Beneath the surface of a certain planet, Archbishop de Villiers of the Church of Terra continued to devise and direct countless wicked, shadowy plans. In his spare moments, he spoke of his thoughts to the lower-ranking bishops and priests.

"Do you not understand why it was Yang Wen-li we killed, and not Kaiser Reinhard?"

Even his voice was filled with the light of arrogance. Yang's successful assassination had made de Villiers' power and authority preeminent among the archbishops.

"To concentrate the hatred and resentments of the people against Reinhard, we must make him a more absolute ruler, and finally a tyrant. When the time comes to oppose that tyrant, that opposition must be rooted in faith in the Church—not that grotesquerie of spirit men call democracy!"

From a theocratic perspective, democracy is indeed grotesque, being a system and spirit premised on multiple systems of values coexisting side by side. Furthermore, when usurping a system of power, it is always easier to take over one that is unified than one that is divided. Better, too, if the people have little awareness of their rights and are accustomed to being ruled. The Church of Terra did not have an iron arm like the one Rudolf von Goldenbaum had used to topple the Galactic Federation.

"Rebellions by high-placed retainers arouse a tyrant's suspicion and result in purges. These unsettle the other retainers and invite further rebellion. The history of any dynasty is nothing more than the repetition of this cycle, and we will turn this iron law against the Lohengramm Dynasty."

De Villiers, it seemed, was in his own way a historian. The lessons he took from his studies were not philosophical but practical, chiefly concerned with intrigue and conspiracy, but it took a sharp mind to accumulate this much information and analyze it for statistical trends.

"In ancient times, when the great empire of Rome ruled over our beloved Terra, it was induced in a moment of weakness to make a certain monotheism its imperial faith. This allowed it to control history and civilization for many centuries. We should remember this incident and consider it a guidepost."

De Villiers' haughty pronouncements must have made him some enemies among the elderly archbishops, but any who might have spoken out were long gone. On the contrary, it was flatterers who were in the majority now.

"Is that why you seek to provoke von Reuentahl to rebellion, Your Grace?"

"Von Reuentahl is one of the new dynasty's highest-placed retainers, and is rich in experience despite his youthful age. A betrayal by von Reuentahl would shake even Kaiser Reinhard. *Who will be next to turn?*, he would wonder, unable to control his suspicions about his other loyal retainers. All we need do is amplify this."

Other followers spoke, offering a more pessimistic view. "Oskar von Reuentahl is certainly an outstanding general. But will those he commands ultimately accept his orders to hoist the flag of revolt against the kaiser?"

"That is what concerns me. Even if every single one of von Reuentahl's five million men swear fealty to him, that still amounts to less than a fifth of the empire's forces. How could he possibly defeat the golden brat if that is the extent of his resources?"

De Villiers chuckled. There was no need to worry, he explained. Measures had been taken.

"Yang Wen-li is dead. Von Reuentahl will die too. As will the golden brat who dares call himself kaiser. Their bodies will fertilize the realization of our righteousness."

After that, all of human society would be united in a vast empire where religion and politics were one. In the past, when humanity had been restricted to a single planet's surface, a state resembling this had endured for centuries. Now it would be reborn on a galactic scale, with de Villiers as midwife. Long years of patience would come to an end and the time of glory would arrive.

De Villiers laughed once more. It was a black laugh—the laughter of a man who intended to reverse the course of history through his intrigues.

CHAPTER FOUR:

I

HILDEGARD VON MARIENDORF, chief advisor to Imperial Headquarters, reported for duty again on September 7.

"I apologize for the inconvenience caused by my absence. I hope that it can be forgiven, and I will not allow personal matters to interfere with my work again."

Thus spoke Hilda to her only superior in the entire galaxy. That superior, Kaiser Reinhard, responded with an awkward nod. Not speaking, not able to speak, he dismissed her from his office. The interaction revealed anew the immaturity that belied Reinhard's magnanimity as a public figure, but in fact Hilda was grateful that it had been brief. If Reinhard spoke to her, what could she say in reply? She would be paralyzed with embarrassment. And what if he apologized?

That was only a dream, Your Majesty. Please, put it out of your mind, as I have already done.

A different tack, perhaps?

I am Your Majesty's subject. Whatever orders you see fit to give, I shall obey.

Neither reply struck her as ideal. Of course, he had nothing to apologize for in the first place.

Hilda had returned to work simply because she could no longer ignore her official responsibilities. She had not yet decided how to respond to the kaiser's proposal of marriage.

Resign her position as chief advisor? No, a resignation after an absence would surely invite speculation from others. On reflection, it was rather mysterious that the young, unmarried kaiser and his young, unmarried, female advisor were not already the subject of rumors. No doubt it was because Reinhard seemed so aloof from such matters, while Hilda had always kept their relationship strictly professional, never even attempting to charm herself into his good graces. But now a new fact had appeared. What would become of them? What should she do? For all her perspicacity, Hilda had failed to find the answers after an entire week of thinking.

As for the youthful, handsome kaiser, his emotional state was one he had never experienced as a public figure and only very rarely as a private one: he was at a loss.

He had proposed to Hilda. Had her reaction been immediate, even an immediate rejection, he could have put his feelings in order. But he had yet to receive a reply at all, leaving his awareness adrift on the surface of his heart. He understood that his question had not been the sort to which an immediate answer could be expected. And yet.

And yet, if some might jeer at Reinhard's immaturity in private, none could deny his diligence in carrying out his imperial duties and responsibilities. He continued to govern with steadfast reason and judgment. A cynical observer might reasonably conclude that he had thrown himself into his work to escape his private anxieties, but even if so he deserved credit for compartmentalizing those anxieties away from his administration. Reinhard had only once in his life ignored his obligations as a public figure, and that had been immediately after Kircheis's death.

However, even Reinhard's vast responsibilities as ruler allowed the occasional break. At these times he found himself uncertain of what to do. With an air of distraction, he would sip coffee or page through dry tomes with only their thickness to recommend them. Sometimes he played three-dimensional chess with his aide Emil or his secondary aide von Rücke, or took the two of them out riding through the grounds.

Having made little time in the past for the finer things in life, Reinhard had difficulty filling his schedule when neither war nor governance were on it. And, of course, he did not fill the space with romantic adventures.

His senior ministers were uneasy. Not just about the way Reinhard seemed to find himself at loose ends these days, but also out of concern that his repeated fevers might presage a more serious illness.

His condition seemed less like a debilitating disease than a small mass of cloud that occasionally crossed the face of the sun. In the past, though, Reinhard's brilliant vitality had not permitted even the tiniest cloud to dim it. For that reason, and because he was as irreplaceable a presence as the sun, his retainers could not help but fret.

"Perhaps the Westerland incident was a greater shock to His Majesty than we realized…"

Commodore Kissling, head of Reinhard's personal guard, kept his face expressionless as he heard such rumors go by. He knew that Hilda had spent the night in the kaiser's private quarters, and that the kaiser had visited the Mariendorf estate early the following morning bearing a bouquet of flowers, but naturally never spoke of these facts to anyone. While not, perhaps, the equal of Senior Admiral Ernst von Eisenach, the "Silent Commander," Kissling did know how to keep his mouth shut. He would have kept Reinhard's secrets even if the kaiser had visited a different woman every night. His tight-lipped discretion had hitherto gone to waste, but now it was proving useful at last. Personally, of course, Kissling did not see why a man of the kaiser's stature should not be forgiven the odd mistress or lover.

There was an awkward side to Reinhard that was stubborn almost beyond redemption. He had proposed to the countess; this was unshakable fact. Whatever her answer might turn out to be, it would show a lack of integrity to have relations with other women while waiting for it. Of course, he had always viewed such affairs as more trouble than they were worth in the first place, so it may be objected that this talk of integrity was simply a way of justifying his existing position.

"Some insist that, because the kaiser was attractive, he must—*should*— have been a playboy," Ernest Mecklinger once observed. "How they explain the existence of ugly yet libertine men, I cannot say." A cynical view, but it was true that few would have guessed the poverty of Reinhard's romantic life from his evident beauty and power.

In any case, Reinhard made no attempt to pluck any other blooms from the gardens available to him.

In a development that drew a rueful but sympathetic smile from Count von Mariendorf, it eventually became common for Reinhard to go out after completing his official duties for the day. He discovered the worlds of theater, music, and art, in which he had never before shown any interest. Solitude, it seemed, he now felt as a burden.

The kaiser's new interests were greeted with less enthusiasm by the admirals he pressed into service as his companions, although their complaints remained private. Senior Admiral Wittenfeld was dragged to a classical ballet performance in perhaps the most egregious example of suboptimal deployment. Lutz found Wittenfeld's plight hilarious, but was soon ordered to attend a poetry recital himself, from which he returned in despair. Wahlen waited with dread for his turn to come around, giving serious thought to how he might trade places with Mecklinger, the "Artist-Admiral," who was posted to the worlds of the old empire and therefore unavailable.

"His Majesty is himself a masterpiece. Why should he take an interest in more forced expressions of the artistic impulse at all? The only relationship the powerful should have with the world of art is as sources of funding. Their presence in the audience is superfluous and their opinions unnecessary. Such things only breed charlatans, who flatter the tastes of the powerful while claiming to be great masters."

This was Marshal Wolfgang Mittermeier's critique, although this disinterested perspective was perhaps only possible because his duties at the head of the Imperial Space Armada excused him from the kaiser's outings.

"If you know so much about the art world, by all means accompany His Majesty in our place," lamented Müller. "This evening I am to endure some kind of avant-garde concert I have no hope of understanding. Even a war or revolt would be preferable."

This was not, of course, meant as a prophecy. But, in days to come, Müller would recall these words with sadness.

II

As Reinhard applied himself to the tasks of governance, brooded over the uncharted territory he faced in his private life, and swept his admiralty up into an impromptu "Autumn of Art," something was burgeoning deep in the soils of conspiracy.

The rootstalks in question had snaked across the galaxy to reach the bowels of Phezzan. That they had not taken a direct route was unsurprising. This was no single root; it was a tangle that had reached toward the same sun. And the eerie growth was greedy for nourishment.

Junior Minister of the Interior and Domestic Safety Security Bureau Chief Heidrich Lang and former landesherr of Phezzan Adrian Rubinsky were engaged in a discussion. Had Oskar von Reuentahl seen the pair, he would have been gripped by the urge to shoot them on the spot, but their meeting was not a public affair. The venue was a room in one of Rubinsky's many safe houses in which the deaths of several people had been decided in the past. The lighting in the room shone through crystal glass, illuminating key tones of green like an artificial forest. The two conspirators differed in appearance and age, but they did share one thing: mutual contempt. Although Rubinsky was, perhaps, more aware of this than Lang.

Lang mopped his brow with a handkerchief. This was one of the many ways he concealed his expression from those he spoke to. Not allowing his sneer to reach the surface, Rubinsky continued to explain.

"If the kaiser does not visit the Neue Land, it will be difficult to ensure that Marshal von Reuentahl launches his revolt. As I am sure that you appreciate, minister, we must bait the marshal with an opportunity so inviting that it clouds his reason."

"That may be so, but is it wise to prepare such advantageous circumstances for the man?" Lang replied. "What if—what if, you understand—his revolt succeeds?" He could not help feeling apprehensive about this prospect, which must be prevented at all costs. Lang was not noted for objective self-assessment, but even he knew that if von Reuentahl carried off a regicide and seized control of the galaxy, Lang would be the first to be purged. It would be both tragedy and farce.

"No need to worry," Rubinsky said. "The assassination attempt on the kaiser will only be for show. A performance. Everything has been precisely calibrated to ensure that he will escape unscathed and determined to strike von Reuentahl."

"You're certain of that?"

"Would you like it in writing?"

Lang replied with pointed silence.

His aim was to devour the sumptuous dish that was the Galactic Empire, with his loathing of von Reuentahl as knife and his greed for power as fork. In an age where military force reigned supreme, achieving this goal would not be possible without borrowing the authority and power of the Kaiser.

If Reinhard became suspicious of his loyal admirals and made his enlightened rule a reign of terror, Lang would wield absolute power as the kaiser's special prosecutor—and executioner. Rebellion by von Reuentahl would be an unmissable opportunity to bring about this state of affairs.

After all, how could Reinhard maintain his faith in Mittermeier and the others after a rebellion, even if it were put down? Mittermeier was von Reuentahl's closest friend, and would be the greatest tactician alive once he was dead. If Lang could somehow maneuver Mittermeier and von Oberstein into mutual annihilation, nothing would remain to bar him from power. Hildegard von Mariendorf was just a girl, with no power of her own. Her father was a sincere but talentless nonentity. And, away from the battlefield, the senior officers from Müller on down worried him no more than a box of toy soldiers.

But there were certain things that Lang did not realize.

First, that his plan, or rather fantasy, had been conjured up and nurtured within his psyche by Rubinsky's subtle machinations. Second, that he was to Rubinsky nothing but a tool, useful enough in his way but cheap, vulgar, and entirely disposable. Rubinsky had taken care not to allow Lang's attention to alight on these facts.

If anyone was aware of them, it was not Lang but the Galactic Empire's minister of military affairs, Marshal Paul von Oberstein. Certainly von Oberstein's artificial eyes, with its onboard optical computers, saw far more than Lang did. Equally certain, however, was that even von Oberstein did not understand everything he saw. If Lang was a tool Rubinsky used to advance his intrigues, he was also a tool von Oberstein used for political purposes. Rubinsky, of course, considered both of them part of his tool kit. Van Oberstein was his superior and the benefactor who had appointed him to his current position, although this was not widely known. But van Oberstein's most generous act as Rubinsky's benefactor was yet to come—when he would be the sacrifice that ensured his protégé's success.

Both Rubinsky and Lang wanted von Reuentahl's rebellion to take place, but their motivations and goals were entirely different. Where Lang expected a controlled fire, extinguished according to plan, Rubinsky hoped to spark an all-encompassing inferno. Rubinsky was aware of this gap between them, but Lang was not. He had his suspicions, but had failed to confirm them. He was no more a match for Rubinsky than he was for von Oberstein. Rubinsky could at least sneer at himself in the mirror. For Lang, this was impossible.

In the end, Lang would go down in history as a dishonorable and unfaithful minister to the Lohengramm Dynasty. He was not devoid of redeeming qualities—at home, he was a good husband and a caring father—but these were not nearly sufficient for him to avoid criticism of his acts as a public figure.

It was undoubtedly the Age of Ambition that some later labelled it. Kaiser Reinhard himself, born to a poor household that was noble in name only, had risen to become an admiral of the old dynasty while still a teenager, and been crowned emperor in his early twenties.

For the past five centuries, humanity had been ruled by the descendants of Rudolf von Goldenbaum—some enlightened, some less so; some direct descendants, others members of branch lines. Only two men in history had defeated the despotism of that bloodline: Ahle Heinessen and Reinhard von Lohengramm. Their methods and beliefs had differed, but neither man's name would ever be erased from history.

One original can inspire a legion of imitators. Even Reinhard's goal of ruling a unified galaxy had been inspired by Kaiser Rudolf's achievements. Of course, Reinhard aimed not to imitate Rudolf but to exceed him, and by the age of twenty-five he had largely succeeded.

The scale of Reinhard's achievements filled the multitudes with awe.

Lang was surely among their number, but unlike them he did not view the young, handsome conqueror as infallible or holy. An infallible Reinhard would not have let Kircheis die, or himself be defeated by Yang Wen-li.

Lang intended to make Reinhard his puppet. The first step was to rob him of his faithful and capable retainers, isolating him amid suspicion and distrust. As inexorably as the kaiser's fortunes sank, Lang's own would rise.

III

It was late August when bizarre rumors began to circulate on Phezzan, but in September these underground streams bubbled to the surface and an unceasing flow of ominous stories reached the ears even of imperial officials.

"Governor-General von Reuentahl plans to betray the kaiser."

"Von Reuentahl knows he's no match for the kaiser in battle, so he's going to invite him to Heinessen on the pretext of inspecting the Neue Land and assassinate him on the way."

"After assassinating the kaiser, von Reuentahl will produce the missing Erwin Josef II and declare the restoration of the Goldenbaum Dynasty— but he'll act as regent, so that he can stay in control of the government and military. And from what I hear, not long after that he plans to crown himself kaiser."

"No, he's not going to assassinate Kaiser Reinhard. He's just going to force the kaiser to write a statement of abdication and retire from public life, so that von Reuentahl can take his place."

"In any case, the kaiser's so afraid of von Reuentahl that he can't even leave Phezzan."

"I hear von Reuentahl's going to send the kaiser an invitation to Heinessen, but of course the kaiser will never accept it."

"If anything, he'll probably recall von Reuentahl to Phezzan for questioning."

Rumors of rebellion had swirled around von Reuentahl before, in late winter of the same year, but he and Reinhard had held a public dialog to ensure that they ended as just that—rumors. But would an amicable resolution be possible this time? None had the confidence to make such a prediction.

Baron Wenzel von Hassellbag, Reinhard's grand chamberlain, was the younger brother-in-law of Viscountess Schafhausen, a friend of Reinhard's elder sister the Archduchess von Grünewald. Von Hassellbag had inherited his barony after being adopted into the family. He was not noted for his shrewdness, but he was warm and sincere and devoid of ambition, which perfectly qualified him for his position. As grand chamberlain, he was expected not only to assist the kaiser in the realm of governance, but also to ensure that His Majesty's private life went smoothly—although Reinhard lived so plainly that his bodyguard Emil von Salle could usually handle such matters alone.

It was von Hassellbag who brought the rumors racing around Phezzan to the kaiser's attention. It was not a slip of the tongue. A missive arrived from von Reuentahl requesting that Reinhard visit the planet Heinessen, and von Hassellbag noticed it on the table in the library at Reinhard's new residence and brought it to the kaiser personally. Noticing the uneasy expression on his grand chamberlain's face, Reinhard forced him to explain. Or, at least, this is how von Hassellbag described it in the memoirs he wrote in his twilight years.

The following day—September 10, to be precise—Reinhard convened a meeting of his top navy officials at Imperial Headquarters. They arrived to find him already in a dark mood, with unseen storm clouds gathered at his brow. He reported the invitation from von Reuentahl and declared his intention to accept it.

His eyes fell on the minister of military affairs, Marshal von Oberstein, who stepped half a pace forward. "Your Majesty is, I trust, aware of the peculiar rumors circulating at court and among the people. Until it can be ascertained what truth, if any, lies behind them, would it not be better to remain on Phezzan?"

"Idiotic drivel!" Reinhard was visibly enraged, his ice-blue eyes blazing like flame through sapphire. "Von Reuentahl would never harm me. I do not doubt him. Nor do I fear him. Do you mean to drive a wedge between me and a trusted retainer for the sake of these preposterous lies?"

Von Oberstein's cybernetic eyes gleamed.

"In that case, I hope that Your Majesty will at least consider traveling with a fleet of ships."

"And invite further uncertainty and fear? Why should an emperor need a fleet of ships to travel within his own empire? If these useless comments are the best you can offer, keep them to yourself."

Reinhard calmed his breathing, then fixed his gaze on another attendee.

"Senior Admiral Müller."

"Yes, Your Majesty."

"You are hereby appointed chief of my retinue. Begin the preparations for our departure."

"Yes, Your Majesty." Müller bowed his sandy-haired head slightly.

There was a brief silence, and then another man opened his mouth to speak: Senior Admiral Kornelias Lutz.

"Your Majesty, might I have permission to join your retinue? My younger sister is married to a civilian officer in the Neue Land governorate, and I have not seen her in some time. This would give me the opportunity to do so."

With this attack from the flank, Lutz successfully broke through the wall of Reinhard's hitherto impregnable fortress. One reason for his success was the fact that the official change of capital and accompanying military restructuring had rendered his temporary post as fleet commander for the Phezzan region somewhat moot. Until he received a new assignment, Lutz was effectively without duties, only active as a counselor at Imperial Headquarters and the Ministry of Defense. Under the circumstances, his request to accompany Reinhard on his journey was a reasonable one.

Later, after they had left the kaiser's presence, Wittenfeld lamented, "What a disappointment! Why doesn't His Majesty take me with him?"

Lutz flashed him a grin, a hint of purple in his blue eyes. "I'm sure His Majesty would take you if he actually expected to grapple with Marshal von Reuentahl," he said. "Let's hope this trip is a peaceful one."

More mystifying to Lutz and his fellow admirals was the fact that Countess Hildegard von Mariendorf, usually a permanent fixture by the kaiser's side, would be remaining behind.

"Fräulein von Mariendorf has not been entirely well of late. Exposure to warp would be inadvisable in her weakened state."

This was the explanation offered by the kaiser himself, and so his admirals accepted it. Now that they thought about it, the sagacious countess had not been called to today's meeting either. So that was the reason for her recent string of absences, they thought.

In truth, however, Reinhard had another, far more personal reason for not taking her with him. More than ten days had passed since their night together, and although Hilda had resumed her duties at headquarters, she had yet to give him an answer to his proposal.

She had never suffered from such indecision before, but every time she considered it, she found herself miserably standing before the same question, unable to find the answer: Would marrying her bring Reinhard happiness?

Reinhard summoned her to his office to inform her of his decision.

"Fräulein," he said, adopting a crisply businesslike manner. "At the end of this month, I will depart for the Neue Land."

"Yes, Your Majesty. The news had reached me."

"You are to remain on Phezzan."

A pause. "Yes, Your Majesty."

"I would like you to use this time to decide on your answer to the matter I raised the other day." The young kaiser evaded the countess's gaze, keeping his eyes fixed on her smoky blond hair instead. "I refer to my proposal of marriage, naturally."

This unnecessary clarification was arguably an example of Reinhard's immaturity. But it also showed his sincerity, and in any case Hilda was just glad he had given her until his return. A more impatient man, a man who put himself above others in all things, might have demanded her answer before he left. Reinhard was, after all, an absolute ruler. He could have done anything he pleased, without regard for Hilda's will at all. The way he had chosen to act caused the balance of Hilda's heart to tilt more deeply in a certain direction.

As an administrator, Hilda had been as efficient as ever since returning to imperial headquarters, but her creative thinking had lost some of its brilliance. Her ability to concentrate and maintain her mental energy had not, it seemed, entirely recovered its former level.

Hilda was aware of this, and so could not argue with Reinhard's decision to leave her behind. She had also heard the rumors about von Reuentahl, of course, but considered them an uninspired rehash of the nonsense of spring. This conclusion itself might constitute evidence of her temporarily weakened intellect and will. On the other hand, she also trusted Müller and the others in Reinhard's retinue.

Furthermore, there was something Hilda herself wanted to do.

"I shall visit the kaiser's sister—the Archduchess von Grünewald."

This idea had been with her since her fateful night with Reinhard, but no opportunity to put it into practice had presented itself. Reinhard's absence might make it possible. Hilda had no objection to Reinhard's sister knowing the entire situation as her father did—indeed, she wished this were so. Annerose had, after all, raised Reinhard with tenderness and care, and knew all his strengths and weaknesses.

Reinhard had lived a life rich in splendor but not in variety. In fact, his life had been rather simple. His values were clear, his goals unambiguous; it had remained only for him to keep his eyes fixed on the latter as he advanced.

A simple life is inevitable for those who must turn their full intellect and ability to the task of defeating a mighty enemy. In Reinhard's case, the impossibly vast goal of toppling the Goldenbaum Dynasty had always helped him find the shortest route through the uncharted wilderness before him.

Yang Wen-li, on the other hand, had trod a far more complicated and winding intellectual path. His faith in democracy had never wavered, but he had certainly experienced its worst abuses, both directly and indirectly.

There had always been a spiral of ambivalence in Yang's life, thought, and values. His apparently eccentric but actually stable character and unfailing broadmindedness had helped him retain control.

In brooding over the Westerland Atrocity, Reinhard was, perhaps, a frailer ruler than the "Steel Giant" Rudolf von Goldenbaum had been.

But it was not strength in the Rudolfian sense that Hilda sought from him.

Reinhard had only an imperfect perception of Hilda's thoughts and feelings. Once he had said what needed to be said, he raised an awkward hand and tried to leave the room first. As his motion raised a whisper of wind, Hilda spoke.

"Your Majesty."

"Yes?"

"Please be careful."

The young emperor looked at his beautiful advisor as if puzzled. When he digested the meaning of her words, a smile almost appeared on his face. He nodded once, and then turned to leave.

Hilda had a sympathizer and advisor in her father. Setting Yang aside as a special case, who did Reinhard have? None of those who had supported him this way in the past were close enough to hear him call now. Or if they were, they were not visible to mortal eyes.

Even loyal retainers like Mittermeier and Müller could never act as confidants of this sort. The exposure of his immaturity and vulnerability to the Mariendorfs had been an inevitable result of events, and the prospect of approaching Mittermeier or Müller to discuss his private life—of allowing them to learn of his weaknesses—held only unease.

IV

As for Mittermeier, he was too busy with his multiple key positions in the military to volunteer for the kaiser's retinue like Lutz, but he did invite Müller into his office and grill him on the matter, from the broadest outlines to the smallest details. Müller was just two years younger than him, and he trusted his friend and comrade deeply.

"I think I know what concerns you," Mittermeier said. "In June, Yang Wen-li was assassinated while traveling to meet the kaiser. You fear that this tragedy may be repeated."

"I do." Müller nodded, a hint of anxiety in his sand-colored eyes. Those who tasted success always sought to re-create it; this was simply how the human mind worked. "I would have preferred that the kaiser remain on Phezzan, but with the situation as it is, a cancellation would only encourage worse imaginings among the people."

"Well said. Still, the craft of all this!"

With rumors circulating that the kaiser was afraid to leave the capital lest he fall victim to von Reuentahl's rebellion, Reinhard's personality all but guaranteed that he would refuse to remain in a safe place. This, in turn, would prove other rumors true. It was a trap designed to drag him to the Neue Land no matter how he responded. A simple, effective, and utterly brazen trap. Mittermeier shuddered.

Had this conspiracy been in preparation since von Reuentahl's relationship with Duke Lichtenlade's daughter had been revealed, some six months earlier? If so, was the distasteful weasel Heidrich Lang pulling the strings?

This seemed unlikely. Lang's mastery of intrigue aside, he did not seem to Mittermeier the sort who could organize and execute something on this scale. It seemed more likely that Lang himself was under the influence of another, still more cunning figure. It would not be long before this suspicion was proven correct.

"That said," Mittermeier continued, "These conspirators cannot have much in the way of military capacity. If the kaiser travels with fifty or a hundred ships, this should be sufficient to deter them without aggravating von Reuentahl."

"True. But whether His Majesty will agree even to that…"

"Let me make the request. I'm sure he will approve a force of that size."

The two young admirals shared a rueful smile. The kaiser's willfulness and pride could be vexing, but were also among the reasons they loved him.

"By the way, has the minister of military affairs offered any further opinions about all this?" Mittermeier asked, an ironic gleam in his lively grey eyes. They all knew that von Oberstein viewed von Reuentahl's invitation with suspicion, and when the topic of conversation turned to the minister, Mittermeier's feelings were expressed directly in his physiology.

If von Reuentahl does rebel, he will muster his forces for a decisive frontal assault. He is not the type to use intrigue and deception to get close enough to the kaiser to stab him in the back—unlike some I could mention.

But Mittermeier could not say this, no matter how much he might want to. Too much was at stake. A higher rank was not always license to speak one's mind.

"As far as I know, the minister has said nothing more since the original meeting," Müller said. "Nor is his name on the retinue list."

"Good to hear."

Mittermeier did not want von Oberstein to accompany Reinhard to the Neue Land, of course, but this was not out of personal animosity. It was because he knew that there was a magnetic repulsion between von Oberstein and von Reuentahl, far sharper and deeper than its surface manifestations. It seemed all too probable to him that von Oberstein's presence alone might aggravate von Reuentahl in precisely the wrong way.

Had von Oberstein been the kind of man to prioritize self-preservation, he would not seek to accompany the kaiser on a mission like this in the first place. But even Mittermeier had to admit that the minister was not content by nature to protect his own interests and safety. A goal he considered important might drive him to act in unexpected ways, even at his own expense. Mittermeier could not help feeling uneasy at this prospect—for von Reuentahl's sake, of course, not von Oberstein's.

At that time, there were aspects to the unfolding conspiracy that Mittermeier simply did not see. This was because he had always strived to live a life free of intrigue and contrivance, and largely been successful.

Indeed, at that point, to grasp the full extent of the web of intrigue that the Church of Terra's leadership had spun across the galaxy would have been a near-supernatural feat of insight. No mere human is in a position to attack Mittermeier for his limitations in that area.

However, even without any talent for conspiracy, Mittermeier's judgment as a high-placed state official revealed to him the essential danger of the situation. If the rumors of rebellion turned out to be true, even after it was put down mutual distrust would remain between the kaiser and his officials. The former would think, *Even von Reuentahl betrayed me—who will be next?*; the latter, *Even von Reuentahl was purged—who will be next?* An endless chain of purges and revolts would be the inevitable result.

"No matter," Mittermeier said. "Whatever the minister's opinions may be, I have my own way of doing things. I will concentrate the forces of the space armada in the sectors around Schattenberg."

Schattenberg, which meant "City of Shadows," was the name of a fortress slated for construction in former alliance territory, at the Neue Land end of the Phezzan Corridor. It would not compare to Iserlohn Fortress, but it would block the entrance to the corridor and play a major role not only in defending the new imperial capital but as a base for sorties, supplies, and communications.

Incidentally, the fortress to be constructed at the other end of the Phezzan Corridor, in imperial territory, was to be called Drei Großadmiralsburg. This name meant "City of the Three Marshals," and commemorated the three imperial marshals of the Lohengramm Dynasty who had already fallen in battle—Kircheis, Fahrenheit, and Steinmetz.

"If someone else dies, are they going to rename it Führ Großadmiralsburg?" was Wittenfeld's joke, so unfunny it drew only grimaces from his friends—but, in any case, the construction of these two new fortresses would have great import for the continued existence and expansion of Reinhard's fledgling dynasty and indeed empire, whose two halves were connected by the Phezzan Corridor. The kaiser's grand vision of galactic unity was steadily being realized in practical efforts such as these, Mittermeier, in his capacity as military leader, was responsible for overseeing and directing the project, which was another reason why he could not join the kaiser's retinue.

It was a new age. Mittermeier was adapting to his new duties and finding success dealing with the new challenges that came his way. He was the bravest general in the Galactic Navy, but he was more besides. His flexibility and broad-mindedness were rated extremely highly by Oskar von Reuentahl, among others, although he was not aware of this himself. Reinhard, of course, saw this side of Mittermeier too, which was why he had always entrusted the Gale Wolf with such important duties.

If relations between Reinhard and his officials truly did descend into a cycle of purge and rebellion, Mittermeier thought, for what would they have risked their lives to overthrow the Goldenbaum Dynasty and crush the Free Planets Alliance? What purpose would the trail of bloodshed they had left across the galaxy have served? The Lohengramm Dynasty had brought peace and unity to the galaxy, and established a more progressive and just government across at least half of it. One mistake could stain those dazzling achievements the dark red of a reign of terror in a development that later ages would view with contempt and derision.

That could not be allowed to happen. The kaiser would have to show broad-mindedness, and von Reuentahl would have to exercise self-control.

"Admiral Müller, I place His Majesty's very life in your hands. Be sure that you and Lutz work together to bring him safely home to Phezzan."

"I will spare no effort. Come now, though, surely you don't think any-thing will actually happen?"

Müller's relaxed smile was presumably an attempt at reassuring the friend he loved and respected that all would be well. As the two men shook hands, Mittermeier prayed that Müller was correct.

U

"However diabolical the conspiracy from which it resulted, the shoots of rebellion can only grow from fertile soil. We must conclude that there was already enough distance between Kaiser and von Reuentahl for the conspirators to work with."

Although rather materialist in tendency, historical criticism of this nature is at least partly correct.

Reinhard had always planned to tour the Neue Land once the war was over. Precisely because it was a new addition to the empire, he would have to seize every opportunity to demonstrate his dignity and benevolence to his subjects, even creating more opportunities to do so if necessary. As a result, it was not suspicious in and of itself that von Reuentahl should invite him there.

For von Reuentahl, the situation was more complicated. Just before sending the invitation, the antennae he had left on Phezzan conveyed to his ears a peculiar rumor:

"His Majesty the kaiser remains troubled by frequent outbreaks of unexplained fever. Worse, Minister von Oberstein and Junior Minister Lang are taking advantage of the kaiser's illness and growing more despotic by the day. Von Oberstein behaves more like a prime minister, and Lang treats his ministry as a personal possession, much to the people's dismay. Furthermore, Lang bears such a grudge against von Reuentahl that he slanders him at every opportunity, endlessly petitioning the kaiser to recall him to Phezzan and purge him. Worst of all, he claims that von Reuentahl means to invite the kaiser to the Neue Land and assassinate him there…"

The fact that Lang himself was the source of this information was part of the plot's craft. Von Reuentahl was capable of utterly unsentimental strategic observation, but he did not realize that Lang's exaggerations and fabrications were specifically for von Reuentahl's benefit. Because he was by nature a ruler, he thought of rebellion as purely negative for those in power. The idea of inciting a revolt intended to be suppressed was alien to him. He had confidence in his skills as a military leader, and was alarmed by this threat to the relationship of trust between him and the kaiser.

His view of Lang was also colored by preconceptions. He did not believe that Lang truly respected the kaiser, and suspected him of malicious intent toward von Reuentahl himself. It did not help that these preconceptions were true. The result of all this was that he was taken in by Lang's scheming.

"His Majesty is not the type to be led astray by a worthless sycophant like Lang," he told himself. "He surely remembers that only this spring Lang attempted to capture me in that wretched snare—and failed miserably."

Still, a degree of unease stayed with him. He called in his close friend Bergengrün, inspector general of the military, and asked what he made of the rumors circulating on the new imperial capital.

"I agree that our kaiser is unlikely to be moved by Lang's flattery," Bergengrün said. "What concerns me is the possibility of another actor in all this intrigue. Someone for whom Lang simply serves as a ventriloquist's dummy."

Bergengrün intentionally mentioned no names, but the prime suspect he had in mind was all too clear to von Reuentahl. He saw the minister of military affairs' unnaturally brilliant cybernetic eyes in his mind. It was not the first time that an apprehensive von Reuentahl had considered the unpleasant possibility that von Oberstein might not have the kaiser's best interests at heart.

"What a disappointment it would be to learn that *mein Kaiser* has sunk to the level of a puppet for men like von Oberstein and Lang," von Reuentahl said. Such would be a pathetic end for a life of such spectacular ambition. And so the marshal's own ambitious nature led him to a new idea: What if he were to take over from von Oberstein and Lang, and protect the kaiser himself?

Reinhard would arrive for his tour of the Neue Land with only the lightest of guards. Von Reuentahl could refuse to let him leave, and announce the transfer of Imperial Headquarters and the kaiser's court to Heinessen. Von Oberstein and Lang, still on Phezzan, would be helpless to stop him.

Was this not the ideal opportunity to gather the entire galaxy into his own hands?

Naturally, Reinhard could not be expected to meekly acknowledge von Reuentahl's superiority. He would no doubt struggle to escape from custody and start a war to win back his position and authority. But that would be interesting in itself. As a military opponent, not even von Oberstein posed a serious threat to von Reuentahl, much less Lang. Even if von Oberstein was behind the current plot, it relied on the kaiser's power to function. He was not a worthy adversary for von Reuentahl's five million troops and strategic genius.

In the Goldenbaum Dynasty, purges of capable retainers had not been rare. Some had returned in triumph from campaign victories only to be stripped of their authority upon arrival and sent straight to the execution grounds. If Reinhard's illness was clouding his judgment, this undesirable practice of the former dynasty might be revived for use against von Reuentahl.

Nor, indeed, was von Reuentahl's own transparency complete or uncolored. He had his own ruthless side, and since accepting his post as governor-general he had been exploring how much political and military pressure the Neue Land's production capacity would allow it to bring to bear on the empire's original territory. Of course, he had always envisioned his enemy in these scenarios as von Oberstein.

For this reason, historians of later ages who were critical of von Reuentahl made assertions like the following:

"As a retainer to Kaiser Reinhard, Oskar von Reuentahl lacked loyalty; as the leader of a revolt, he lacked decisiveness. Ultimately, rather than a traitor, he was simply an eternal dissatisfied element."

"With a little more awareness of where he stood in the course of history, he would surely have perceived that his contributions were needed most of all in the establishment of peace and order. Did the reason and intellect that had helped him succeed and flourish up to that point abandon him when he reached his highest position as retainer?"

"By betraying Reinhard at the final stage, he left the impression that the loyalty he had shown the kaiser up to that point had all been a lie. This was nobody's fault but his own..."

Nevertheless, no historians dared bend the truth enough to call him incompetent. On the contrary—the consensus was that it was precisely a surfeit of genius and ability that drove him off-course.

We might also examine the views of Julian Mintz, a contemporary witness from the camp permanently opposed to the marshal:

"...Oskar von Reuentahl was a man of towering achievement. His abilities qualified him for any position, whether as military leader, governor-general of vast territorial holdings, or even prime minister. But there was one position in that age to which he was not suited: ruler of a newly founded empire. In a dynasty that had reached its third generation, for example, it is difficult to imagine a more outstanding candidate for emperor. Inheriting the policies of the preceding administration, he would doubtless have cultivated their merits, corrected their flaws, enforced discipline, reconstituted state organizations, suppressed military rebellion and protected imperial authority and the people, and in all things used his mighty powers of leadership to maintain an unshakable central unity. There is no question that he would have been a greater ruler than the majority of the Goldenbaum emperors.... However, in his empire, the capital would surely have remained on Odin. Among his contemporaries, however, there was a youth whose incomparable genius shifted the center of galactic rule to Phezzan. From this perspective, von Reuentahl comes to appear a conservative man in a foundational age. Was it simple ill fortune that he shared the age with Kaiser Reinhard, the founder himself? Or..."

Julian chose not to write further. He appears to be wordlessly stating that, as a contemporary, he also saw von Reuentahl's rebellion as something arising in the domain ruled by truth, not by fact. However, if this analysis is correct, a clear mismatch can be seen between its conclusions and the subjective views of von Reuentahl, who never stopped thinking of himself as living through an age of unrest. Or perhaps we should say that his desire to be the hero of such an age outweighed whatever preference he had for stability.

In any case, von Reuentahl had no intention of yielding to von Oberstein and Lang in any matter, even at the expense of his own future.

He had sent his invitation despite the unpleasant rumors partly to see how the kaiser would respond. If Reinhard refused to leave Phezzan, this would show that he believed the rumors and doubted von Reuentahl's loyalty—that he had become von Oberstein and Lang's puppet. As painful as it would be to have this confirmed, at least the situation would be clear.

On the other hand, if Reinhard accepted the invitation and prepared for a tour of the Neue Land, would this prove his faith in von Reuentahl? The answer, regrettably, was no. He might simply mean to lull von Reuentahl into complacency, the better to capture and eliminate him. Such dissimulation would be out of character for Reinhard, but it would not be beneath von Oberstein and Lang.

And so, on September 22, Kaiser Reinhard left Phezzan and set off for the Neue Land. As governor-general, it fell to Marshal von Reuentahl to prepare His Majesty's welcome.

CHAPTER FIVE:
THE URVASHI INCIDENT

I

LATE AUGUST, YEAR 2 of the New Imperial Calendar, SE 800.

The summer had been a warm and peaceful one for the Galactic Empire's subjects. The long and all-consuming war appeared to have reached its end at last. Fathers, husbands, brothers, lovers, and sons returned from duty. Soldiers went straight from spaceport reunions to weddings with their sweethearts—tens of thousands of them, all told.

But beyond the known horizons of the people, dark clouds gathered.

The people were not responsible for the clouds. But should those clouds fill the sky and unleash a storm, the people would be soaked. The people had no right to participate in causes, but were obliged to endure effects. This was the sin of autocratic governance, which differed from open democracy in being founded on exclusion and discrimination. Yang Wen-li had spoken to Julian Mintz of this in life, and with time Julian would come to see his words as a valuable prophecy.

Sealed in Iserlohn Base, Julian received his most valuable information from two sources: public communications networks, and Boris Konev's "Blockade Busters."

Konev, who would be thirty-one that year, was neither a formal member of the Iserlohn Republic nor a holder of public office there. He had been born a citizen of the Phezzan Land Dominion, but with Phezzan's unique political position shattered by the Imperial Navy, no existing authority legally guaranteed his rights as an individual.

But the brash independent trader showed no sign of unease at his status as a man without affiliation. On the contrary, he reveled in it, taking the greatest pleasure in risking his life to breach the Imperial Navy's blockades, gather information, and smuggle supplies—all on no one's orders, but solely according to his own whims. For Konev, to be someone's friend and equal was a far finer thing than being their superior or vassal as a matter of law. Just as Dusty Attenborough was passionate about waging revolutionary war, so Boris Konev proudly proclaimed his status as a free and independent trader. He was free to act as he chose to rather than out of obligation, but in his comments like "Spiritual profits are more important than material ones," there were those who saw more of the adventurer in him than the trader. Olivier Poplin's assessment, however, rendered the distinction moot: "He's just a thrill seeker."

Sarcastic comments about Konev and his relatives were stock in trade for Poplin. "I just don't get along with that family," he'd say. "There's something in their genes that's just not compatible with good sense." And yet, although the green-eyed ace pilot showed no concern for his own family members—at least not on the surface—he made sure to inquire about the safety of Ivan Konev's family, who were still on Heinessen following Ivan's death.

In the years to come, historians would place Olivier Poplin alongside Dusty Attenborough as one of the best representatives of the Iserlohn Republic's cheerful "festival mood." Excluding the short period in which Poplin had allowed his grief full reign, this was an accurate evaluation. But Dusty Attenborough records that, after Yang's administration gave way to Julian's, he sometimes sensed that Poplin's heart was not truly in the festive mood he promoted. Poplin was not so shallow that this could be discerned by just anyone, but if Attenborough was able to see it, this was surely because of commonalities between the two men in how they thought and acted.

Where all contemporary accounts agree is on Poplin's popularity among the younger generations. Cheerful, stylish, and dashing, he was followed by crowds of fresh-faced soldiers and little children who hung on his every word. Many also imitated the way he wore his beret or strolled down the corridors, although many parents no doubt discouraged their sons from following his example in the romantic arena. However, as it was widely known that Poplin was interested in women, not girls, parents trusted him to a perhaps surprising degree around their daughters.

"And so, my young comrades, from now on make sure to call me Poplin the Far-Sighted and Respectable."

"Don't you mean Poplin the Lady-Killer?" asked a young wag.

"Who did you hear that foolishness from? Admiral Attenborough?"

"No, Admiral Caselnes."

"To be misunderstood by the older generation is the fate of every young revolutionary. Let us rise together, comrades, and sweep them into our memories of the past."

Given Poplin's responsibility of turning the republic's hapless new recruits into fighter pilots, his popularity among the younger set was a valuable asset. He inhabited the role of leader and mentor with ease. Watching him lead a platoon of boys and girls to the pilot training center, Attenborough folded his arms and muttered, "If he'd been born in an age of peace, I think he'd have become a kindergarten teacher. Strange how well the company of children suits him."

The mixture of sarcasm and genuine admiration in Attenborough's voice drew a laugh from Julian.

"If Commander Poplin can go from lady-killer to kindergarten teacher, perhaps you can relinquish bachelordom, too, Admiral Attenborough."

"Ms. Celibacy shows no sign of relinquishing *me*. We've been together such a long time—you can't just throw that away."

Had Attenborough been so inclined, he could have long since had a family or lover fitting his position and personal charm. But he did not yet feel the need to harbor his ship anywhere in particular.

Attenborough disappeared into his office with an armful of paperwork, and Julian entered his own office next door. On his desk he found a handful of letters. He encouraged this as a way of venting dissatisfaction or sharing opinions. Some were constructive, but others were simply torrents of personal abuse.

But Julian had never frowned on even the letters that criticized or censured him. He believed that a society whose members could not speak ill of their leaders did not deserve the sobriquet "open." Only when Yang was the target of abuse did he lose his temper, as the accounts of Katerose von Kreutzer and countless others show.

When Yang was alive, simply standing beside him had apparently made Julian seem a kind of quiet genius, even richer in military sense than the black-haired magician himself. Today, with Yang gone, Julian made a different impression. Only the sensibilities of the observers had changed, not Julian himself, but it seemed that another side of the sensitive-featured youth was revealing itself to others: a diligent missionary with the *Record of Yang Wan-li* as his bible.

Even so, Julian was neither brooding nor overbearing. Lacking the radiant, feverish self-confidence of Kaiser Reinhard, he appeared to have simply allowed the natural flow of events to carry him into his current position as Yang's successor.

At this point in their history, his fundamental approach as a public figure was simple: wait.

"The empire's subjects have spent almost two thousand years growing accustomed to *being* governed, *being* ruled. They think of government as something done *to* them, or at best *for* them. Why shouldn't they support the Lohengramm Dynasty, which promises to do better things for them than ever before? With time, the dynasty will be eroded and start down the slope to self-destruction. That is the moment when democratic republican governance will begin to have meaning."

Which is why Julian believed that the right thing to do for now was wait. The Iserlohn Republic was still too weak to serve as the core around which circumstances might change, must less to actively seek to become that core. Julian did not expect that to be within their power for generations.

On the other hand, he knew both emotionally and intellectually that circumstances could change with shocking speed. As a result, while he managed the republic's military with an eye to the long term, he was constantly pondering how they might respond to short-term change. In the final months of SE 800, this approach would yield highly effective results.

"Julian Mintz has never once spoken for himself. His every utterance and opinion is drawn from the *Record of Yang Wen-li*. He is a plagiarist, creating nothing, and simply by virtue of having outlived Yang unjustly monopolizes all the glory."

Dusty Attenborough's response to cruel slander of this nature leveled at Julian is instructive:

"Julian Mintz was a performer, not a composer—a translator, not an author. This was what he wanted, and indeed he became a performer and translator of the very highest caliber. Never once did he conceal his models, and in no way does he deserve the label of plagiarist. No music is sublime enough to move an audience without being performed."

Julian never spoke in his own defense. He refused to indulge the desire for self-justification—remained, to the very end, successor to and evangelist for Yang Wen-li. This was precisely what some historians felt set him above the common herd. Certainly no one can deny his achievements in ensuring that Yang Wen-li's life, achievements, and thought were recorded in near-perfect form for later generations—even if the occasional doubt is raised about the accuracy and objectivity of those records.

But if Julian's strategy was to wait, he would not have to wait very long. In mid-October, Boris Konev arrived at Iserlohn with the most explosive news since the May revelation of a plot to assassinate Yang Wen-li:

"Marshal von Reuentahl, governor-general of the Galactic Empire's Neue Land, is in revolt against Kaiser Reinhard!"

II

"Before proceeding to Heinessen, the kaiser and his suite will stop at the planet Urvashi in the Gandharva system for a memorial service at the cenotaph to those lost in the Great Campaign."

Thus was the itinerary for the imperial tour of the Neue Land. Nothing after the visit to Urvashi was yet fixed except the kaiser's return to the capital in early February. This was partly because Reinhard did not care to be bound to schedules.

The primary members of his retinue were Senior Admirals Müller and Lutz, Vice Admiral von Streit, Commodore Kissling, Lieutenant von Rücke, and Emil von Selle. The lack of civilian officers was noteworthy, and could be considered a flaw. Reinhard's team of doctors were also to accompany him, as were, of course, the crews of his flagship *Brünhild* and the squadron acting as his escort.

Reinhard had always had a tendency to be "less warrior-kaiser than kaiser-warrior," as historians put it. Since his days as one fleet commander among many in the Goldenbaum Dynasty, he had always been happier among the troops on a warship's deck or a military facility than surrounded by beauties at court. No doubt his soldiers, too, found their kaiser more resplendent in his black and silver uniform than any daughter of the nobility bedecked in silks and jewels.

The imperial suite arrived at Urvashi on October 7, one day ahead of schedule.

Urvashi's conditions as an inhabited planet were similar to Phezzan's. The climate was chilly and water resources precious. However, since only enough water was needed to meet the needs of the troops stationed on the planet, in effect the only inhabited part of the planet was the oasis covering six hundred square kilometers that had been constructed around an eighty-square-kilometer artificial lake. In the past, Marshal Karl Robert Steinmetz (now deceased) and his fleet had been stationed there, but it was currently home to five hundred thousand troops from the Neue Land Security Force. Should an emergency break out on Heinessen, home of the Neue Land governorate, Urvashi would have to act as the core military base until relief arrived from the imperial capital on Phezzan. As a result, roughly a tenth of the Security Force was posted to this cold, half-desert planet.

The kaiser and his retinue were welcomed to the planet by Urvashi base commander Vice Admiral Alfred Aloys Winckler. After dinner with the base's senior officers, they adjourned to the state guesthouse next door at 2110. Despite its somewhat grandiose name, the guesthouse was true to Lohengramm Dynasty style in offering virtually no luxuries. Even the oil paintings in the hall were the winners of various competitions held for the troops garrisoned on the planet. This could verge on the sarcastic if taken too far, of course.

Müller and the others left the kaiser in the combined library and parlor at 2240. Not yet hearing the sandman's approaching tread, Reinhard took the first volume of *The Foundation of the Free Planets Alliance* down from the shelf and sat on the sofa to read it. His bodyguard Emil von Selle placed a glass of lemonade on the table and left the room. But at 2230, the door burst open and Emil reappeared with a tense expression.

"What is it, Emil?" the young kaiser said, offering the boy a smile. *He worships the ground Your Majesty walks on*, Mittermeier had once said, and although he meant it as a joke it was very close to literally truth.

"Your Majesty, Admirals Lutz and Müller say they must speak with you urgently. May I show them in?"

It seemed to Emil that the kaiser actually welcomed this interruption of his idleness. The tall form of Kornelias Lutz appeared in the doorway.

"My apologies for the interruption, Your Majesty, but we must prepare to leave right away. The base guards are acting suspiciously."

Lutz's eyes had a violet cast to them, as was often the case when the typically composed and trustworthy strategist grew agitated or tense. Wittenfeld called him "a man who needs sunglasses to play poker"—but this was no time for banter. Reinhard turned his ice-blue gaze to Lutz, closed his book, and rose to his feet. Emil held out his jacket.

Loyal Neidhart Müller had stationed himself outside the door to protect his young liege. When Reinhard emerged, he switched his blaster to his left hand to salute with his right.

"At ease, Müller," Reinhard said, sweeping his golden hair back from his brow. "Just tell me what in heaven is going on."

Müller explained that a short time earlier they had noticed troops running hastily to and fro, both inside and outside the base. Furthermore, visiphone communications had been cut off. It seemed best for the kaiser to return to his flagship *Brünhild* for the time being.

At 2337, Reinhard, Müller, and Emil climbed into the back seat of a landcar. Kissling took the wheel, and Lutz rode shotgun. There were two other vehicles available, and these quickly filled with members of

Reinhard's personal guard. Those who did not get a seat were forced to remain behind.

As soon as the landcars began to move, Reinhard asked, with some urgency, "Where is von Streit? And von Rücke?"

Müller looked grave. "I don't know, Your Majesty," he said. "Even our own situation is unclear at this point."

"But you do know that we're in danger," Reinhard said, not without a hint of irony—just as a searchlight swept across his face.

Energy beams were fired on the landcar from every direction, raising plumes of white smoke. Kissling's driving and the evasive systems of the landcar itself spared them a direct hit, but Reinhard could no longer deny that Müller and the others had judged things correctly.

In the headlights and infrared monitor, a group of armed soldiers swam into view up ahead, followed by the headlights and sirens of other vehicles.

Kissling let out a low whistle. "Looks like a whole regiment."

"They sent a single regiment to take out the kaiser of the Galactic Empire and two senior admirals? I'm never felt so disrespected," muttered Lutz, albeit with somewhat forced humor. The violet cast was long gone from his eyes. With the danger they were in no longer hypothetical, his tension had actually eased, and he was recovering the almost everyday equanimity and resoluteness that befit a front-line soldier.

Their headlights suddenly revealed five armed soldiers directly in their path.

The landcar began to slow, but as soon as it detected the soldiers leveling ion beam rifle barrels at them, it accelerated again. The passengers felt soft impacts and, through the windows, saw the soldiers' bodies tumbling back down around and behind them.

Müller said, "Excuse me, Your Majesty!" and hurled himself bodily over Reinhard and Emil. Half a moment later, a single beam pierced the car through from right to left at window height. The back of Müller's jacket and a few strands of sandy hair on the back of his head were carbonized.

"Müller! Are you all right?"

"Yes, Your Majesty. Not to worry—I'm quite thick-skinned, especially on my back." As he delivered this terrible joke, he drew his blaster and raised himself enough to see out of the window. "I think we have to conclude that the entire base is out to get Your Majesty."

"You say von Reuentahl has betrayed me, then?"

Reinhard's voice was cold as ice. Strong passions do not always take the form of fiery winds or rumbling thunder; some are more like a blizzard.

But Müller answered without flinching. "I don't want to cast aspersions on a colleague," he said. "But Your Majesty has an obligation to avoid danger. If I have slandered him unfairly, let me make amends later. For now, Your Majesty's safety must come first."

He had the same earnest look in his eyes as Emil. Reinhard glanced at his young bodyguard and forced a smile.

"Do not trouble yourself with needless concern, Emil," he said. "I have already resolved to die in a more scenic location than this. A kaiser's grave on Urvashi—it simply does not sound right."

The landcar swerved to avoid colliding with another vehicle barreling directly toward it. Reinhard's flowing hair hit the window glass. Müller fired his blaster from the window on the landcar's right. Straightening up, the kaiser spoke again.

"If this is indeed von Reuentahl's rebellion, he will have accounted for everything, to a molecular level. Is it possible we are already trapped?"

Lutz and Müller were silent. Reinhard appeared to be holding a dialogue between his reason and his sensibilities, and even if the words were directed at them, it would have been strange to sympathize with one side or another.

Blaster drawn, Lutz used the other hand to adjust the communications system on the passenger's side of the dashboard. Finally he succeeded in contacting the flagship *Brünhild*. Through heavy static, they heard the voice of Commodore Seidlitz, the ship's captain—who reported that *Brünhild*, too, had come under attack from the surface of the planet, and was currently returning fire.

III

The military spaceport was already under rebel control. As soon as this became clear, their landcar turned sharply toward the artificial lake.

They were alone now, having lost the other two landcars at some point behind them.

Orange light rippled up ahead, providing further evidence that the attack on Reinhard and his admirals was not a small-scale operation.

"*Brünhild* will take off from the spaceport and then land on the lake for boarding," Lutz explained.

When they finally reached the lake, they found it churning furiously as flames and smoke poured into the night sky from the surrounding forest. But dominating even that sky was the elegant form of a spacecraft, shining pure white as it glided across the unseen surface of the water toward them. The beautiful, invincible warship *Brünhild* had come for its only master.

They abandoned their landcar close to the lakeshore and ran toward the *Brünhild*, which had touched down on the water, only to see a silhouette leap out of the shadowy forest before them. Müller and the others raised their weapons.

"Your Majesty! Your Majesty! Thank goodness you're safe. Odin All-father has kept you from harm."

The man's voice revealed his identity. Under his mask of black soot, he was Lieutenant Theodor von Rücke, secondary aide to Reinhard. Had this revelation come a second later, this loyal retainer to the kaiser would have been shot dead by a colleague of no lesser loyalty—but there was no time for even a rueful grimace at this idea.

Von Rücke's party had received a false report that the kaiser had already escaped. Upon discovering the lie, he had begun a frantic search for his liege, eventually making his way to the lake—"just in case."

"Admiral von Streit and the others are waiting up ahead."

"Then *Brünhild* shall depart at once."

"Wait, Your Majesty!" Lutz's tone was sharp, and the purple light was back in his eyes. "If this rebellion was not spontaneous, the enemy may already be waiting in orbit."

A heavy silence followed as the party digested this observation. Finally, Reinhard spoke in a voice pointed with displeasure.

"Who, may I ask, is 'the enemy'? Von Reuentahl, I suppose, even if you refrain from speaking the name for lack of evidence…"

"To borrow Admiral Müller's expression from earlier, as governor-general of the Neue Land, Marshal von Reuentahl is responsible for guaranteeing Your Majesty's safety. And yet these are the events that have come to pass. Unfortunate as it may be, I cannot agree that he is unworthy of criticism for this."

Lutz was not by nature inclined to think this way. Without question, the stories of von Reuentahl planning a rebellion had cast their shadow even on this upright soldier. He was not by any means on bad terms with von Reuentahl, but this was precisely why he had to draw the line in his official capacity.

"In any case, let us continue to the ship," said Müller. "Even if she remains on the surface, Your Majesty will be safe aboard *Brünhild*. Any response to these events, I feel, can come afterward."

The soundness of Müller's proposal saved both Lutz and Reinhard from further confrontation. The group pushed further into a chaos of black and orange bombarded by alternating cascades of freezing and scorching air from the atmosphere above. The flames called the wind, the wind carried the smoke, and the wild dance of sparks and cinders assailed their ears with menacing song.

A shout went up, and dark figures that seemed cut out of the forest's shadows emerged to surround them. Soldiers from the Neue Land Security Force. When Reinhard's five companions formed a wall around him, his dazzling golden mane caught the soldiers' eyes.

One, standing directly in front of them, gasped, "The kaiser!" His awe was evident not just in his voice but in his entire body. He kept the barrel of his weapon raised, but the finger on the trigger seemed to weaken even as they watched.

Reinhard took a step forward. "You have retained some portion of your senses, then," he said. "Indeed, I am your kaiser."

Müller tried to stop him, but the kaiser held him back with one arm as he opened his jacket before the soldiers' weapons. In that moment, light and darkness themselves seemed his subordinates, existing only to emphasize the young emperor's beauty and authority.

"Shoot me, then. There is only one Reinhard von Lohengramm, and only one man will go down in history as his killer. Who will become that man?"

"Your Majesty!" Müller tried once more to interpose himself between

Reinhard and the soldiers. Reinhard quietly but firmly pushed his loyal admiral back.

The noble-born military leaders of the Goldenbaum Dynasty had coerced obedience through arrogance and bluster, but until this moment Reinhard had never had the slightest need to follow suit. His incomparable achievements and strategic genius had been enough to win the full faith and loyalty of his troops. His streaming golden locks and semi-divine appearance had even made him the object of ardent worship.

"Had Kaiser Reinhard been of loathsome appearance, his men would not have shown him such reverence." Malicious opinions of this nature could be answered simply: none of those who faced Reinhard in battle had any reason to let him win simply because he was beautiful. His soldiers worshiped him to a degree and in a manner commensurate with his abilities.

In any case, at that moment in the forest on Urvashi, the men of the Neue Land Security Force were clearly overwhelmed by Reinhard's authority. The barrels of the weapons pointed at his chest trembled so fearfully that they no longer seemed even capable of hitting their intended target.

A gust of searing wind cast waves of orange light across the stand-off. The moment the black shadows gave way to this, somebody yelled, "What are you waiting for? The kaiser has a billion-reichsmark bounty on his head!"

This incitement galvanized several soldiers into action. Just as a few of the gun barrels appeared to stop trembling, a lone soldier at the back forestalled his colleagues with a cry:

"Sieg Kaiser!"

Even as he shouted the words, he opened fire on the men who a second earlier had been his allies.

When the chaotic firefight died down, seven bodies lay dead on the ground. Seven men were still standing: Reinhard, his party, and the soldier who had yelled "Sieg Kaiser." Müller had been shot through the right arm protecting the kaiser. Kissling was bleeding from his right cheek, and von Rücke had light wounds on his left hand, but none had been killed— a small stroke of luck amid great misfortune.

The soldier from the Neue Land security force threw down his weapon and prostrated himself before Reinhard in abject apology.

"What is your name?" Reinhard asked him.

"Yes, Your Majesty. Lance Corporal Meinhof, Your Majesty. I was instigated by others, but even so I deserve death for the crime of leveling a weapon at your person. Have mercy, I beg of you..."

"Very well. You are promoted to sergeant, effective immediately. I trust you can lead us to *Brünhild*, Sergeant Meinhof?"

Meinhof led the way, walking as if in a dream, religious exultation in his face. There was, he explained, a shortcut to the lake, impassible to landcars.

Flames and smoke at their back, they ran through the forest for a minute or so before the newly promoted sergeant was struck by a beam fired from somewhere up ahead that bored a hole into the middle of his face. Lutz returned fire before unlucky Meinhof hit the ground. The man who had shot him took a beam to his own face, and toppled over with a scream.

Lutz leaned closer to Müller, whose right arm was wrapped in a bloodied handkerchief. "We were lucky he was alone, but there will be more," he whispered. "I'll stay here and hold them off. You get His Majesty safely aboard *Brünhild*."

"With respect, Admiral Lutz, don't be a fool."

"A fool? In case you'd forgotten, I'm five years older than you. You owe me more respect than that. I'm only going to carry out the responsibilities of a senior officer."

"My apologies," said Müller stiffly. "But the responsibility is mine too. And you have a fiancée, where I have no such ties at all. I'm the one who will stay behind."

"And what use would you be with one wounded arm?"

"Admiral..."

"Concern yourself with the responsibilities that only you can fulfill. Now, enough formalism, unless you want me to shoot you through the other arm too."

Müller gave in. Time was of the essence, and he had to admit that Lutz was right. There would be no end to the enemies that pursued them. Someone had to stay behind and buy the others time, even if only a few minutes. If only they had not become separated from the kaiser's personal guard during the landcar chase—but it was too late for that now. It also pained Lutz that they had lost Meinhof before finding out who had "instigated" him.

Lutz waved away offers by Kissling and the others to remain behind in his place, accepting new energy capsules for his blaster instead.

Seeing that Lutz's mind was made up, Reinhard took his admiral's hands in his own. If he succumbed to sentiment here, all Lutz's loyalty would go to waste. The kaiser had his own path, and only he could walk it.

"Lutz."

"Yes, Your Majesty."

"I do not wish to promote you to marshal posthumously. Take as much time as you need, but be sure to follow."

"Your Majesty, I have every intention of accepting the marshal's staff from you alive." Lutz retained his composure as he spoke. He even smiled. "I had the honor of sharing the founding of Your Majesty's empire. With luck I will also share the ease and flourishing to come."

Lutz glanced at Müller. The "Iron Wall" nodded, then respectfully took Reinhard by the arm. "We must go, Your Majesty," he said.

Reinhard's golden hair shone even more splendidly in the firelight.

"Lutz, when you are no longer able to fire, surrender. Von Reuentahl knows how to treat a hero."

Lutz saluted, but spoke neither *ja* nor *nein* in reply. He watched Reinhard and the others leave, offering a final salute when the kaiser turned back one last time, and then strode unhurriedly into the trees by the path to take cover.

The limits of Lutz's patience were not tested. Ten seconds later, roughly a platoon's worth of pursuers turned up. Lutz opened fire.

The pursuers visibly shrank from him. They knew Lutz as a great general, but had never imagined that he was such an accurate marksman.

In just two minutes, Lutz's blaster felled eight men, half of whom died instantly. Despite the flames and the relentlessly approaching enemies, he remained flawlessly composed. Half-concealed behind a great tree, sometimes even taking the time to brush off the sparks that showered down on him, Lutz held the line grimly. When he heard calls for him to surrender, he unflappably replied, "Surrender! And rob you of the chance to see how a senior admiral of the Lohengramm Dynasty dies? Whether you come with me or not, why not watch and learn?"

Then he extended an arm as unbending as his spirit and pulled the trigger again.

It was as if his own will poured forth from the barrel in streams of pure energy. The pursuers seemed to forgot their numbers—each of them returned fire desperately, as if facing him alone. They dove into the forest to escape his deadly accuracy, only to be chased out again by the flames.

As he loaded his third and final energy capsule into his blaster, Lutz wondered when exactly *Brünhild* would take off. He felt irritation not for himself but on behalf of Reinhard and the others.

The flames flickered wildly. The red and black and darkness and light that had struggled for supremacy above him were pushed aside by an all-illuminating silver gleam. Looking skyward, Lutz saw a warship that every soldier in the Galactic Empire knew. A great bird of purest white, spreading its wings amid a thicket of energy beams rising uselessly toward it from the planet's surface. The sight was magnificent.

The transcendental moment passed. Lutz saw a thin beam of white light pierce him beneath his left clavicle, and then felt it emerge from his back just beside his left shoulder blade. Pain exploded from the point of impact, spreading to fill his body. Lutz staggered just half a pace backward, frowned slightly, and brought down two more pursuers with two more pulls of the trigger. He pressed his left hand to the breast of his uniform and felt an unpleasant stickiness. Tiny snakes of a dark, wet color trickled from between his fingers and crawled downward.

Still upright, he once more pulled the trigger, which now felt very heavy. As his target spasmed before a backdrop of flame in a brief dance of death, the left side of Lutz's skull was pierced by a diagonal blast of return fire. A gout of blood poured from his ear. The flames disappeared from his field of vision, leaving only darkness.

"*Mein Kaiser*...I am afraid I cannot make good on that promise to accept the marshal's rod alive. I shall await my reprimand in Valhalla—but let it not be for some time yet..."

The soldiers in the forest saw the indomitable general collapse against the roots of a great tree that had just begun to burn. They knew he was mortally wounded, but none dared approach to confirm his death. Only when a mass of fire in the shape of a branch fell onto him from above were they finally sure that their fearsome opponent was gone.

IV

Word of the disturbance on Urvashi, of course, soon reached von Reuentahl on Heinessen. If he was stunned for a moment, it was at least a moment too short for any of those present to notice.

"Find the kaiser and his retinue as quickly as possible and keep them safe. Besides that—Admiral Grillparzer, take a fleet to Urvashi with all speed to restore order and clarify the situation."

There were no other orders to give. If he had the kaiser in hand, he could argue in his own defense. If Reinhard returned to Phezzan, he would summon von Reuentahl to be judged as a criminal. Punishment aside, to be treated this way over events he had no knowledge of was something von Reuentahl's pride would not permit—particularly when unpleasant figures seemed certain to insinuate themselves between him and the kaiser.

The reports from Urvashi were both few in number and wildly inconsistent, but one horrifying detail was soon confirmed: the fate of Senior Admiral Kornelias Lutz.

"Lutz is dead?"

Von Reuentahl's voice cracked for the first time. At that moment, he distinctly heard doors closing behind him. Not only had his retreat been cut off, he had lost one possible route from present to future. Any possibility of clearing up the misunderstanding, of letting bygones be bygones and reconciling with the kaiser, had been lost forever. He could not see it any other way.

"What will you do, Your Excellency?" asked Senior Admiral Bergengrün. Bergengrün was inspector general of the military and fearless enough to unflinchingly accept an order to die on the spot, but even he was barely keeping his fear in check. His face appeared utterly devoid of blood.

"It's just as you heard, Bergengrün. Turns out I'm the first traitor in the history of the Lohengramm Empire."

"Your Excellency, I know this is a disaster of unprecedented proportion, but surely if you explain to His Majesty that you had no knowledge—"

"It's too late for that!" Reuentahl snapped, as if pushing his own fate angrily away.

He was innocent. Why should an innocent man have to grovel, desperate and humiliated, to explain himself? *Ridiculous*, he thought, and the idea filled him like a rising tide. Was this how his service under the kaiser was to be rewarded?

"I don't mind bowing my head to the kaiser," he said. "I'm his vassal, so that much is only natural. But…"

Von Reuentahl did not finish the thought, but Bergengrün could supply the unuttered words: *But bow my head to von Oberstein and Lang?* As he shared his superior's antipathy to the minister of military affairs, Bergengrün did not dare voice his own opinion. A melody of silence played for about three bars before von Reuentahl spoke again.

"Becoming a traitor is one thing. I can live with that. Being turned into a traitor by others doesn't interest me."

The black of his right eye had an almost mournful cast to it, but ferocious drive glittered in the blue of his left. He was not thrown into confusion by the unexpectedness of the situation, and this lack of endearing vulnerability meant that he was often misunderstood. In this respect, he resembled von Oberstein, although he would not have been pleased to hear the comparison.

"By the way, Bergengrün, what will you do?"

"Do, sir?"

"If you intend to stay loyal to the kaiser, kill me here and now. I'm going to be a disaster for him. Or perhaps I already am…"

Bergengrün watched with apprehension as von Reuentahl's mouth bent into a self-mocking grin. "I see only one thing I can do," he said. "Accompany Your Excellency, unarmed, to an audience with His Majesty, to report that you played absolutely no part in this plot."

"Bergengrün, I have been suspected of treason against the kaiser once before. Twice is too many times. And I'm sure the kaiser agrees."

"If a suspicion is false, it must be dispelled, be it twice, thrice, or a hundred times. This is not an area where efforts should be spared."

Von Reuentahl's reason saw the truth in what his inspector general said. But that reason could not control the flames that rose in his breast and gleamed in his heterochromatic eyes.

"Suppose that we do set out to visit the kaiser, unarmed. Are you sure that we will not be murdered by the minister for military affairs, or the junior minister of the interior, whether somewhere along the route or right before arrival?"

Bergengrün had no reply.

"I will not abide the pity of future generations for being the first name on von Oberstein's purge list."

If that is to be my fate, better by far to... But even von Reuentahl knew to bite his lip and leave those words unuttered.

"In any case," he said, "If I'm unjustly condemned, it can only be a plot by that walking vermin Lang. I don't even care if that's the truth or not. It's what I want to think, so let me. A master strategist like Yang Wen-li would be one thing. To be handcuffed by a man like Lang and live out my days in shame would be more humiliation than I can bear."

Suddenly he wondered: What fate awaited them once the fighting was over? Would they be dogs with jeweled collars, arrayed at court in golden cages to grow old in dissipation and idleness? Was he doomed to rot away bit by bit amid peace and lassitude?

In an age of peace, Yang Wen-li could have lived a peaceful life. Apparently this was what he himself had wanted, although he had died before achieving it. Meanwhile, he was survived by those who found peace to be unbearable idleness. Perhaps the Creator was evenhanded after all—in treating all his creations with equal malice.

You were born to make me and your mother unhappy.

So von Reuentahl's father had told his young son. There was no arguing with it, because it was true. His existence alone brought unhappiness to his parents, even if that was not his will.

Von Reuentahl wondered if another path had been open to him. Could he have started a family, lived in peace and comfort?

Unlikely.

Enough women had sincerely loved him over the years to form several platoons. Virtually all of them had been possessed of beauty well above the standard, and at least a platoon's worth had met all the qualifications to be wives and mothers.

It was he who was not up to standard. His qualifications as husband and father were sorely lacking, and he did not strive to make up for them.

"The von Reuentahl line ends with me. No brothers or sisters, thankfully. No more of our kind to trouble future generations."

Von Reuentahl had spoken these words to his friend Mittermeier while drunk. The following day, he brought Mittermeier a bouquet of flowers. "For your wife," he muttered. He had remembered that the Mittermeiers were childless, and regretted his thoughtless remarks. Mittermeier accepted the flowers gravely on his wife's behalf, knowing that his friend's psychology would not permit him to apologize frankly, no matter how clear his meaning.

The Mittermeiers were married but childless. Von Reuentahl was not married and did not even want children, and yet he was a father. This alone was proof of a malicious creator. His mismatched eyes viewed his life with cold detachment. Would the same be true for his death? Von Reuentahl had a desire to witness the moment of his own death. The idea reminded him of the brutal tale from ancient history of a great general who dug out his own eyes so that they could witness the fall of his former homeland.

"If childhood seems a happy time, that's only because you can spend it not knowing your true self."

Von Reuentahl spoke these words to Mittermeier when the two of them were surrounded by children with feverish admiration in their eyes. The Twin Ramparts of the Imperial Navy were visiting the Children's Academy to speak to the students. Both of them had felt self-conscious about delivering formal speeches from the podium, so they had finished up early and sat down under an elm tree in a corner of the schoolyard to mingle with the children.

Mittermeier flashed a gray-eyed glance at his colleague but said nothing. He continued shaking the hands of excited children until the line finally dwindled away.

"Does that mean it's like being intoxicated?" he asked then. "Or like sobering up?"

"Good question. Either way, you're luckier if you can die drunk."

This was how von Reuentahl truly felt. Of course, by "drunk" he might have meant to include other kinds of intoxication, like love and allegiance. He had never gone into detail about this idea with anyone.

"The nobles are beyond redemption. They must be destroyed."

This idea had taken root in von Reuentahl's inner world while he was still a child. He knew how harmful the tepid swamp of noble society had been to his mother's psyche. The knowledge had been forced on him against his will.

But the Goldenbaum Dynasty had spent five centuries cultivating a subject mind-set among those it ruled, brainwashing them to believe that it was both holy and immortal. This had kept von Reuentahl in unseen fetters of iron, able to kick the ground but not to fly.

When he learned that Reinhard aimed to overthrow the dynasty and usurp the position of kaiser for himself, von Reuentahl had been shocked. The psychological barriers that had proved insurmountable to him were nothing to this boy nine years his junior, who meant to soar high above and far beyond them on wings of gold.

This was the moment he had realized how vast the difference in ambition was that separated great men from the common herd.

One part self-mockery and nine parts admiration changed the course of von Reuentahl's life. Alongside his close friend Mittermeier, he staked his life on that golden-haired youth, and found success. But would that success last forever? Even before these new developments, too much had been uncertain. After the attack on Reinhard and the death of Lutz on Urvashi, how could what had been lost ever be restored?

His one hope was to find and protect the missing kaiser himself. Otherwise, his chance to explain that the attack had not been by his will would be lost forever. Well, perhaps not forever, but he would rather stand on equal footing with Reinhard and explain things rationally than beg for mercy as a prisoner of war.

"I wish we could have had one last drink together, Mittermeier. Even though I have only myself to blame for being unable to…"

He felt a pang of sorrow. *Mein Freund, honey-haired Gale Wolf, you will surely risk your life to defend me to the kaiser. But the malice at work between the kaiser and me outweighs even your benevolence. My pride leaves me no choice but to fight.*

And if I must fight, I will fight with everything I have. I will spare no effort to secure victory. To do any less would be an insult to the kaiser...

It did not pain him to think of Kaiser Reinhard. On the contrary, he felt a rare elevation run up his spine. It was accompanied by a kind of shudder, but von Reuentahl managed to check the enthusiasm within him and reorient his attention by force.

"What is Trünicht doing?" he asked.

"Do you have need of him, Your Excellency?" asked Bergengrün, somewhat pointedly, after a moment's surprise. Von Reuentahl had always shown distaste at even having to speak his high counselor's name aloud. Why do so now, when the man's presence would be less welcome than ever?

"Even Trünicht has his uses. Not noble ones, of course. Let's get the unpleasant business out of the way first. Bring him in."

"I will have to clear it with the director general of civil affairs first."

"No, there's no need for that." Even the fearless von Reuentahl blanched slightly at this prospect. Director General Julius Elsheimer was married to Lutz's younger sister. He could not be expected to maintain equanimity given von Reuentahl's culpability for his brother-in-law's death.

During the assault on Iserlohn, Lutz had served as von Reuentahl's subcaptain. He had always deserved the faith people placed in him. Von Reuentahl was sure that he had died on Urvashi protecting the kaiser. A fine, upstanding man who had lived without a hint of dishonor.

Half an hour later, his exact opposite arrived at von Reuentahl's office—a man who seemed smeared head to toe in dishonor somehow made liquid. Every time von Reuentahl saw Trünicht, he felt new disdain for the political system that had nurtured and rewarded his malfeasance.

"The glacial pace of republican democratic governance often frustrates the masses," von Reuentahl had once said. "If I can satisfy them with swiftness, they will soon forget their affection for democracy."

On the front lines of his administration, this jaundiced and contemptuous view was already being proven correct. In government offices and public institutions, citizen services that had once been all but moribund were making a recovery. Every day, reports reached his desk of successes so minor it pained him to read them: "The high-speed underground railroad now runs according to schedule." "Once-arrogant ward office staff have started treating citizens with kindness."

Do you see?, he thought. *Those who call themselves public servants only fear punishment from those with authority. They certainly show no devotion to the citizenry, the supposed rulers of a democracy…*

Trünicht greeted the governor-general with his usual impeccable gentlemanly demeanor. Von Reuentahl's return salute was formally perfect too.

"I have a small job for you," he said.

"Your wish is my command."

"Before we get into that, let me ask you a question I've wanted to for some time now. You make no claim, I hope, that your deplorable behavior was designed to sound the alarm for future generations and promote the healthy development of democratic republicanism…?"

"Marshal von Reuentahl, you are as perceptive as ever! How gratifying it is to have my true intentions recognized."

"What…?"

"A joke, of course. I have no interest in playing martyr. I hate to disappoint, but the behavior you refer to was for my benefit and no one else's."

The man was mob rule in a necktie. What else might one call him? And yet, von Reuentahl was unable to shake the suspicion that Trünicht was more than just a corrupt politician. He had outlived Yang Wen-li—would he survive von Reuentahl too? Having let democracy rot and sucked the marrow from its bones, would he blight autocracy, too, and finally feast on its corpse? The prospect was all too plausible—unless someone took responsibility for disposing of him.

Von Reuentahl turned to Bergengrün. "Inspector general, find a suitable cage for this rat." He jerked his chin at Trünicht as if indicating something unclean; even his superficial courtesy was gone now. "It may squeak like a man, but you don't have to listen. Be sure to feed it occasionally. We might feel a twinge of guilt if it starved to death."

Trünicht was surrounded by soldiers and dragged away. Not a flicker of fear showed in his eyes, which might be thought worthy of admiration even if it was only false bravado.

Von Reuentahl frowned and bowed his head in thought for a moment. Then he looked up. "Bergengrün!"

"Your Excellency."

"Send a messenger to Iserlohn Fortress. Tell them that if they deny the Imperial Navy use of the corridor, I'll give back the alliance's entire former territory."

A look of astonishment rippled across Bergengrün's usually impassive face.

Von Reuentahl laughed. "Why so surprised?" he asked. "The empire's what I want to rule. If those republican holdouts want the former alliance territory back, they're welcome to it."

His face shone with a vital energy that could only be called ruthless. This was the moment at which he took his first step forward, without even a glance at the door behind him.

"In any case, there's no reason to put ourselves at a military disadvantage. Make the offer. I'll even throw in that traitor to democracy Job Trünicht as a bonus—or just his head, if they prefer. Make sure you mention that."

Bergengrün appeared about to speak, but then thought better of it and closed his mouth. With a salute, he left the governor-general's office. Von Reuentahl ran one hand through his hair, so dark a brown it was almost black, and returned to his meditations.

∪

Not all of these details were in Boris Konev's report. His information was more basic: Reuentahl in revolt, kaiser missing. But it was valuable even so, and the relative ease with which he had broken the blockade was proof of the confusion among the Neue Land Security Force.

For Iserlohn's leadership, Konev's report hinted at the exciting possibility of change. They were eager to see the situation develop further.

Julian had once told Caselnes that Iserlohn Fortress had strategic value only when each end of the corridor was home to a different political and military power—and that it might be half a century before that happened again.

Half a century! It was less than half a year since Yang Wen-li had died. The time frame had shrunk to one hundredth its former size. How rapidly things were changing! Of course, a moment's reflection reminded

Julian that Kaiser Reinhard himself had first appeared on history's page, as Count von Lohengramm, less than half a decade earlier. Was history in the process of revealing itself in a new form—not a broad, rolling river but a raging torrent swallowing all in its path?

Julian ran a hand through his flaxen hair. A profound foreboding passed through his breast. The whole of history seemed to be accelerating, and so many of the people he knew, both directly and indirectly, seemed to be living fast and recklessly, hurtling toward early deaths. Could this be the road that Kaiser Reinhard and Marshal von Reuentahl would take as well? Enemies though they were, they were such radiant, singular figures.

"What are you going to do, Julian?" said von Schönkopf. "Do you think this chaos will give us a chance to improve our position?"

"I hope so, but…"

But if he erred in his judgment, all Iserlohn would be knocked off course. The fate of democracy itself could be affected. The clash between Reinhard and von Reuentahl was, in the end, a power struggle within an autocratic system, nothing more. What Iserlohn needed was a way to play both ends against the middle. Even so, Julian had one reservation he could not ignore.

"Marshal von Reuentahl is a master tactician, but can he really win against Kaiser Reinhard? What do you think, Admiral von Merkatz?" He turned to the older man, who sat with his arms folded in silent thought.

"It seems to me," said von Merkatz, "that von Reuentahl is the type of man who grows richer in ability as he rises in rank and responsibility. Before the Lippstadt War, I did not expect to lose to a man with so much less experience. Nor, of course, did I think him any sort of rival to Kaiser Reinhard. But if he can avoid a two-front war and outlast the kaiser's supply lines, he may just have a chance."

"Avoid a two-front war…" murmured Julian. Based on this hint from the respected older admiral, he attempted to construct a pyramid in his thoughts. Noticing a large stone which should be included, he spoke to himself in the form of a question.

"The marshal's own abilities aside, will those he commands go along with his decision to raise the flag of rebellion against Reinhard?"

As it happened, this question also occupied the Terraist fanatics who had staged this masque of intrigue. Reinhard was not a foolish or cruel leader, and his soldiers revered him as a martial god. Von Reuentahl might have more than five million troops under his command, but what percentage would put their loyalty to him ahead of their faith in the kaiser?

If only Yang were alive, Julian thought, then caught himself and shook his head internally. A reliance cultivated over long years was a stubborn thing. "You have to think for yourself, Julian"—how often had Yang reminded him of this, ruffling his hair affectionately?

Julian sank into thought. His staff officers, Caselnes, von Schönkopf, Attenborough, Poplin, and von Merkatz, waited patiently. Frederica, too, and others not in the room, both living and dead, also doubtless followed the tracks of his thought.

October, year 2 of the New Imperial Calendar, SE 800. Word of the Reuentahl Revolt tore through inhabited space like lightning. Far from bringing lasting peace to the galaxy, Yang Wen-li's death seemed on the verge of plunging humanity into the howling abyss.

CHAPTER SIX:
REBELLION IS A HERO'S PRIVILEGE

I

THE CONFUSION OF THE SITUATION and the disorder of the information twisted into a helix that sent ever-widening ripples of misfortune across the galaxy.

Kaiser missing!

The news, which of course was not made public, sent shudders through the upper levels of the empire. Communications were exchanged with the Neue Land governorate, some polite and some heated, but this merely piled up more fuel in the form of frustration, suspicion, and concern, waiting only for a spark to set it ablaze.

Then, on October 29, *Brünhild* was discovered and brought under protection by the Wahlen Fleet, which had launched from the area around Schattenberg.

The good news was immediately sent to the imperial capital of Phezzan. Once the situation became clear, there would surely be other grave problems to trouble everyone anew, but for now Müller felt that he had at least fulfilled his obligations to Lutz. Of course, Müller had no way of knowing that Reinhard's rescue by friendly forces was also according to the plans laid by the conspirators, who arrogantly believed that they were free to manipulate the fates of men as they pleased.

Conspiracy is entirely uncorrelated with intellect and incompatible with character. That Müller failed to detect a conspiracy which could contribute only negatively to his humanity would actually raise his estimation among later generations. But losing Kornelias Lutz, a trusted senior colleague, grieved him far more than any evaluation of himself could.

When the transmission confirming Lutz's death reached *Brünhild*, Reinhard had closed his eyes, brought his folded hands to his brow, and remained motionless for some time. Finally, just as a concerned von Streit was about to say something, the kaiser lowered his hands again and spoke in a voice like the melody of a requiem.

"Lutz is hereby promoted to imperial marshal. He might not like it, but that is his punishment for breaking his promise."

Reuentahl in revolt!

These words reminded the leaders of the Imperial Navy that however many battlefields they had visited in this restless age, however mighty the enemy forces they had distinguished themselves against, they were not free from the demon of surprise.

At the same time, however, there was an odd kind of sense to the news. They lived in an age that had seen a man of vigor, ability, and capacity rise from the lowest ranks of the nobility to claim the highest crown. Countless others would surely leap at the temptation to rule the entire galaxy, given the opportunity. Von Reuentahl's position and self-confidence were commensurate to his ambition. He could not be accused of failing to know his limits.

Of course, some did not believe the reports—or, perhaps more accurately, did not wish to believe them. When the news reached von Reuentahl's dear friend Mittermeier, he was furious. "I thought that nonsense had vanished in early spring with the year's snows!" he shouted. "Apparently I was wrong. Are you among the wretches who would have it snow in summer?"

The bearer of the news did not flinch. "That was only rumor, but this is fact. Even if Marshal von Reuentahl had no connection to the conspiracy, what of his responsibility to ensure the kaiser's safety?"

As commander in chief of the Imperial Space Armada, Mittermeier had directed the search for the kaiser around Schattenberg. A muddy stream of intelligence flowed in as he carried out this task. Some reported that the kaiser had died. Others brought news of von Reuentahl's coronation. The only news that could be confirmed was the death of Lutz. None of what Mittermeier heard brought him much comfort, whether true or false, until Wahlen sent word that the kaiser was alive and well.

November 1. Escorted by the Wahlen Fleet, *Brünhild* entered the Phezzan Corridor, where it was met by Mittermeier. The Gale Wolf boarded the ship, rejoiced to see the kaiser safe, and thanked Müller and the others for their part in protecting him.

"I have matters to discuss with the commander in chief," Reinhard said to Müller and the others. "Leave us."

They obeyed, but were unable to hide their conflicted expressions.

"Mittermeier."

"Yes, Your Majesty."

"I am sure you understand why I had you remain in the room. Von Reuentahl is one of the greatest military minds of his generation. In all the Imperial Navy, only two men could even hope to prevail against him. One of those men is me. The other is you."

Mittermeier was silent.

"That is why you are still here. Is my meaning clear?"

Mittermeier did not need to be told twice. He hung his head, rivulets of near-freezing sweat trickling down his forehead.

"I know it is too much to ask," Reinhard continued. "Your friendship with von Reuentahl goes back over a decade. And so, on this occasion only, I grant you the right to refuse an order from me. Although I suppose you might only find this more insulting…"

Mittermeier once more perceived Reinhard's meaning. If Mittermeier refused his orders, the kaiser meant to lead a punitive expedition against the rebellion himself.

"Please, Your Majesty, wait."

Mittermeier's voice trembled. He had denounced the evils of Duke von Braunschweig, head of the most distinguished noble family in the Goldenbaum Dynasty, despite the threat of death, but now it seemed that even his heart had gone pale.

Reinhard lowered himself into his chair and crossed his left leg over his right knee. His eyes were like ice-blue novae, and never left Mittermeier's.

"I would give up every honor I have won in battle if it would convince Your Majesty to reconsider. Is there any hope this request might be granted?"

"Reconsider?" Furious emotion colored Reinhard's fair cheeks a pale crimson. "Reconsider what, pray tell? Are you sure you do not misunderstand this situation, Mittermeier? The one who should reconsider is von Reuentahl, not me. He betrayed me—I did not betray him!"

The kaiser's entire form seemed to gleam golden, ablaze with indignation and rage.

"Your Majesty, I cannot believe von Reuentahl meant any betrayal. His loyalty and record of service dwarf my own. Please grant him an opportunity to explain himself."

"An opportunity, you say! And how many days passed between my escape from Urvashi through Lutz's sacrifice and my rescue by Wahlen? If von Reuentahl wished to protest his innocence, could he not have done so a hundred times over?"

On Urvashi, the kaiser had if anything been inclined to reject the view of von Reuentahl as chief conspirator. But the death of loyal Lutz and the escape that followed had wounded his pride deeply. A key retainer had been killed in his own territory, and he, the kaiser, had been forced to flee lest he become a prisoner of war.

"Your Majesty, when von Reuentahl was slandered in February, your faith in him never wavered."

"Is an attack on my person and the loss of Lutz's life mere slander?" Reinhard shouted. His fair hand swept a glass off the table. It shattered against the wall in a spray of crystal shards and droplets of wine.

Black clouds of despair crowded hung low on the horizon of Mittermeier's heart. The kaiser had set out virtually unarmed to visit von Reuentahl, and his magnanimous gesture had been rewarded with perfidy. His trust in one retainer had resulted in the death of another. Small wonder that he could not remain calm. And, of course, when grief and self-reproach over the dead flow back toward the living, an increase in severity is always the result.

Reinhard had no reason to lash out at Mittermeier. In light of his friendship with von Reuentahl, it was all too possible to guess at his anguish. The kaiser did not fail to understand this, but he had psychic pain of his own, and he could not keep it from gushing forth. In truth, Mittermeier's lack of anger at von Reuentahl for forcing Reinhard into this difficult situation also fueled the displeasure and anger that mixed with frustration within him.

"Do you think it is my wish to put down von Reuentahl? No doubt there are indeed things he would like to explain. There was friendship between us, too, if not as deep as the one you and he shared. In which case, why does he not appear before me to explain himself? While I was fleeing in dishonor, what was he doing? Has he sent even a single line of apology? A single word of condolence over Lutz's death? On what grounds would he have me recognize his sincerity?!"

Mittermeier could not reply. Everything Reinhard said was correct. Von Reuentahl's actions were more than deserving of criticism. In the back of his mind, Mittermeier saw his friend pushing deeper into a maze, but he could not speak of this to his liege. He felt that he *must* not speak of it, in fact, for both the kaiser's sake and von Reuentahl's.

What he did say was something else entirely.

"Your Majesty, this is difficult to say, but the reason von Reuentahl has not presented himself before you may be that he fears he will be intercepted by others before he can arrive."

"Others?"

"I fear Your Majesty will take this as slander, but I mean Marshal van Oberstein and Heidrich Lang."

"You say they would ignore my wishes and prevent von Reuentahl from arriving?"

"Your Majesty, please. Could these two men not be dismissed from their current positions, as a show of Your Majesty's willingness to reconcile with von Reuentahl?"

Reinhard was silent.

"Only give Your Majesty's word on this matter, and I vow to convince von Reuentahl to bend the knee before you, even at the cost of my own life. I beg you, forgive him this momentary madness. I know it reverses the correct order of things, but there is no other way."

. "Am I obliged to concede so much to him? Instead of putting down a subject who has betrayed me, you order me to dismiss other, loyal retainers to win him back? Who is it who sits on the throne of this empire—me, or von Reuentahl?"

Still enraged, Reinhard all but spat out the question, which was surely the most agonizing Mittermeier had ever been asked.

"Your Majesty, I admit I have never been on good terms with Marshal von Oberstein, but it is not for that reason that I call for his dismissal. He could be relieved of his position temporarily, and restored to it later with his honor reaffirmed. But if we let this opportunity pass, von Reuentahl may never have another chance to return to Your Majesty."

"Do you believe this logic will convince the minister?"

"I do not propose that he alone should be dishonored. I will also give up my role as commander in chief of the Imperial Space Armada. This, I believe, will mollify the minister to some extent."

"What are you saying? Who do you propose I have command my armada instead? Must I lose all three of my marshals at once?"

"The armada may be safely left to Senior Admiral Müller. As for von Oberstein's replacement, I know it is not my place to offer suggestions, but I believe that Kessler or Mecklinger could act as minister of military affairs. There is no need for concern."

"I see how it is. You wish to retire before the age of thirty-five. I confess I did not expect the most fearless general under my command to take life lessons from Yang Wen-li."

Reinhard began to laugh at his own joke, but this ray of sunlight was blocked by clouds before it could reach the ground. His mood having worsened, if anything, his eyes bored into Mittermeier again.

"I will take your opinion on advisement. For now, I need your response to my orders. Ja, or nein? If the latter, of course, then I will simply lead the expedition myself."

Mittermeier bowed his head deeply. His honey-blond hair concealed his expression from the kaiser's gaze. For long moments, the music of silence played.

At last Mittermeier said, "I humbly accept Your Majesty's orders."

I have no other choice, he thought, but did not say aloud.

II

When Mittermeier returned to Imperial Space Armada Headquarters from the sectors around Schattenberg, his staff officers could not look him in the eye. He disappeared into his office enshrouded in a pale magnetic field. Thirty minutes later, however, when he called in his youngest staff officer, Admiral Karl Eduard Bayerlein, his expression and voice were clad in the armor of officialdom.

"Contact Wahlen and Wittenfeld. They'll probably be shoring up the flanks on this expedition."

"Yes, Your Excellency. What about Admiral Müller?"

"Müller's wounds aren't fully healed yet, and he's needed by His Majesty's side anyway. If I'm defeated, he'll be the last line of defense."

Bayerlein frowned. "In that case, he'll play no role at all. There's no chance of Your Excellency being defeated, after all."

At this show of faith and respect, Mittermeier's expression softened. "To be honest," he said finally, "I'd rather let von Reuentahl win."

"Your Excellency!"

"No, even that is my vanity speaking. Even if I pushed myself to the limit of abilities, I could never defeat von Reuentahl in the first place." Mittermeier's sour chuckle dismayed Bayerlein by how poorly it suited the commander he loved and respected.

The Gale Wolf was young, fast, and bold. He kept his eyes forward, neither flattering those above him or mistreating those below. There was a bright clarity to him that made him an aspirational figure for everyone from Bayerlein to the students at the Children's Academy. The children assigned to be his orderlies would brag with eyes agleam to envious classmates. Some even went to the trouble of bring the treats they received from Mrs. Mittermeier to school, making sure everyone saw them. But now that magnificent blue sky was filling with black clouds that threatened a terrible storm.

"It does not seem that way to me," Bayerlein said.

"You're free to believe what you wish, but I am no von Reuentahl."

"Your Excellency—"

"There is no comparison to be made. I am just a soldier. Von Reuentahl is more. He is..."

Mittermeier stopped himself. Bayerlein, sympathizing with his commander's inner turmoil, could not help but hesitantly press him further.

"Suppose that what Your Excellency says is more than modesty. You intend to fight Marshal von Reuentahl anyway, don't you? So that the kaiser will not lead the expedition himself..."

Mittermeier fixed Bayerlein, who was quite correct, with a gaze that was piercing but somehow lacking in force. He did not praise his young subordinate's insight, or scold him for overstepping his place. He simply said, "The kaiser's hands must stay clean," and that was all.

It took some time, but Bayerlein eventually understood his import. If Reinhard led the expedition to put down von Reuentahl, his hands would be stained by the blood of a traitor. This would cloud the faith of those who believed in the "soldiers' kaiser," eventually cracking this once-perfect icon far more deeply than his stalemate against Yang Wen-li ever could. For Mittermeier, this was something that had to be prevented, even if that meant riding roughshod over his own feelings.

"If von Reuentahl falls—even if I fall with him—the Galactic Empire will survive. But if the worst were to happen to His Majesty, the unity and peace he worked so hard to bring about would collapse overnight. It may be that I cannot win this fight, but I must not lose it."

Bayerlein found Mittermeier's calm tone paradoxically unsettling. "Your Excellency, I must protest. If you and Marshal von Reuentahl fell together, Marshal von Oberstein could act as despotically as he pleased with no one to stop him."

Bayerlein's invocation of von Oberstein was an attempt to inspire his commander, but Mittermeier did not seem affected. "Not to worry," he said. "The minister might be so satisfied to have us out of the picture that he retires from the public eye himself."

"Your Excellency, even as a joke—"

"In any case, enough hypotheticals. Contact Wittenfeld and Wahlen."

Still looking at his superior with concern, Bayerlein saluted and left.

Von Oberstein I can live with, von Reuentahl thought. *But the other one—he alone is beyond forgiveness. For the kaiser's sake, before leaving for battle I will have to exterminate that particular pest.*

Although Heidrich Lang had no official post at the Ministry of Military Affairs, it was not unusual for him to visit Minister von Oberstein there.

Today, a gleeful Lang had come to report that the hated von Reuentahl had finally sunk to the level of traitor. The news had, of course, already reached von Oberstein, who said, with his usual dispassion, "I may be sent as special envoy to von Reuentahl as a result of the disturbance in the Neue Land."

"Oh, dear, what a burden for you. And dangerous, too."

"No need for sympathy. You will come with me, after all."

Despite the calmness of von Oberstein's delivery, panic slapped Lang hard enough to knock him off balance.

Von Oberstein ignored this embarrassing display and sipped his coffee. "Be prepared to depart at any time," he said. "I have finished my preparations already."

"I-if I show my face around von Reuentahl, he will kill me on the spot. He despises me, after all, for what reason I do not know."

"I am fairly certain he despises me more." Von Oberstein's voice had no echo of irony or mockery. It was a factual observation, delivered with scholarly detachment.

Stuttering a feeble excuse for postponing his reply, Lang fled from the minister's office just as Commodore Ferner entered. Lang thought he detected a sneer on Ferner's face, but had had no time to check.

This was no joke. He had no objection to von Oberstein being slain by von Reuentahl. If anything, such an outcome would benefit his own future prosperity yet. The two marshals dying at the same time would be even better—ideal, in fact. But he had no interest in appearing in that tableau himself.

At this time, Lang's ego was as obese and distended as a goose liver made into foie gras. He did not realize that others viewed him as von Oberstein's inferior.

He went around to the rear staircase, hoping at least to reduce the number of people who saw him, and had just begun descending when he froze on the spot, entire body rigid. A young man in the black and silver uniform of the Imperial Navy was climbing the stairs toward him from below. The man's gaze was fixed on him, and the light that brimmed in those gray eyes was the polar opposite of goodwill.

"M-Marshal Mittermeier…"

"Well, well, the man of the moment even knows my name. I'm honored beyond words."

Mittermeier's voice was uncharacteristically venomous. Lang took two unthinking steps back, still fixed by that gray-eyed stare. This was the first time he had confronted Mittermeier without anyone else to hide behind.

"I-if you have business with the minister, he is in his office on the fifth floor…"

"My business is with you, Junior Minister Lang." The change from hostility to harmful intent seeped into Mittermeier's voice. "Or do you prefer Domestic Safety Security Bureau Chief Lang? Either way, your title in life won't do you much good where you're going."

Lang heard himself swallow loudly. The color faded from his vision, with only Mittermeier's honey-colored hair floating vividly before him.

Mittermeier began to climb the stairs, military boots ringing out with each step. His right hand was on his blaster, but he did not hurry. The spirit that radiated from his body drove unseen iron nails through Lang's feet, pinning him where he stood.

"Stay where you are until I get there," Mittermeier said.

Lang's mind rejected the order, but not his body. He wanted to run, but his impulses were crawling through his nervous system slower than snails. Both eyes and mouth open, the former wide and the latter not, he found it difficult even to struggle in the viscous air. The people nearby were as overwhelmed by Mittermeier's spirit as Lang, and only stopped and stared.

No—there was one man who could still move, and who climbed

the stairs after the Gale Wolf to place a hand on his shoulder just as he reached the top.

"Stop this, Marshal Mittermeier. The junior minister is an imperial official."

Mittermeier turned, murder in his eyes, to see Senior Admiral Ulrich Kessler, commissioner of military police and commander of capital defense.

"You have accomplished incomparable things on the battlefield, marshal," Kessler continued, "but you may not bring your personal grudges into the ministry, and I have the authority and the duty to stop you from doing so. Do I make myself clear?"

"Personal grudges?" Mittermeier expression and voice overflowed with bitterness. Fury boiled from his gray eyes. "I disagree with that characterization, commissioner, but if you insist on it I will not object. But if I am to set off on this expedition with confidence, I cannot allow this termite in human skin to ravage the empire any further. You may not realize this, but—"

"Lang's abuses will be punished according to law. To do otherwise would undermine the very foundations of the Lohengramm Dynasty. You are one of the dynasty's most important officials, and one of its most respected military commanders. You cannot fail to understand this."

"A fine position to take, commissioner, but what power has law ever had over that quivering termite there? Punish me if you wish. Just let me give him his just deserts first."

"Calm yourself, marshal. You are wiser than this. If anything happened to you, who would protect the Goldenlöwe's glory in your stead? Is the Gale Wolf himself such a slave to private passions that he would abandon his responsibility to the entire empire?"

Kessler's voice was not loud or impassioned, but it struck a deep chord within Mittermeier. In his violent passion, sweat trickled from his disheveled, honey-colored hair, rolling down from temple to cheek. Watching this with pain and sympathy, Kessler adopted a more conciliatory tone as he continued.

"The kaiser is a wise ruler. If the junior minister has done wrong, he will surely be corrected under imperial authority and national law. Please, marshal, put your faith in me, and fulfill the duties that fall to you."

After a long silence, Mittermeier said, "Very well. I leave him in your hands." His voice was low and drained of vitality. "I'm sorry you had to see that. I'll make up for causing this unpleasant scene another time."

His spirit broken, Mittermeier walked away. Kessler watched in silence, then shifted his gaze to Lang, still transfixed on the stairs. The look that crossed the commissioner's face was one of visceral disgust.

III

October came, and then November.

The Church of Terra's conspiracy had succeeded to an artistic degree. However, in a sense this was like a child's scribbles receiving high critical praise. Among what was later reported by the church's leadership was the comment "If we had failed with von Reuentahl, we intended to advance our plans with Mittermeier and von Oberstein as target," which surely proves a tendency to overestimate the perfection of the conspiracy based on the success of its fruits.

"The Reuentahl Revolt," "the Heinessen Upheaval," "the Neue Land Conflict," "the War of the Third Year": this vast disturbance, which would be known by many names, was disproportionately personal in nature.

Von Reuentahl knew that he would never be Reinhard's equal. The kaiser's usurpation of the Goldenbaum Dynasty had been a creative ambition, but for von Reuentahl to usurp the Lohengramm Dynasty would be an imitation. It was the Church of Terra forcing him into a dangerous position that had led him to raise the flag of rebellion regardless, but even at that point the catastrophe might have been averted. Had he taken Bergengrün's advice and traveled unarmed to the new capital on Phezzan to explain himself to the kaiser, Mittermeier would have taken his side, ending the revolt before it began. He would have been forced to accept final responsibility for the death of Kornelias Lutz, but later historians were agreed that his punishment would likely have been removal from his position as governor-general and temporary reassignment to the reserves.

However, in another corner of the galaxy, circumstances were developing in a way that von Reuentahl could not have foreseen.

Grillparzer restored order on Urvashi before October was out. His methods were severely militaristic, and more than two thousand were killed in battle or executed on the spot for not immediately obeying orders to lay down arms and return to their postings. Once he had taken control of the planet, Grillparzer set about piecing together the full picture of what had happened there. This proved no easy task.

The Urvashi base commander, Vice Admiral Winckler, was missing. His body had not been found and no reliable testimony about his whereabouts could be obtained. Observations of symptoms suggesting a drug addiction were discovered in his on-base medical records, but Grillparzer's investigators could not ascertain why a senior officer whose abilities and achievements had been rewarded with such heavy responsibility should have fallen into addiction.

Testimony from the soldiers who had participated in the unrest was highly confused. Some even claimed that their superiors had ordered them to rescue the kaiser before he could be harmed by Admirals Lutz and Müller, who had been brainwashed by the Church of Terra.

The church did seem to be behind the plot. Its scriptures and emblems were discovered in the possession of more than ten dead soldiers and several living ones. But Grillparzer chose not to reveal this information publicly for the time being.

While Grillparzer was untangling the snarl of barbed wire on Urvashi, or pretending to, the surrounding situation deteriorated. A wall of enmity, great and high, was rising between the imperial government and the Neue Land administration. Accordingly, when Grillparzer returned to Heinessen and pledged his allegiance instead of fleeing to Phezzan, von Reuentahl could not hide his surprise.

"You genuinely intend to ally yourself with me?"

"That is my intention. However..."

"However?"

"I have ambitions of my own. I want a promise that I will be made minister of military affairs and an imperial marshal the morning after Your Excellency's victory."

"Agreed." Particles of derision flecked von Reuentahl's heterochromatic eyes as he nodded. "I thought you would seek a slightly higher position, but if minister of military affairs will satisfy you, I will grant that wish. As of now, you are fighting for your own hopes too. I expect you to spare no effort."

Von Reuentahl and Grillparzer were both warriors in a turbulent age. They should have been able to find common cause and values founded on shared ambition. The fact that Grillparzer had revealed particularly unscrupulous ambitions might have strengthened von Reuentahl's trust in their alliance as one based solely on calculation. Even if he had harbored suspicions, there was no evidence to justify acting on them. Eliminating Grillparzer as a precautionary measure ran the risk of unsettling his other subordinates. Von Reuentahl had no choice but to proceed as he did.

Meanwhile, Admiral Bruno von Knapfstein, all but under house arrest in his official quarters, was soon surprised by a visit from Grillparzer.

"Why did you return to Heinessen?" he demanded indignantly of his colleague. "Are you so eager to go down in the history of the new dynasty as a traitor?"

Grillparzer said nothing.

"In fact, from what I hear, you did more than return. You voluntarily swore fealty to von Reuentahl, and even demanded rank. What are you playing at?"

"Calm yourself, Knapfstein," the young geographer said, as if ridiculing his colleague's simple-mindedness. "Surely you don't think I'm sincere about my allegiance to the marshal's flag of rebellion?"

Von Knapfstein looked four parts disgruntled and six embarrassed. "You say you aren't? In that case, I'd love to hear what you *do* mean by all this. After all, unlike you, I am an uneducated man. Complex theories are beyond me."

Grillparzer ignored this attempt at sarcasm. "Think, Knapfstein!" he said. "How is it we were able to become admirals in the Imperial Navy while still in our twenties?"

"By the kaiser's benevolence, and by distinguishing ourselves in battle."

"And could we have distinguished ourselves without an enemy *to* battle? The Free Planets Alliance is vanquished, Yang Wen-li is dead. Throughout the galaxy, war will soon be a thing of the past. If we let that happen, we will be stranded in an age of peace, with no way of proving our valor or bettering ourselves. Agreed?"

"Well—I suppose so. But—"

"Which means that we must perform feats of arms, even if some wiliness is required to arrange them. Do you understand yet?"

Grillparzer was smiling. When von Knapfstein saw through that painted-on grin to the skeleton of ambition beneath, he recoiled with an unconscious shudder.

"So…you mean to feign allegiance to von Reuentahl for now, and then betray him in the end?"

"Betray? I wish you'd take more care when you speak, Knapfstein. We are still subjects of His Majesty Kaiser Reinhard—we simply happen to be posted under Marshal von Reuentahl. Isn't it self-evident where our ultimate loyalty should lie?

Von Knapfstein groaned. There was no error in Grillparzer's logic. But didn't that mean that they should state their allegiance clearly from the beginning, denounce von Reuentahl, and go to join to the kaiser? By turning his back on the kaiser now and von Reuentahl later, Grillparzer would only achieve a double betrayal. He seemed confident that he could use von Reuentahl's revolt to further his own interests. Would things truly go as smoothly as he expected? Still, despite these misgivings, in the end Grillparzer had his colleague's sympathy. No other options seemed immediately available to him.

By contrast, Julius Elsheimer, director general of civil affairs for the Neue Land governorate, flatly refused to swear fealty to the governor-general. Voice shaking, face white with fear, collar soaked with cold sweat, he told von Reuentahl that he could not take part in any rebellion against the kaiser, not backing down even before the marshal's intimidating presence and glittering mismatched eyes.

"Furthermore," he added, "if I may speak in a personal capacity, Your Excellency bears responsibility for the death of my brother-in-law, Kornelias Lutz. I cannot ally myself with you with this matter still legally and morally unresolved."

Von Reuentahl frowned very slightly. After a prolonged silence, he spoke, grave composure in his voice.

"Your opinions as a public figure are trite and undistinguished, but your position as a private individual is both brave and fair. If you refuse to join me, fine. Remain in your residence and do not actively oppose me, and you and your family will be safe."

Von Reuentahl wrote out a short document on the spot and gave it to Elsheimer to take home with him. The document was addressed to Marshal Wolfgang Mittermeier, commander in chief of the Imperial Space Armada. It declared that Elsheimer had refused to support the rebellion, vouched for his unwavering loyalty to the kaiser, and asked that he be spared any rebuke or reprisal.

Von Reuentahl's magnanimity toward Elsheimer showed the noble element fixed in his character. At the same time, however, he had to do what was necessary to survive—and prosper.

I may be defeated by mein Kaiser, may be utterly vanquished, but not until I have done all I can to win.

Thus was the resolve in von Reuentahl's black right eye—but his blue left eye raised an objection.

If you choose to fight, you must desire victory. What good does it do to think of defeat before you begin? Or is that what you truly want? Your downfall— your destruction?

There was no answer. The possessor of these two eyes gazed at himself in the mirror on the wall.

"Beyond redemption, if I say so myself."

As he muttered the words aloud, he was grateful at least that no one was around to hear.

IV

There was, of course, no formal declaration of war. With no clear point of departure, the hostility and tension between the worlds of the old empire and the Neue Land continued to rise. Von Oberstein in the Ministry of Military Affairs and Mittermeier in the space armada command center, though differing in demeanor and frame of mind, were both preparing for mobilization.

Meanwhile, in Imperial Headquarters, a reunion took place. Returning to Phezzan from the sectors around Schattenberg, Reinhard entered his office to discover a familiar figure standing beside his massive walnut desk. Her name came unbidden to his lips.

"Fräulein von Mariendorf…"

"Welcome home, Your Majesty. I'm so happy to see you safe."

Hilda's tone was even, but her voice was rich with tender feeling. That Reinhard realized this was perhaps a sign of his growing sensitivity, but his reply of "Yes, my apologies for the concern" indicated that his expressive powers remained at a standstill.

"Lutz is dead," he said flatly, after a pause. He indicated that Hilda should sit on the sofa, and took a seat beside her. "How many have died for me in all? Three years ago, I thought there was no one left whose absence I would mourn. But this year alone, I have lost Fahrenheit, Steinmetz, Lutz… Even as punishment for my own foolishness, it strikes me as excessive."

"Your Majesty's marshals are not tools used by fate to punish you. Nor do I think they set out for Valhalla with resentment in their hearts. You must not torment yourself."

"I know. Still…" As if suddenly realizing his own thoughtlessness, the kaiser changed the subject. "And you, fräulein, have you been well?"

"Yes, Your Majesty, by your leave."

The response was slightly curious, but Reinhard nodded in apparent relief.

Hilda was one year younger than Reinhard, but sometimes she had to take on the older, wiser role. There was no discontinuity in Reinhard's psyche in terms of the noble and the base, but he did contain both a perfected, unsentimental man of action and a dreamy, pure, and vulnerable boy who could only see what lay directly before him, and these two coexisted in an endless cycle of fusion and separation. Particularly when the latter was ascendant, Hilda had to treat him with care.

If Reinhard's birth and life were historical miracles, the same was surely true of Hilda's. Where Reinhard had been born to a poor family, noble in name only, she had been born the daughter of a count, albeit not in the family's main line. In this sense, Hilda may have deserved more credit for remaining a unique presence in her sealed, hothouse milieu.

Hilda had originally aligned her family with Reinhard's camp during the Lippstadt War to ensure that the Mariendorf County would not get caught up in the battle between the Coalition of Lords and the Lichtenlade–Lohengramm axis. It was a political decision, but the diplomatic and strategic sense behind it was so remarkable that Reinhard had been moved to offer her a position as his chief secretary.

Hilda had not seduced the young conqueror with her feminine wiles. She was beautiful, but beauty was not seduction. In any case, Reinhard was frostily indifferent to sensual allure; had seduction been her strategy, it would have failed her. The truth was that such an approach had not even occurred to her, meaning that the synchronization of their mental wavelengths was not solely her achievement. Had Reinhard seen only the surface manifestations of her intellect and character, he would have judged her an impertinent know-it-all and banished her from his thoughts. Which would have cost him his future at the Vermillion War, and altered the history of all humanity.

"Von Reuentahl sent a communication—addressed to the imperial government. Were you aware of this, fräulein?"

"Yes, Your Majesty."

The message had been delivered to Phezzan at around the time of Reinhard's arrival. Von Reuentahl's choice to address it not to the kaiser but to the government itself revealed certain complexities in his thinking. This alone would have displeased Reinhard, but the message's content was more unpleasant yet:

> Minister of Military Affairs Paul von Oberstein and Junior Minister of the Interior Heidrich Lang have seized control of the state. They ride roughshod over His Majesty's wishes with the freedom to eradicate those who oppose them. I, Marshal Oskar von Reuentahl, will not sit by and permit this to happen. I hereby declare my intention to end their tyranny—if necessary, by force of arms…

Particularly aggravating to Reinhard, Hilda suspected, was a reference elsewhere in von Reuentahl's message to the two alleged villains "taking advantage of His Majesty's debilitating illness and weakened state." It was as if von Reuentahl were intentionally provoking the kaiser.

"Tell me, when did I allow von Oberstein or Lang to seize control of the state? If von Reuentahl is correct, how is it he became governor-general of the Neue Land in the first place? Did he have to denigrate me so viciously to justify his betrayal?"

To submit to another, to be ruled by another: these were what Reinhard hated most. His anger over this insult to his pride was fierce, deep, and entirely natural. His Majesty's weakened state! The words were like a hot wind fanning the flames of his fury.

Von Reuentahl had reasons for making the claims he did. Since Kaiser Reinhard himself was not guilty of misrule, a rebellion against him had no choice but to denounce "disloyal subjects" instead. The antipathy for von Oberstein among Reinhard's courtiers might be mingled with awe, but Lang was simply despised. Vowing to eliminate both could be expected to elicit a certain amount of sympathy at court, which made it only natural, on both diplomatic and strategic grounds, for von Reuentahl to do so. Further, diplomacy aside, von Reuentahl's own antipathy against von Oberstein and Lang was genuine.

However, even if judgment were passed against both men, Hilda did not believe that von Reuentahl would call off his revolt. Ultimately, she suspected, he sought a position higher than either of them currently held.

The existence of sycophants and petty tyrants like Lang was an unavoidable flaw in the autocratic state. Throughout history, even the greatest rulers and wisest kings had placed such malefactors in positions of authority, time and again. Because they were not worthy of the ruler's attention, they were underestimated and ignored until they grew into a severe threat to their fellow subjects. The animus against Lang among Reinhard's court could become sympathy and empathy with von Reuentahl's betrayal. Hilda had to make Reinhard see this much at least.

She turned her gaze on the ice-blue suns that smoldered in his eyes, and opened lips as beautiful as his own to speak.

"If I may, Your Majesty—Minister von Oberstein aside, Lang's crimes against the state, and against you personally, far outweigh any good he might do. Surely Your Majesty is aware of the enmity his deeds and character attract?"

Reinhard, his fury seemingly dampened, put a hand to his shapely chin and thought. "As you say, fräulein, I am well aware that Lang and men like him are of little worth," he said. "But a single mouse helping himself to the storehouse grain does little real damage. The Galactic Empire must be large enough to tolerate even irritations like this."

These were not necessarily Reinhard's true feelings on the matter. Reinhard had a peculiar complex about being seen as a just ruler. Since ancient times, the sages had agreed that a king must be tolerant and broad-minded enough to accept even the most worthless wretch. Aware of this idea, Reinhard could not banish Lang, who had after all not broken the law or committed lèse-majesté. Beyond that, Lang simply did not command Reinhard's attention. The kaiser might admire a winter rose, but fail to notice the pests that troubled it.

Lang was well aware that his life was lived on these terms. In Reinhard's presence, he showed scrupulous deference; in his position at the ministry, he worked diligently to carry out the imperial will. Indeed, this was the reason for his sycophancy. On this point he differed radically from von Oberstein, who spoke his mind with almost callous frankness, even when this meant contradicting Reinhard directly.

Privately, Hilda wanted to urge Reinhard to remove von Oberstein from his position as well. But precisely because she knew how different he was from Lang, she could not take advantage of her special bond with Reinhard to criticize the minister.

"There are any number of capable officials, not to mention those not currently in official service, who could take Junior Minister Lang's place," she said. "Dismissing him would immediately eliminate one of Marshal von Reuentahl's excuses for rebellion. The other admirals will surely accept the measure."

Reinhard's golden hair was almost imperceptibly ruffled by the air in the room. "But Lang has committed no crime," he said. "I cannot punish him simply for being despised."

"No, Your Majesty, his crimes are very real. Please consider this report."

The document she held out had been compiled by Senior Admiral Kessler in his capacity as military police commissioner. Its topic was Nicolas Boltec, former acting secretary-general of Phezzan, and his suspicious

death after being arrested and imprisoned for his alleged role in the explosion that killed Secretary of Work Bruno von Silberberg. Specifically, the
document showed that the accusations against Boltec had been falsely
concocted—by Lang.

"Did you commission this report, fräulein?" Reinhard asked.

"No, Your Majesty. Before his death, Marshal Lutz took note of Lang's
domineering ways and, recognized the danger he posed to the empire,
requested that Admiral Kessler investigate him."

"Lutz...I see."

A shadow passed over Reinhard's eyes. He began to read. As he turned
the pages, his fair cheeks turned crimson, like the glow of the evening sun
appearing in virgin snow. When he finished the report, he sighed deeply.
His monologue came after a short, almost mystical silence.

"Lutz never gave up on me, I see. And then, in the end, he cast away
his life to save my own."

His fair fingers went from his chin to his brow. Their slight trembling
expressed without words what lay in his heart.

"I was a fool. To think that I protected the rights of that nullity while
capable, loyal retainers were left dissatisfied and discontent."

He bit his lip with pearl-white teeth.

"In von Reuentahl's case, it is already too late. But we can still ensure that
Lutz's loyalty was not in vain. Will that suffice, do you think, fräulein?"

Hilda rose from the sofa and saluted. In that moment, she was not
entirely free of the desire to be kissed and embraced, but Reinhard's
expression of faith in her felt like an even greater reward.

V

As she left Reinhard's room, Hilda felt a sudden nausea rise within her.
Her hand went hand first to her chest and then covered her mouth as
she ran into the restroom, feeling the curious stares of the soldiers who
saluted her as she passed.

She leaned over the white porcelain basin and vomited. After washing
the result down the sink, she cleansed her mouth with a cup of water.
The physical urgency had passed, but mental agitation had taken its place.

Surely not—not after just one night… But what else could it be?

Then she remembered that her menses had been absent the previous month. Her mouth dropped open in shock. It had been two months since her night with Reinhard—not too early for the first signs of morning sickness. She wanted to believe that it was just mild food poisoning, but she had been so anxious and eager to see Reinhard safely back today that her only breakfast had been a glass of milk. Even if that had not been the case, her reason would have rejected such escapism.

Hilda was at a loss. Becoming a mother, Reinhard becoming a father— these were far beyond the horizon of her imaginative powers. But she did make one decision: to keep this from Reinhard for the time being.

Bringing her breathing and facial expression under control, she left the bathroom at an even pace and walked back to her office.

Not far from this reunion, a separation was at hand. Evangeline Mittermeier did not like to think it might be permanent, but after just two months with her husband following a year of living apart, they were to be dragged from each other again.

"I won't be coming home for a while," Mittermeier said. It was not the first time this apologetic tone had been heard in their household. He was not just a warrior but the commander of a great navy, and it was not rare for him to lead expeditions across hundreds, even thousands of light years.

But the circumstances this time were unique. A simple "Be careful" would not convey her feelings, and so she spoke to her husband in the living room of the new residence they had just settled into.

"Wolf, I have nothing but affection and respect for Marshal von Reuentahl. He is a close friend of yours, after all. But if he becomes your enemy, then I can despise him unconditionally."

Her emotions were too high to say any more.

Wolfgang Mittermeier felt his wife's small hands placed lightly on his cheeks. His grey eyes gazed into her violet ones, which brimmed with tears.

"Come back safely, Wolf," Evangeline said. "If you do, I promise to cook bouillon fondue for you every day. Your favorite."

"Make it once a week," Mittermeier said. "I don't want to get fat." His body was trim and muscular, without a hint of obesity, and this awkward joke failed to make his wife laugh. Removing her hands from his cheeks, he gave her a kiss that was rather more adroit than any Yang Wen-li might have ever been able to manage.

"There's no need to worry, Eva," he said, even as he considered the possibility that she might have more than sufficient reason to loathe von Reuentahl before long. He embraced her girlish form. "After all, it's not even certain there'll be combat. His Majesty has taken Lang into custody. Von Reuentahl might be satisfied with that."

It seemed that deception was sometimes unavoidable in love. But the next request he made of his wife was sincere to the molecular level.

"So if you do pray, I hope you'll pray that all this will end without any fighting. That's all I want, Eva."

November 14, year 2 of the New Imperial Calendar.

The sectors around Schattenberg were filled with ships under Mittermeier's command. There were 42,770 in all, with 4,608,900 troops aboard. The two senior admirals under Mittermeier were Wittenfeld and Wahlen.

CHAPTER SEVEN:
LIVE BY THE SWORD...

I

MARSHAL WOLFGANG MITTERMEIER, commander in chief of the Imperial Space Armada, invited senior admirals Wahlen and Wittenfeld to a strategy meeting aboard *Beowulf*, his flagship. Their basic course of action, of course, was already decided. They had been dispatched to bring von Reuentahl to heel; their only option was to seize the initiative and strike a single, decisive blow before their enemy (an unpleasant term, under the circumstances) could develop his strategy. Von Reuentahl's forces were already pushing against their physical and mental limits. An initial victory would decide the conflict's final resolution.

The meeting was concluded in short order and coffee brought in. Wittenfeld chose that moment to raise an important if somewhat tactlessly put question: "Strategic matters aside, what has made von Reuentahl so disgruntled with the kaiser that he would commit such an outrag—pardon me—engage in such reckless behavior?"

Wahlen sent Wittenfeld a sharp glance and a low rebuke. Given the friendship between von Reuentahl and their commander in chief, the latter's pain was all too easy to imagine. Wittenfeld's line of questioning seemed less ruthless than simply insensitive.

"Thank you, Admiral Wahlen, but your solicitude is unnecessary," said Mittermeier. "My friendship with Marshal von Reuentahl is ultimately a private matter, and one which my official duties far outweigh."

Those who did not know Mittermeier personally could never have guessed at the depth of emotion in every word of this mild response. Wahlen was so affected that he could not even bear to look Mittermeier in the eye.

"That's right, Admiral Wahlen," said Wittenfeld. "Our commander in chief is doing his duty. To tiptoe around what we imagine he might feel privately would be frankly insolent, in my opinion."

The force of this assertion surprised Wahlen, but he realized that his fierce, orange-haired colleague was, in his own way, just as concerned about their commander as he was. This did not go unnoticed by Mittermeier, either, and something just short of a wry smile appeared on his face as he answered his own questions internally.

Von Reuentahl will bend the knee to one man in all the galaxy, and that is His Majesty Kaiser Reinhard. He will not abide being made to kneel before the minister of military affairs first. Nor do I blame him…

It was said that von Oberstein had called von Reuentahl a caged bird of prey, and Mittermeier had to concede the accuracy of this assessment. Was it simply that this particular eagle, after swearing loyalty to a single white swan in all the galaxy, was now trying to fly away from that other on the winds of a storm?

After Wahlen and Wittenfeld left *Beowulf*, Mittermeier stood by the observation window for some time. As a subject of that beautiful white swan, it was his duty to bring down that eagle. He had never imagined that their friendship might end this way. His honey-colored hair gleamed in the starlight as he wondered just how many mistakes had been made throughout the history of the Galactic Empire—not excluding, of course, his own.

Would the sagacious Siegfried Kircheis have been able to untangle the snarl of wire between Reinhard and von Reuentahl, had he lived to this day? Or had the present situation always been inevitable, beyond the power of even Kircheis to avert?

Immediately after Mittermeier's forces departed, Kaiser Reinhard left Phezzan himself, traveling aboard his flagship *Brünhild* to the sectors around Schattenberg. Senior Admirals Eisenach and Müller accompanied him as his staff. "Iron Wall" Müller's wounds were not fully healed, and his right arm was in a sling.

Reinhard had offered him the Siegfried Kircheis Distinguished Service Award and a promotion to marshal, but the sandy-haired young admiral had respectfully declined. "I cannot accept the marshal's rod before I have proven myself worthy of it," he said. "With Your Majesty's permission, I look forward to gratefully receiving it at a later time, once my achievements merit such an honor."

Reinhard nodded. It was true that, unlike Lutz, Müller would have more opportunities to distinguish himself in battle. "Is there no other way I can reward your valor?" he asked.

"In fact, Your Majesty, I do have one request…"

"Oh?"

The expression that came down over the kaiser's fair, graceful face like silk gauze was less cynical than miserable. But that, too, was but a storm passing over one corner of the ocean, and did not compromise the young conqueror's beauty. (Was it the aftermath of the storm, perhaps, that sent a ripple through his golden hair?)

"I believe I know what you intend to ask of me," Reinhard said. His voice retained its musical rhythm despite the bitterness in his words. "You would have me spare von Reuentahl's life."

"Your Majesty's powers of observation remain unsurpassed."

The kaiser stirred with obvious displeasure. Ice-blue sparks seemed to fly from his eyes.

"Müller, you are one of my most experienced admirals, and I owe you my life. I would grant you any wish within my power. But this one is not."

"Your Majesty…"

"The difficulty does not lie with me. Von Reuentahl is the man you should ask. Not about what he has already done. No, you must ask him what he means to do in the future."

"In the future, Your Majesty?"

"He has raised the flag of rebellion. When the fight is over, is he willing to come to me, head bowed, and beg for his life? Should you not be asking these questions of him, not me?"

Müller was both chastened and shocked. At times like this, he could not help wishing that Countess von Mariendorf were there. She would surely agree with him, and appeal to both reason and emotion in helping to persuade the kaiser. How unfortunate that the beautiful high counselor had been too ill to leave Phezzan!

Müller could not know the real reason for her absence. Indeed, not even Reinhard knew it. She had remained on-planet to protect the child in her womb from the effects of warp…

Reinhard's feelings regarding Wolfgang Mittermeier were based on deep faith in his abilities and character. How he felt about von Reuentahl was more complicated—a helical tangle of emotion. Von Reuentahl presumably suffered from an even graver version of the same psychology, but Reinhard had recognized his gifts and placed deep trust in him all the same. The sense of betrayal was searing. On Urvashi, Reinhard had sought to reject Lutz's argument for von Reuentahl's responsibility for the attack, but after Lutz's sacrifice, Reinhard seemed to have inherited his opinion. Reinhard began by reproaching himself over Lutz's death, but when that feeling turned toward von Reuentahl, a subtle chemical reaction began.

But will bringing down von Reuentahl bring peace to my heart?

The answer, Reinhard knew, was nein. But when he asked himself if that meant he should let von Reuentahl be, the answer remained negative. The first answer was born of emotion, the second of reason. If he forgave von Reuentahl unconditionally, Reinhard's authority as ruler would be lost. The hierarchy of the empire would crumble. What standing would he have to punish the next person who rebelled or otherwise broke the law?

All he has to do is come to me in humility, and I would be spared the obligation to bring him down. The greater responsibility for this situation is his.

To protect the authority of the kaiser and the order of the state, Reinhard had no choice but to bring von Reuentahl to heel. This much was solidly within the bounds of rationality and principle, but in the abyss of emotion beyond, another question boiled: *Why is he so* unwilling *to humble himself before me?*

Yang Wen-li had maintained his equal footing alongside Reinhard without any particular fanfare, and Reinhard had never found it unpleasant or unnatural. This was partly due to Yang's personality, but also because he had never accepted a fief from Reinhard. Not so for von Reuentahl. Was he simply tired of showing deference? Or could it be (could it possibly be?) that he was doing as Reinhard had suggested he should, three years ago? If so, was the fault Reinhard's own? But no—even if the rebellion had been inspired by Reinhard's words, he had no obligation to concede victory to the rebel commander. Conquest must be achieved by superiority of ability; amicably transferred supremacy was a laughable idea.

Meanwhile, 11,900 ships under the command of Senior Admiral Ernest Mecklinger were approaching Iserlohn Corridor from the empire's traditional territory. Their mission was to force a two-front war on von Reuentahl. To do so, they would need to petition Iserlohn Base for safe passage through the corridor. Mecklinger was acting not only as fleet commander but also as ambassador and diplomat, invested by the kaiser himself with full authority to negotiate.

Admiral Grünemann, along with the fleet whose command he had inherited from Lutz, was posted to keep the peace in the old imperial territory that Mecklinger had vacated. Injured almost fatally in the Vermillion War, Grünemann had finally recovered enough to resume active duty. Lutz's faithful lieutenant, Vice Admiral Hotzbauer, had requested a transfer to Marshal Mittermeier's command. No one needed to ask him why.

The galaxy was alive with will, with action, countercurrents swimming across the void. Strategically, the situation must have been a fascinating one, providing rich fodder for the analyses and discussions of historians in later generations.

"How would the Magician have turned this situation to his advantage?" Reinhard mused aloud. Without waiting for his two senior admirals to reply, he pursued the thought further. "Yes, I see. How his successor answers that question will reveal his true capacity."

In truth, there were more pressing matters to consider. If the Iserlohn Republic came to an agreement with von Reuentahl so that both left their rears unguarded, they could launch a war on two fronts, however imperfect. The imperial forces coming the long way from Phezzan would be met head-on by von Reuentahl, while the Iserlohn fleet would advance from the corridor into imperial territory. The kaiser would have to return first to Phezzan and then to the heart of imperial territory to battle the invading army. It seemed unlikely that the old capital of Odin would fall to Iserlohn's forces, but if the unlikely event did occur it would severely harm the new dynasty's authority.

"My apologies for raising such an ominous scenario, Your Majesty, but how would you respond in that case?" asked Müller, who may have had Yang's successor Julian Mintz somewhere in his mind.

"In that case…" Reinhard's ice-blue eyes glittered so fiercely with internal light and heat that they were hard to look on directly. "In that case, I would simply treat it as a hostile act directed at my person and therefore justifying an attack on Iserlohn Base. After eliminating von Reuentahl, I would turn immediately to crushing Iserlohn with our full military might. The temporary tactical disadvantage we would be under is not worth considering."

Müller and Eisenach exchanged glances. The kaiser's conquering spirit burned bright as ever. He was not even considering the possibility that he might lose to von Reuentahl. His field of vision was so broad and his sight so far-ranging that it covered the entire galaxy.

"If Yang Wen-li's successor lacks strategic vision and simply seeks to profit from the confusion unfolding before him, he surely will throw his weight behind von Reuentahl. Either way, the decision is his to make."

With this observation, the kaiser turned his ice-blue gaze to the stars.

II

On November 16, the Galactic Empire issued a decree in the kaiser's name stripping Oskar von Reuentahl of his rank of marshal and position as governor-general. Having lost his authority to lead the five million troops under his command as a result, he was now a perfect traitor in the legal sense too.

Had Lang been a free man, he would surely have clapped his hands with glee, but at that time he was in military police custody being interrogated about his role in Nicolas Boltec's unjust arrest and death. Von Reuentahl was not aware of this, but even if he had been it would have been unlikely to persuade him of the justice of fate. He had never viewed Lang and himself as the same class of being.

When he heard about the imperial decree stripping him of his rank, a wave of wry amusement washed across his mismatched eyes. It was the first time he had been without rank or position since entering officer's school. It felt odd not to have a status backed by power. Before the wryness had faded from his eyes, an FTL transmission arrived from *Tristan*, the warship of his "enemy," Wolfgang Mittermeier. For Mittermeier, the new circumstances meant that he could finally speak to von Reuentahl directly.

After a moment's consideration, von Reuentahl directed his communications officer to patch the transmission through to his private chambers.

In his chambers, the grayish-white on his screen gave way to his friend's grim expression.

"Von Reuentahl. Sorry to bother you at such a busy time."

A strange greeting, considering.

"Nothing to apologize for. It's you and me we're talking about."

There was no irony or sarcasm in von Reuentahl's tone. Mittermeier had been the one man with whom he could remove the armor from his heart when they spoke. Von Reuentahl had thrown this bond away with his actions, but he was happy to see it restored, however briefly and in whatever form.

"What do you say, von Reuentahl? Will you come see the kaiser with me? I don't want to fight you. I'm sure it's not too late."

"I don't want to fight you either, Mittermeier."

"In that case—"

"But I will anyway. Why, you ask? Because unless I fight you, and win, the kaiser won't deign to fight me himself."

The casually offered remark left Mittermeier speechless. Quiet but fierce emotion shone in von Reuentahl's eyes, making their odd colors even more vivid.

"For a long time, I didn't know why I'd been born into this world," von Reuentahl continued. "I knew the melancholy of a man without wisdom. But now I finally understand. I've lived my whole life in order to go to war with the kaiser, and find my satisfaction there."

Mittermeier tried to argue, but found his throat blocked by a formless door. After a few seconds of struggling that felt like an eternity, he finally forced the door open and tried another appeal to common sense.

"Think it over one more time, von Reuentahl. You can trust me to make sure your rights are protected, even if it's at my own expense. The kaiser's had Lang taken into custody. Things are getting better. Slowly, but surely. Now it's your turn to accelerate that process through your sincerity. You have my promise. Trust in me."

"A promise from the Gale Wolf. That's worth more than gold." There was gratitude in von Reuentahl's voice, but he shook his head as if to cut it away. "But no, Mittermeier. Your life is worth too much to trade it for my continued existence. You always tread the righteous path. I can't do that. All I can do is…"

Von Reuentahl closed his mouth. He felt the impulse to reveal all to his loved and respected friend. What had happened after the Lippstadt War and the tragic death of Siegfried Kircheis, when von Reuentahl had brought the news of Duke Lichtenlade's capture to then-Marquis Reinhard von Lohengramm. The words Reinhard had spoken, as an inorganic smile filled exquisite features that seemed carved from crystal: "If a conqueror lacks ability, it's only natural that he be overthrown himself. If you have the confidence and you're ready to risk everything, go ahead. Challenge me anytime." Von Reuentahl had understood in that moment what Reinhard craved most of all: enemies. Powerful, competent enemies…

The moment passed. Adopting an intentionally ambitious expression, von Reuentahl changed the subject. "What about you, Mittermeier?" he asked. "Are you ready to join me?"

"Even by your standards, that's a terrible joke."

"It's no joke. I'll be kaiser and you can be viceroy. The other way around would be fine too. Or we could divide the universe up and rule separately. Even Trünicht managed that one."

On the screen, he saw a mournful shadow appear in Mittermeier's gray eyes. His friend's youthful face, always so vital and spirited that it gave the impression of a willful boy, now seemed to fill with achromatic clouds.

"You're drunk," Mittermeier said.

"Stone cold sober."

"Not on liquor. On blood-red dreams."

Now it was von Reuentahl's turn to be speechless. Mittermeier sighed so deeply that von Reuentahl felt it through the screen. Then he continued.

"We have to wake up from our dreams eventually. What happens when you wake from this one? You hope to find satisfaction in war with the kaiser? And if you win, what then? When the kaiser is gone, how will you feed your starving heart?"

Von Reuentahl closed his eyes and opened them again. "Maybe I am dreaming," he said. "But either way, it's *my* dream. Not yours. It doesn't look like we're going to find common ground here, so there's no need to waste any more of each other's time."

"Wait, von Reuentahl. Hear me out just a little more."

"So long, Mittermeier. Take care of the kaiser. However strange that sounds under the circumstances, I mean it sincerely."

The transmission cut out. Mittermeier, about to say more, swallowed his words and silently exhaled his frustration and sorrow before hurling the entire boiling mass of his emotional state at the screen, shouting, "Reuentahl! You imbecile!" It was the voice not of an imperial marshal but a newly minted officer. Mittermeier glared with genuine loathing at the screen, which had faded back to ashy white, as if this merciless barrier were what stood between him and his friend.

Mittermeier knew he would remember von Reuentahl's face the moment before he cut the transmission for the rest of his days. It was a memory that, along with his own life, he would be forced to take back to Phezzan.

Mittermeier left his private chambers and returned to the bridge to sit in the commander's chair. A student orderly brought him a coffee. He thanked the orderly mechanically, sinking into thought. The thought of a tactician.

Von Reuentahl's weakness is his lack of trusted lieutenants. He'll have no problem coming up with plans for battle, but will he have the admirals to execute them?

Mittermeier had seen the truth of the situation. The issue was not some flaw in von Reuentahl's personality but the fact that his rebellion was against the kaiser and the empire itself. Forcing his subordinates to join him in it risked robbing their loyalty of its direction.

Given von Reuentahl's character, there was a chance he would divide his own forces, swap his main force with a diversionary force, and lure Mittermeier into a vast trap. In that case, too, though, he would need a second—someone to act as another von Reuentahl. Mittermeier mentally ran down the list of officers who might play this role. Bergengrün? Barthauser? Dittersdorf? Sonnenfels? Schüler? Or one of the two admirals who had been posted to the Neue Land at its establishment, Grillparzer and von Knapfstein?

Thinking, brooding, moving at a pace that no would-be pursuer could possibly match, Mittermeier led his fleet deeper into the Neue Land.

On the bridge of von Reuentahl's flagship *Tristan*, the Goldenlöwe still hung on the wall, catching every visitor's eye with its splendor.

Von Reuentahl had received the banner from the kaiser himself, and had no intention of taking it down. Perhaps he wanted to believe that he was the true defender of the new dynasty's standard. This way of thinking was one point on which he had to recognize that he was beyond redemption, and one reason why his rebellion was glorious to behold but ultimately hollow.

His troops picked up on these ideas in their commander's mind, and took to debating the justice of their cause and their reasons for fighting right where they stood, weapons still in hand.

"We'll just have to follow where Marshal von Reuentahl leads. What else can we do?"

"So you're going to fight the kaiser? *That* kaiser?"

In this case, the demonstrative "that" expressed a sense of mythic awe. Young and beautiful, the kaiser had piled victory upon battlefield victory, led vast armies across the sea of stars, and now ruled more territory than anyone in the history of humanity. To his troops he was a martial deity.

"Won't fighting against His Majesty make us traitors?"

"We're not fighting against His Majesty. We're freeing him from the disloyal and treacherous courtiers that have his ear and twist his wishes."

"Like the minister of military affairs? I don't like the man, but they say he's not the type to act out of selfish motives."

"How do we know that? I hear that lately His Majesty has been ill, and the minister has started running the empire as he pleases."

"Either way, our first opponent isn't His Majesty or the minister. It's the Gale Wolf."

At this the soldiers fell silent. As they exchanged glances, they sensed something resembling excitement rising hotly within each other.

"A terrifying thought..." somebody whispered.

"When the Twin Ramparts clash, who wins?"

In the abstract, the question would surely have interested every single recruit in the Imperial Navy. But the prospect of seeing it played out from within the formations involved turned their shudders from hot to cold.

At this point, von Reuentahl's forces had not yet produced deserters in any great number. Von Reuentahl himself had shown his mettle as a commander and warrior. But that had always been as the *kaiser's* warrior. Whether the troops he commanded would willingly follow him as an independent warlord was a different matter. Having explained to them that they were not betraying the kaiser but freeing him from the disloyal courtiers that troubled him, he would next have to raise their morale by securing a victory on the field of war.

III

In November of year 2 of the new imperial calendar, the galaxy seemed to exist for the sake of von Reuentahl and Mittermeier alone. Yang Wen-li's demise had not, it seemed, sounded the death knell for battles between great commanders at the height of their powers.

Von Reuentahl's initial strategy was roughly as follows:

1. Reorganize the troops stationed across the Neue Land into multilayered defensive lines to slow the advance of Mittermeier's fleet while forcing the heaviest losses possible upon it.
2. Draw the main enemy force toward Heinessen, and then either cut off its rear or feign such a maneuver so plausibly that it began to retreat anyway.
3. Bring together disparate forces to block the enemy's main route of retreat, coordinating to form a pincer formation whose other point was von Reuentahl's main force, to be scrambled from Heinessen.

It was a sweeping but fine-grained operation that would stand as testament to von Reuentahl's strategic vision and tactical prowess for generations to come. However, perfect success could only be achieved on two conditions. The first was that no enemy forces arrived from the direction of Iserlohn to open up a second front. The second was that von Reuentahl could find people to lead and then reintegrate the individual units to be stationed across the Neue Land.

To ensure that the first condition was met, von Reuentahl sent an emissary to Iserlohn Base. And not just any emissary. The individual he selected was, in a sense, an extreme symbol of both von Reuentahl's strengths and his weaknesses.

Turning to the second condition, von Reuentahl assigned this duty to a man in whose character and ability he had the utmost faith: Bergengrün. Bergengrün silently set about preparing to play his role—but in the end these preparations were all for naught.

This was because Mittermeier, true to his sobriquet, advanced at a pace that would have been utterly impossible for other tacticians, denying von Reuentahl any time to lay the groundwork for his ambitious strategy.

None knew better than von Reuentahl the true value of Mittermeier's preternaturally rapid maneuvering. He had expected Mittermeier to move swiftly, but the reality exceeded his most pessimistic predictions. On the other hand, no one but von Reuentahl could have responded so adroitly to Mittermeier's arrival, recalling the ships in the process of separating from the main fleet and reuniting the whole into a dense formation just in the nick of time. As a result, von Reuentahl's forces entered their first battlefield with far higher offensive potential than Mittermeier's.

The Duel of the Twin Ramparts was fought on a higher level than lesser commanders could even imagine. Terrible sparks began to fly before the two sides had even physically met.

When von Reuentahl received a report that Mittermeier's fleet was already halfway through the Neue Land, his heterochromiac eyes first flashed with admiration: "His maneuvering, his development—the sheer *pace* of it!" But when he saw how thinly Mittermeier's fleet was stretched, this admiration was replaced with a hard gleam more befitting a tactician. "Only to be expected, I suppose," he muttered. "Those mediocrities can't keep up with the pace he sets."

Von Reuentahl decided to defeat the enemy in detail.

He felt an exquisite excitement at the prospect of facing a worthy opponent on the battlefield. His affection and respect for Mittermeier had lessened not a molecule, but coexisting with those emotions was genuine elation—clear proof of just how far beyond salvation those beings known as tacticians are.

Mittermeier felt the same excitement. A voice whispered inside him, asking, *Isn't it the heart's desire of every warrior to square off with a brilliant commander like von Reuentahl?* But, in addition to the bitterness of fighting to the death with a friend, Mittermeier had concerns of a different nature.

The troops under von Reuentahl were all subjects of Kaiser Reinhard. Mittermeier hoped to avoid killing them as far as that was possible. The alternative, after all, was to slaughter brothers and colleagues who should be their allies. There was an officer of Mittermeier's acquaintance with two sons. The older served beside him under Mittermeier's command, but the younger had been posted under von Reuentahl in the Neue Land. Who knew how many others were in similar situations?

Mittermeier expected von Reuentahl to throw his entire fleet into the coming battle. There were two reasons for this. The first was positive: if von Reuentahl could overwhelm Mittermeier with sheer military might, the tactical victory would position him better for a strategic victory in due course. The other reason was negative: if he left part of his fleet on Heinessen, and they mutinied against him—or, from the empire's point of view, ceased their participation in the rebellion—von Reuentahl would lose his home base. Von Reuentahl's need to use his full fleet together was a stark representation of his Achilles' heel in this fight: a lack of allies he could truly trust.

November 24.

The Reuentahl and Mittermeier fleets confronted each other in the Rantemario Stellar Region, where Free Planets forces had once held the line under Alexandor Bucock (now deceased) against Reinhard's Imperial Navy. This was not a coincidence. The strategic importance of the region was clear at a glance.

At 0950, when the two sides had approached to within 5.4 light-seconds of each other, a half moment of silence filled their communications circuits before fierce cries pushed this into the past.

"Fire!"

"Fire!"

The same order, issued in the same language.

The field of stars vanished, outshone by myriad beams of light. Vessels cloaked in energy-neutralization fields glowed like colossal fireflies. Those unable to endure the burden exploded in all directions, spattering the vivid paints of death and destruction across a rampageous canvas of shadow and light. Balls of light and fire erupted without rhyme or reason, as if the goddess of war were shaking them off a broken necklace. This continued with the second exchange. Warships were torn open with exhalations of energy that sent animate beings and inanimate objects hurtling into the vacuum together. Space filled with silent screams; heat and flame enfolded the casualties in a blazing shroud. However noble a military unit's commander may be, it exists for one purpose: to secure supremacy by force. The most effective means of doing so is murder. To kill and to die are the duties of a soldier.

Beams and missiles created pockets of ghastly day in their corner of the endless night. Holes opened in hulls and vomited motive components into the void. Soldiers being burned alive rolled screaming across floors, watching blood and innards spill from their dying forms.

At the outset of the Second Battle of Rantemario, also known as the Clash of the Twin Ramparts, the Reuentahl fleet was 5,200,000 soldiers strong while the Mittermeier fleet had 2,590,000, giving the former the numerical advantage. Accordingly, von Reuentahl went on the offensive and Mittermeier defended. By rights these should have been the basic battle postures of the two sides, but Mittermeier made skillful use of the mobile forces under his direct command to repeatedly block the Reuentahl fleet's attempts at penetration. It was clear that any victory would be hard-won. Mittermeier had opened hostilities knowing that he had the numerical disadvantage in order to create a situation in which von Reuentahl would choose defeat in detail rather than a protracted war of resistance. Strategically, he expected a short and decisive confrontation; at the tactical level, he only needed to hold the line against Reuentahl's fleet until his own allies arrived in force, leaving the final stages of the conflict for later. Such was Mittermeier's basic position.

The balance of military force shifted with surprising speed.

At 0830 on November 25, Senior Admiral Fritz Josef Wittenfeld arrived with his fleet on the scene. The frenzied pace of his advance had left a few ships behind, but he still had more than ten thousand, which would have no small effect on the state of the conflict.

"Further, harder, bolder, tougher!" This was the motto of the Black Lancers, to whom cowardice, passivity, and hesitation were anathema.

"Charge!" shouted Wittenfeld on the bridge of his flagship *Königs Tiger* as it took its place at the head of the Black Lancers' offensive. "Let's give Mittermeier a break for breakfast!"

Legend has it that Wittenfeld had skipped breakfast himself that day, and was eating a frankfurter with extra mustard even as he stood before his bridge's main screen. If this was an intentional act of bravado, it is hard to avoid criticizing it as overdone.

On the bridge of his flagship *Tristan*, von Reuentahl made a noise of disgust. "The Black Lancers are here, I see." While fighting alongside them as allies, he had not, in all honesty, thought the Black Lancers especially intimidating. Now that they appeared before him as the enemy, he could not deny the sinking feeling of being explosively overwhelmed. Each and every one of the overlapping points of light charged toward him with its fangs bared in open hostility.

A chain of explosions lit up the area, expelled energy surged across the field in waves, but the *Königs Tiger* led the Black Lancers toward the Reuentahl fleet without slowing or weakening. They had an almost arrogant air about them, and the Reuentahl fleet's left flank was so intimidated and unnerved that their formation slipped a fraction. Mittermeier's largest formation responded by focusing its main cannons there, firing three volleys, and began a relentless approach under cover of concentrated firepower. It was 0915.

IV

Wittenfeld's Black Lancers had lost half their number during the Battle of the Corridor in April and May of that year. Since then, however, they had been merged with the former Fahrenheit fleet, and in purely numerical terms were 10 percent larger now than they had been at the founding of the Lohengramm Dynasty.

Both the original Black Lancers and the former Fahrenheit fleet had been renowned for daring and valor under skilled leadership, but in military organization fifty added to fifty does not necessarily make a hundred. And the more capable and individual a unit is, the more difficulty it has integrating with others.

At Rantemario, the original Black Lancers moved in lockstep with Wittenfeld's orders, flooding the battlefield with their usual ruthlessness: everything before them was the enemy, and every enemy was to be annihilated. Members of the former Fahrenheit fleet, however, were a fraction slower to advance. This opened a gap which part of the Reuentahl fleet was able to slip into, setting off chaotic dogfights that rippled outward in waves.

With imperial forces on both sides of the battle, ships of the same make mingled together, making it difficult to distinguish friend from foe. This confusion was one of the defining marks of the Second Battle of Rantemario.

"Don't embarrass yourselves!" roared Wittenfeld. "We've fought imperial forces before—remember the Lippstadt War? This is no time to get squeamish about it!"

With their distinctive lacquer-black exteriors, Wittenfeld's ships were in no danger of being misidentified by either side. The exact same paint job had been given to the ships reassigned from the Fahrenheit fleet, of course, but their crews could not escape the lingering feeling that they had been the victims of a takeover. Some still believed that Wittenfeld's mad rush at the Battle of the Corridor had been partly responsible for Fahrenheit's death, and although this was in the past now, they remained unhappy with how things had turned out. Fahrenheit had enjoyed the confidence of his fleet, and some of his former troops who were now in the Black Lancers had indeed served under him in the Lippstadt War three years ago—battling von Reuentahl and the rest of Reinhard's forces. Now, reassigned to Wittenfeld's command, they were fighting von Reuentahl again, this time on Reinhard's behalf. This must have inspired no small number to reflect on the bitter ironies of fate.

At 1700 on November 25, the Wahlen fleet joined the Black Lancers on the battlefield, bringing roughly equivalent might to bear. Until that point, Mittermeier had shown patience; the entry of Wahlen's ships should have granted him security in the superiority of his forces. But, as he considered the overall arrangement of the two sides on his sub-screen, he noticed one enemy unit that was moving oddly.

"What do we have here?" he wondered aloud.

Lieutenant Commander Kurlich, one of his staff officers, replied, "They must be under the direct command of Marshal von Reuentahl."

"Obviously. Irregulars, perhaps?"

What concerned Mittermeier was what the maneuvering of the unit, presumably the enemy's most elite force, might indicate about its intentions. Its lines of activity were neither simple nor straight, and it took some time before Mittermeier made a noise of irritation. "I should have known," he said.

The Bayerlein fleet, which was already ahead of the rest of Mittermeier's forces, advanced further as if dragged out by a partial enemy retreat, and its retreat was partly cut off.

Mittermeier had warned Bayerlein not to fall for any traps that von Reuentahl might lay, but the commander's youth and ferocity rendered him incapable of applying the brakes to an attack that had begun to accelerate.

Von Reuentahl watched the approaching fleet with fierce coldness, then turned to his own aide, Lieutenant Commander von Reckendorf, with a smile.

"What do you say, von Reckendorf? Shall we show our inexperienced comrade what tactics are?"

Von Reuentahl was young enough to be called inexperienced himself, but the difference in dignity and formidability between him and Bayerlein was far greater than would be expected from the five years separating their actual ages.

The Reuentahl fleet drew Bayerlein's ships into the center of a dense ring of fire, showering them with beams and missiles from close range. Bayerlein tried to retreat even as he returned fire, but with every alternation between the two actions von Reuentahl pressed his advantage further, and by the time Mittermeier came to the rescue the losses were severe. Bayerlein's second-in-command, Vice Admiral Remar, was killed, along with three other admirals.

"They got us," said Bayerlein, visibly regretful on the communications screen. "My sincere apologies."

"They're still getting us," Mittermeier replied unsmilingly. "It's too soon to use the past tense. Let's hope we can add a contrastive conjunction soon."

The metaphor would have suited Mecklinger more, but the Gale Wolf let it be, sinking back into thought.

Von Reuentahl may be perfect, but his subordinates are not. Therein lies the key to victory.

Of course, Mittermeier could not have known about Grillparzer's betrayal, or that von Knapfstein had gotten caught up in it, but even so he found it difficult to believe that either of them were willing to die for von Reuentahl, so he decided to concentrate his firepower on these weak links in the enemy chain of command. It was an unremarkable idea, but the sheer volume of fire he brought to bear on them, and the speed with which he did so, were remarkable indeed. In just moments, the Knapfstein fleet was all but overwhelmed. Unable to bear up under Mittermeier's ferocious offensive, von Knapfstein pulled his ships back, formations in tatters. He worked desperately to rebuild the command structure, but Mittermeier did not allow him time to finish. Von Knapfstein's defensive line fell apart like a crumbling sandcastle.

"Damn that Grillparzer! When is he going to turn on von Reuentahl?"

This was the formless chain that restricted von Knapfstein's judgment and actions. He was not without ability of his own, having been appointed by Reinhard and trained as a tactician by the late Helmut Lennenkamp. He was viewed as one of the officers who would bear the Galactic Empire on his shoulders five or ten years from now.

For his own, internal reasons, however, he was unable to exercise his full abilities. He was a puritanically serious man by nature, and part of him was uncomfortable with betrayal and deception, no matter how it was explained away as loyalty to the kaiser. Furthermore, the enemy he faced was simply too powerful. By the time he heard his operators screaming, his flagship was already trapped in a mass of fireballs, each explosion setting off the next. Death battered his ship's energy-neutralization field with crimson sparks and, with vast and unseen hands, began to pry open the cracks that appeared in its hull.

"Preposterous! This cannot be!" Von Knapfstein's scream was directed at both a higher power and at man. Space-time was full of injustice. He was neither an active rebel against the kaiser nor an active betrayer of those who were; why did he have to be the first to die in this meaningless battle?

In the next moment, a column of fire tore his flagship apart, and von Knapfstein's flesh and spirit were reduced to atoms along with his ship in a vast sphere of white-hot light. The practically infinite microscopic grains that make up time sucked the dying man's objections into the unfathomable dark.

It was 0609, November 29.

Von Knapfstein's death was surely the most senseless in the whole civil war. What was more, only one other person knew this: Grillparzer, the very man who had talked him into his double betrayal. The accomplice paid for his crime long before the ringleader.

The report of von Knapfstein's death was brought to von Reuentahl ten minutes later.

"I see," von Reuentahl said. "A shame. I wish that could have been avoided."

Von Reuentahl did not, of course, have a complete picture of the circumstances. His sympathy was simply what common courtesy required. Of course, even if he had known all the details, he might well have said exactly the same thing.

Grillparzer received the report of his colleague's death silently and without expression. Whether he shook his head internally at von Knapfstein's bumbling, or rejoiced that he would be able to claim this dark achievement all for himself in the near future, no one would ever know.

That moment might have been the most favorable one for his betrayal, but he failed to take the decision. Under Mittermeier's punishing offensive, he had no breathing room. If he abandoned his resistance, he would be torn to shreds in an instant, before he could even begin his betrayal.

Without a commander, the Knapfstein fleet's chain of command was in tatters, and the best it could manage was a despairing and largely ineffective counterattack as it wavered to and fro.

Despite the worsening situation, von Reuentahl's tactical mastery allowed him to successfully create an imbalance in the Mittermeier fleet's formation. By carefully balancing areas of sparseness and density in the distribution of his firepower, he created a fault line between the Black Lancers and the rest of Mittermeier's fleet.

Under a barrage of missiles, the Black Lancers had their weakness as defenders exposed. For a moment it seemed as if they would descend from half panic to full rout.

"Hold the line! Hold the line, damn you!" Wittenfeld stamped his foot on the floor of *Königs Tiger's* bridge, his orange hair in flying. "If anyone falls back, blow them away with *Königs Tiger's* main cannon. A true warrior would prefer that to living on as a coward!"

Such an order would never be carried out, but when his vice chief of staff, Rear Admiral Eugen, broadcast it on the comms circuit, his ships froze in horror and the disorderly rout was ended before it began. Meanwhile, *Königs Tiger* not only had not frozen, it continued to advance through the storm of fireballs and light. Even inorganic objects like beams and missiles seemed to give it a wide berth, as if fearing its savagery.

"Who knows what Wittenfeld might do, eh? I suppose notoriety has its uses."

Von Reuentahl laughed, and it did not seem entirely cynical. Whatever their motives or aims, it was true that the Black Lancers had stepped back from the brink to reestablish their fighting spirit and formation. Even von Reuentahl's masterful offensive was blocked by their iron arm.

This in turn set off a positive chain reaction in the near-antagonistic attitude of the former Fahrenheit fleet.

"Remember Marshal Fahrenheit, and do him proud!" said Vice Admiral Hofmeister, once known as one of the fiercest leaders under Fahrenheit's command. "We can't let those raging Black Lancer boars steal the show!" And he led his colleagues in switching from a defensive posture to an offensive one.

Nothing upsets the calculations of a commander like morale igniting such as this, in a plane irrelevant to the dictates of strategic logic. The awe and admiration among the Imperial Navy for Yang Wen-li had not just been because of the countless miracles he produced from his magician's hat. He also maintained morale at the highest level among his subordinates, right up until his death.

The Black Lancers knew little of cooperation or coordination, but they hurled themselves against approaching death and destruction with absolute fearlessness. Von Reuentahl watched the battle unfold in shock, cool and collected manner so rattled that he almost laughed in disbelief. In the end, he avoided the foolishness of facing the zealots head-on, but was forced to retreat on every front. Even then, the way his fleet remained orderly to the last, creating no clear opportunity to attack, was to Wittenfeld and the others another example of his charmless perfection as a commander.

∨

November 30. Combat continued incessantly, relentlessly.

Both sides were led by commanders of equal ability, able to accurately perceive tactical shifts and respond with swift countermeasures. As a result, while both sides took losses, neither suffered a critical blow, and the battle began to resemble a war of attrition.

This did not bode well for von Reuentahl. If both sides lost combat strength at the same rate, his forces would be buried in a bottomless marsh of fire and light. Mittermeier's fleet would be worn down, too, but behind it waited another, completely unharmed and under the kaiser's direct control.

Mittermeier was not a patient man by nature, but he knew how dangerous it would be to act rashly with von Reuentahl as opponent. He imposed double the forbearance on himself, enduring physical and mental consumption that would have made a weak-willed commander faint.

And, of course, his friend and mighty opponent was doing the same.

"I think I finally understand how hard Yang Wen-li had to work," von Reuentahl said to himself with a rueful smile. "Not to mention his true greatness."

Facing an enemy with near-unlimited regenerative power brought fatigue as agonizing as a rasp to the nerves. How stupid those fraudulent tacticians were who prattled of "striking a large force with a small one." Even the bravest, most loyal soldiers had limits to their physical and mental energy. If they were to recover, it was necessary to have enough to allow some to rest and recuperate while others fought the next battle. This was why large armies were so effective.

Von Reuentahl had absolutely no illusions about the morale of his troops this time. In part this was linked to his having no illusions about himself, but as a result he was apparently able to exercise his coolheadedness as a tactician to the fullest.

1600, December 1. Wittenfeld, who had been in the thick of the fighting since it began, was finally forced to temporarily retreat and regroup. For just a moment, von Reuentahl's fleet had the edge in firepower over the enemy's front lines. Von Reuentahl shortened the line and, using concentrated fire to hold Mittermeier's fleet back from advancing, led the agile units under his direct command in an attempt to strike at their enemy's left flank. Success would have left Mittermeier's ships partly encircled, vulnerable to walls of firepower on both left and right

But this dramatic offensive was nipped in the bud by a swift response from Senior Admiral Augustus Samuel Wahlen. The exchange of fire was so furious that it overloaded the sector with the energy it unleashed and created a gigantic energy cyclone that dragged in ships from both sides.

Wahlen's flagship *Salamander* took two direct hits, one destroying its second walküre bay and the other landing under its bridge. On the bridge, sections of the wall and floor went flying, killing eight operators and guards instantly and injuring twenty more. Wahlen himself almost had his left arm torn off. The sleeve of his uniform was shredded, and the gleaming metal bones in his artificial hand were exposed.

His chief of staff, Vice Admiral Bürmering, rushed to his aid, but Wahlen brushed him away. "I've lost this arm before," he said. "Losing it again won't slow me down."

As Bürmering watched, Wahlen ripped the arm from its socket, threw it to the floor, and kicked it away. Glancing at his chief of staff, the usually serious commander could not resist a joke.

"We've cut off our bad luck now. The only thing left to fear is cowardice!"

After three hours of desperate fighting, von Reuentahl finally relented. The final catalyst was Mittermeier punching small breaches through his defensive line and then joining those points lengthwise to advance as a united front. Had this gambit been successful—as, in fact, it almost was—von Reuentahl's fleet would have been swept away by a wave of fire and steel. Especially since the one in that danger zone was Grillparzer.

By contrast with his comrades who had died unwillingly in battle, Grillparzer had made a different miscalculation. His plan had been to wait for the most opportune moment during battle, and then bring his spear about and strike at von Reuentahl from the rear. That moment, however, failed to come. For one thing, not all of his subordinates knew his thinking, and many of them were actively engaged in daring firefights with Mittermeier's ships.

Seeing Mittermeier's fearsome tactics from point-blank range, Grillparzer shuddered even as he marveled. He considered drawing in the Mittermeier fleet's offensive to bring about the total collapse of von Reuentahl's forces, but again hesitated over the decision. The pressure Mittermeier brought to bear was stronger than he had expected, and if he were the one to bore a hole in the dike he could very well drown. As a result, Grillparzer was forced to desperately bear up against Mittermeier's attack simply to keep himself alive, and this bloody, unfunny farce continued until von Reuentahl turned the ships under his direct control around. As he waited, Grillparzer decided to signal his intentions to surrender to Mittermeier—but, moments before the circuit connected, von Reuentahl appeared behind him and he was forced to put the idea aside.

Through precisely concentrated firepower, von Reuentahl closed one of Mittermeier's breaches and launched a counterattack on another, breaking through to fire along the flank of one of Mittermeier's divisions that was in a long column formation. The combat was brief, but so intense that it left both sides with fangs shattered, and Mittermeier was forced to retreat some 600,000 kilometers.

The bloody banquet showed no sign of ending.

VI

Before these events, when Mittermeier and von Reuentahl were still on the verge of their grim battle in the Rantemario Stellar Region, an envoy arrived at Iserlohn Base. He had been sent by von Reuentahl for strategic regions, to request that Iserlohn not permit the Imperial Navy through the corridor. He was not one of von Reuentahl's subordinates but a retired veteran living on Heinessen—and an old acquaintance of Julian and the others.

"Admiral Murai, it's been a long time. I didn't expect to meet under these circumstances, but I'm glad to see you looking well."

Julian shook Murai's hand as he offered this heartfelt greeting, but at the sight of the Thirteenth Fleet's former chief of staff, Olivier Poplin said "Uh-oh" and disappeared, like a wild animal seeing its natural predator.

Dusty Attenborough muttered, "If I'd known he was coming back, I wouldn't have given him that gentlemanly farewell," but bashfully offered his hand. Caselnes and von Schönkopf grinned and saluted, and Frederica bowed her head in sincere gratitude to the man who had been a loyal staff officer to her husband.

Von Reuentahl's choice of his former enemy as envoy was ingenious and cynical, and Murai had only accepted after careful deliberation. Whatever von Reuentahl's true intentions, he had seen value in providing Julian and the others with information about what was currently unfolding in the former alliance territories. This was Julian's guess at his intentions, anyway; Murai himself did not speak of them.

Von Reuentahl's request showed his superior mettle as a villain. Offering to return the entire former alliance territory was not something to be done lightly. It suggested that, if Iserlohn took the offer, even in the worst case they would have little to lose.

But Julian was Yang Wen-li's disciple. When faced with a decision, he spent as much time pondering its historical import as calculating the chances of success. Taken to the extreme, this was no more than imitation, but to Julian it was the torch that guided him through mazes for which he had no map.

"I'll discuss it with Mrs. Greenhill Yang and Admiral Merkatz and give you an answer as quickly as possible. Please make yourself at home while you wait."

"All right, but make it as quick as you can. If I get comfortable, I'll start feeling the urge to complain about what you youngsters are doing. And my place isn't even here anymore."

Raising one hand, Murai headed for the guest room assigned to him.

Won't you come back to us? Julian caught himself just before the words escaped. Provided with his old lodgings, Murai would have laughed and refused.

Julian spent the entire day considering von Reuentahl's proposal.

If von Reuentahl meant to claim political legitimacy against Reinhard and his new dynasty, he would ultimately have to restore the bipolar system from before the New Imperial Calendar began. Would he back Erwin Josef II, who was still missing, and declare the restoration of the Goldenbaum Dynasty? Would he revive the Free Planets Alliance and become a standard-bearer for democratic republican governance? The latter possibility was ridiculous on its face. Furthermore, if von Reuentahl intended to make Reinhard his puppet while wielding true political power himself, there was no reason whatsoever for Julian and the others to get caught up in a struggle for power within the autocracy.

Ultimately, the kaiser's reign might be autocratic in its system of governance, but, judged by his results, Reinhard himself walked the middle path. Julian and the others had to keep this in mind. The fruit of reform could not simply be dashed to the ground, even if it had been born of a system different from their own. What was more, supposing that von Reuentahl did overthrew Reinhard, it was difficult to imagine that the kaiser's senior retainers would meekly bend the knee. Which meant such an eventuality would only mark the opening of an age of war without order or principle.

Marshal von Reuentahl was presumably very nearly Kaiser Reinhard's equal in terms of ability in government and military affairs. Still, in historical terms, he could only ever exist as a reaction to the kaiser. To move history in the best possible direction, would it not be better to ensure that Reinhard continued to rule? Always assuming, of course, that he remained wise and just. Julian's thoughts began to coalesce around this idea.

The problem was the other thing von Reuentahl had offered: Trünicht. This had shaken Iserlohn's representatives, not politically but psychologically.

Julian was no exception, and had felt strongly torn on hearing the offer. Olivier Poplin had whistled and said, "Take him up on that part at least, Julian. I won't ask for Trünicht's head. You can have that. Just leave me an arm."

Julian had not failed to consider a more expedient approach. They could demand Trünicht first, for example, lull von Reuentahl into a false sense of security, and then allow the imperial fleet through the corridor. This would put the empire in their debt while also allowing them to avenge their personal grudges against Trünicht.

But it would disgrace them. However deep their hatred and resentment of Trünicht, if they used his life as a strategic bargaining chip, what right would they have to criticize his own countless betrayals of democracy?

For von Reuentahl to offer such a condition might not be humane, but it certainly made sense in terms of political and military strategy. For them to accept it, however, would be a shameful act.

Julian suddenly thought of asking Murai about von Reuentahl's fundamental approach to this new conflict. Was he dragging the former citizens of the alliance into the fight?

"No, he feels that this is a private battle within the empire, and the citizenry have nothing to do with it," Murai said. "This might be another example of his arrogance, but he is sticking to it."

Julian felt as if he had caught a glimpse of von Reuentahl's pride at work. If the marshal dragged the former alliance citizenry into the war and carried out an uncompromising scorched-earth campaign, he could probably hold out for quite some time. But he was intentionally avoiding this in favor of direct military conflict. Some might ridicule this approach—but let them laugh.

Still, admiration was not a basis for decision-making, and Julian informed Murai that he could not accept von Reuentahl's offer.

"A no, then," Murai said. "Not unexpected, I suppose."

"I'm sorry, Admiral Murai. After you went to all the effort of coming here."

"Oh, I'm just the messenger. I didn't have any obligation to make sure the negotiations succeeded." Murai chuckled before his face grew serious again. "To be honest, Julian, I should be apologizing to you. I was worried that the promise of immediate benefits might lead you astray. And so I was thinking I'd have to stop you, even if it wasn't my place to."

"I can see why you might have worried."

"But there was no need to, was there? You truly are Yang Wen-li's greatest disciple."

For Julian, this was the highest praise possible.

The decision was thus made, but many of Julian's staff officers were disappointed. Von Schönkopf made a public counterproposal, not even bothering to keep it quiet.

"Julian, let me go back to Heinessen with Admiral Murai."

"To visit your lovers?"

"That would be the main purpose of my visit, but there's something else I want to do while I'm there." He grinned with the dangerous dignity and power of an aristocratic, man-eating tiger. "Pose with von Reuentahl's head in my left hand, Trünicht's head under my left foot, and a tomahawk in my right hand, take a photograph, and sell it to the media."

Poplin leaned forward. "Count me in on that one," he said. "You can have von Reuentahl's head. I'll settle for Trünicht's."

"I thought you might say that. Always angling for the easy job."

"No, I just don't have any bone to pick with von Reuentahl. Certainly not enough to risk the ire of all those daughters of the empire."

Julian sighed. "Stop it, both of you. Heinessen is under imperial military rule. Your chances of coming back alive are slim."

"How can you live if you're afraid to die?" said Poplin, putting his black beret on. He wasn't smiling. Julian had started to get the feeling that Poplin wasn't really the frivolous playboy people called him—that he was simply ironically enjoying playing that role.

"Brave words," Attenborough said, "for a man who ran for cover the moment he saw Admiral Murai's face."

Poplin seemed to be about to reply, but Julian's sense of hearing did not register it. Hoping for some solitude to think, he went to the observation deck, but found it already crowded. He was just turning to leave when Karin von Kreutzer saw him and called him over. As they gazed through the transparent wall at the field of stars, the conversation eventually turned to the military decision Julian faced. Of course, it did not expand at all into the area of specialty of the teacher they shared in common.

"Commander Poplin told me that he saw in your face we'd be sitting this one out. Is that true?"

"This one, yes. Just this one…"

Julian's brown eyes were filled with a contemplative light. If he was honest with himself, he wanted to fight. One of the Galactic Empire's greatest admirals was in open revolt against the kaiser. The Imperial Navy must be shaken to its core. *If Iserlohn could take advantage of that…* Julian heard the military adventurer inside him whispering of this sweet dream. The temptation was powerful. It was the same temptation that had led the Alliance Armed Forces to their crushing defeat at Amritsar four years ago.

If Julian had, at that point, formed an alliance with von Reuentahl and fought Kaiser Reinhard together, history would have gone in another direction. The sweet dream would have had a bitter end: an all-out assault on Iserlohn by the vast forces under Reinhard's command.

"Unfortunately, I think you made the right decision," Karin said. "There's no reason to get mixed up in a private war between the kaiser and Marshal von Reuentahl. Have some confidence in your judgment."

"Thank you. For worrying about me."

"What are you talking about? I'm not worried about you—just irritated! If you don't keep it together, you'll embarrass the Yangs and doom us all."

"I understand that."

"You don't understand anything. I'm *not* saying that you aren't keeping it together!"

Julian was still fumbling for an answer when Karin turned and walked away with that strikingly regular tread of hers. At times like this, Julian wished he had even one percent of Karin's father's ability to handle her.

Of course, this did not last long. His hands were already full with responsibility, but another one was about to be added to the pile—another decision that needed to be made. When he returned to the control room, Frederica Greenhill Yang, who was speaking to a communications officer, smiled and called him over.

"It seems this is our day for unexpected guests," she said. "Senior Admiral Mecklinger of the Imperial Navy is asking to negotiate. Will you hear him out, Julian?"

After a moment's surprise, Julian said, "Yes, of course." He could guess what the Imperial Navy were hoping for—the polar opposite of von Reuentahl's requests. As he nodded to Frederica, he had already half-opened the door to his decision.

On December 3, that decision became visible on the battlefield.

The ominous news was brought to von Reuentahl by his aide, Lieutenant Commander Emil von Reckendorf.

"Your Excellency, a large fleet is approaching Heinessen from the direction of Iserlohn Corridor."

"Imperial?"

"Yes, Your Excellency. It seems they are under the command of Senior Admiral Mecklinger. The republicans at Iserlohn granted them passage through the corridor."

The words *tension* and *unease* were printed all over von Reckendorf's face. Von Reuentahl looked away and began speaking to the stars.

"That boy at Iserlohn has a decent eye for strategy, it seems. Either that, or very good staff officers. I wonder if this is old Merkatz's doing."

This guess was incorrect. "That boy at Iserlohn" had weighed, chosen, and announced his decision without help from anyone—or anyone living, at least.

But von Reuentahl did correctly understand what Julian's decision meant. On one hand, he was putting the empire in his debt, creating diplomatic material that could be used in future negotiations. On the other, by allowing Mecklinger through, he was effectively emptying the imperial end of the corridor of fighting strength. If Iserlohn felt the need to, they could invade imperial territory to stir up trouble or worse. Even if they harbored no such intention, they would certainly have freedom of action.

In any case, there was no longer any point in continuing the present battle. If Heinessen fell to Mecklinger, von Reuentahl would stand alone in the void and, furthermore, soon be forced to fight on two fronts.

He ordered his ships to retreat.

This was easier said than done. At this time, Mittermeier had Wahlen and Wittenfeld perfectly under his control on his left and right flank, and was using them alternately to strike von Reuentahl's fleet from both sides, bleeding von Reuentahl as his own ships advanced. But, through cannon fire and feinting by the ships directly under his control, von Reuentahl was able to break up Mittermeier's progress long enough for units to slip out of the war zone, one by one When he saw the opportunity, he beat a hasty retreat himself, thus completing a perfect disengagement for which no one had been sacrificed at all.

"He really is one of the greatest commanders of our age. Retreating even as he fights on, and without a hint of confusion. I don't think even the examples in tactical textbooks are this beautiful."

Thus said Wahlen as he watched the points of light recede on his screen. Mittermeier was silent. He knew this already; there was no need to verbalize it. Gathering on his brow was a sharp, yet heavy resolution. He would end this conflict before the year was out. If it dragged on into the new year, the signal fires would go up across the Neue Land: *the new dynasty is a paper tiger!* If the believers in democratic republicanism convinced themselves of that, there was no guarantee they would not explode in their own rebellion. And then there were the inhabitants of Iserlohn Base—how would they react? No, Mittermeier would have to smash the eggs of danger and confusion before they could hatch en masse.

However, to end the conflict would mean killing his friend. Every commander in the Imperial Navy knew that von Reuentahl was not the sort of man who would beg for his life. Noticing the almost turbulent rise and fall of emotions on the faces of his colleagues, Mittermeier gave his orders.

"All ships, maximum combat speed. We are going to catch up to von Reuentahl before he reaches Heinessen."

Neither his voice nor his expression brooked any argument.

CHAPTER EIGHT:

DIE BY THE SWORD

I

> This miserable civil war will soon bring to us the one slim happiness
> it has to offer: its conclusion. And even this is only a happiness
> by comparison with the alternative...

SENIOR ADMIRAL ERNEST MECKLINGER wrote these
words in his diary after he arrived in the Neue Land, becoming one of
only a handful who had traversed Iserlohn Corridor from the old imperial
side to former alliance territory without braving the fires of war.

Even the strategically oriented Mecklinger, whose gifts of wisdom and
reason were both significant, found it surprising that the Iserlohn Republic
had granted him passage in this way. When he reported their decision to
Kaiser Reinhard in distant Phezzan, the kaiser's initial response had been
several moments of silence. It was not that either of them had underestimated Julian. Indeed, they had been unaware even of his existence,
let alone his capacity as a leader, and unable to harbor any prejudices
about him at all.

"If he says he will grant your request and let you through, then go through," the kaiser said finally. "It appears we owe Yang Wen-li our gratitude for leaving a sensible successor. No doubt he has ideas of his own, but we shall leave that for another day."

Mecklinger complied, but among his staff officers there were, of course, some who had misgivings.

"If Iserlohn fires on us with Thor's Hammer, the fleet will be obliterated. We must remain alert."

A hint of a wry smile appeared under the artist admiral's neatly trimmed mustache. "Will alertness sap Thor's Hammer of its power? If so, I am all for it, but I fear we have rather surrendered our rights in that area…"

As uneasy as Mecklinger's troops were, the residents of Iserlohn Base must have felt an unease of their own. Offering the Mecklinger fleet up as a sacrifice to Thor might bring some temporary satisfaction, but would only call down the wrath of the entire Imperial Navy. And, of course, they had their own nagging suspicions that Mecklinger would attack while Iserlohn's guard was down.

> If I am honest, my mental state was more hopeful than confident, however slight the unbalance. If Yang Wen-li had been alive, that proportion would have been reversed—no, in fact, I would have been able to put near-perfect faith in him. I prayed from the bottom of my heart that Yang's youthful successor would not succumb to his impulses and prioritize ambition over reason.

Julian knew nothing of Mecklinger's prayers, but he did control his impulses. Having granted the empire its request, he knew that he could not allow anything to harm the relationship of trust thus engendered.

"If the fleet tries anything underhanded, we'll just shoot them down. Iserlohn's outer walls can brush off ship's cannon without a scratch. We'll make sure the whole galaxy knows of their dishonor."

Julian was in the base's central control room, eyes fixed on the main screen. The imperial fleet was passing through the firing range of Thor's Hammer in an orderly formation. Mecklinger had plotted a course that put his fleet within point-blank range of the weapon, presumably to convey his trust in Iserlohn's leadership.

Beside Julian sat Dusty Attenborough, slurping coffee from a paper cup. "Almost makes you wish they'd just attack us," he muttered, just loud enough for Julian to hear. "I'd give them a nice pat on the head with Thor's Hammer then."

"I don't ask for much," said Poplin, who was watching too. "I just want to see some fireworks. Not that I'd complain if things escalated, mind you." Beneath the cheer in his green eyes was a hunger for combat. He understood that Julian meant to "sit this one out," but, by all appearances, would not have been dismayed in the least if combat had broken out.

Beside Poplin stood Merkatz, with von Schneider a respectful half pace behind him. Both remained silent throughout. What might they have said to Mecklinger in their hearts?

A communications officer brought Julian a message from the passing fleet:

> From Ernest Mecklinger, senior admiral of the Galactic Imperial Navy, to the Iserlohn Republic's government and military representatives. I offer thanks for your goodwill and anticipate with pleasure the future normalization of relations between us. As we pass, my entire fleet will offer a respectful salute toward the sacred resting place of the great Marshal Yang Wen-li. I hope this gesture will be received in the spirit in which it is offered.

"In other words, the enemy's a pack of sentimentalists, just like us," said von Schönkopf with a sideways glance at Julian. "'Sacred resting place,' was it? I suppose, commander, that this shared sentimentalism is where you expect to reach an understanding and find our hopes for the future?"

"Something like that. But I don't expect the path to be a smooth one."

What was in Julian's mind was less a prediction than an expectation. This was something Yang had always warned against, but at that moment Julian felt that he could sense the direction and speed of history's flow through his skin rather than his reason, and see its final end point more or less accurately.

All the galaxy was a stage, as Yang had once said. Players trod the boards of space-time in tragedies and farces, large and small. The curtain went up, the curtain came down, and one lead gave way to the next. Iserlohn was currently starring in a historical drama colored crimson and gold by staggering bloodshed and resplendent dreams, and Julian sensed the final curtain approaching. As Yang's disciple, however, he was embarrassed by the fact that this feeling was not the fruit of rational, intellectual analysis, and not inclined to speak of it.

Shortly after their imperial guests had finished their passage through Iserlohn Corridor, five thousand light years away in the void, another scene in the drama imagined by Julian would begin.

II

December 7.

The pursuing Mittermeier fleet caught the tail of the Reuentahl fleet in its sights. This should have meant an orderly development of attack and counterattack, but as the Reuentahl fleet prepared to return fire, it suddenly fell into confusion.

"Grillparzer is firing on us!"

The scream from the operator ran through von Reuentahl's auditory nerve. Next came the assault on his optic nerve. Despite controls on the luminosity it allowed through, the screen on the bridge was dominated by pulsing nebulae of light. Voices on the communications circuits repeatedly called the same ship or combat squadron, revealing that contact had been lost with them. *Tristan* was caught in a vast explosion of malicious, murderous energy.

"He must have been waiting for this opportunity all along. That cunning—"

The bitter realization controlled even von Reuentahl's vocal cords. He had crafted his strategy and tactics for Reinhard and Mittermeier alone, never considering the possibility of petty intrigue by a petty traitor.

Grillparzer's betrayal was met with unbridled rage. It can only be called ironic that the ships that returned fire most furiously were those that were formerly under von Knapfstein's command, and now threw the full force of their still-raw grief and anger at Grillparzer. "Coward!" one captain shouted. "Do you think we will sit on our hands and let you have all the glory? No, you are coming with us. When you reach Valhalla, apologize to those who fell!"

The Grillparzer fleet was not entirely unified either. Some unfortunate ships were still hesitating, unsure whether to obey the sudden, unexpected order to attack, when they were blown apart by the response. The situation raced toward the brink of catastrophe, dissolving as understanding clashed with intellect into a rancorous free-for-all of ally versus ally.

Grillparzer's betrayal would leave a large, black stain on the historical canvas of this civil war, otherwise painted in such splendid colors. Until that day, Grillparzer had seldom been criticized on the grounds of ability or morality, and great things were expected from him as a scholar too. Even Mittermeier had once urged Bayerlein to learn from the broadness of Grillparzer's broadness of vision, cautioning him that a warrior must do more than fight.

But while the histories of later ages would describe Bayerlein as the "successor to Mittermeier; a capable soldier of honesty and integrity," Grillparzer was deemed a "despicable traitor." He would join that unfortunate group whose entire legacy is dismissed due to their actions at the very end of their lives—less than one percent of their allotted time.

Mittermeier did not immediately grasp the import of the confusion unfolding before his eyes. But when the word "traitor" began to be heard in the chaos of intercepted messages, all became clear. The Gale Wolf's youthful face reddened with indignation. This was to have been his battle, with his friend, at which they would both exert themselves to the utmost. He had not expected such an ugly development.

Amid the gaudily hued turmoil, firing converged on von Reuentahl's flagship *Tristan*, and a shot from a rail cannon flew toward it from one o'clock. *Tristan* evaded the projectile, but when another flew in from the direction in which the ship had taken evasive action, the increased relative velocity allowed it to breach *Tristan*'s outer hull and explode inside the ship itself.

Von Reuentahl's field of vision shook violently, first up and down and then left and right; it was bleached by dazzling light before subsiding to a glowing orange. Amid the rumbling and howling wind, the commander's chair toppled over, coming down on the leg of von Reuentahl, who stood before it. The sound of explosions battered his eardrums.

Through the scramble of vision and hearing, von Reuentahl's mismatched eyes perceived a presence that was neither light nor shadow descending on him. Had his leg not been caught under the commander's chair, he could have dodged it with ease. But his polished reflexes, ever so slightly, betrayed their possessor's will, and he felt the shock of impact run through the left side of his chest in a straight, narrow line.

A long ceramic shard had pierced him beneath his left clavicle, and the pain went right through to his back.

"Your Excellency!" screamed his aide Lieutenant Commander von Reckendorf, seeing his commander run through amid the smoke and chaos.

"Calm yourself. I'm the one who's wounded, not you." Despite the gravity of the situation, von Reuentahl smoothed down his hair with one hand. "As I recall, screaming on behalf of superiors is not among the duties of an aide."

With an expression more of irritation than pain, von Reuentahl pulled the forty-centimeter ceramic spear from his chest. Blood gushed forth in a thin but powerful stream, immediately soaking the front of his uniform. His hands, too, looked as if he had wrapped them in vermillion silk.

Von Reuentahl snorted. "Whatever the color of our eyes or skin, it seems we all bleed the same color," he said.

He threw the fragment away. By now the blood had reached the tips of his shoes and begun to pool on the floor. The small wound that had opened in his back also formed a vermillion stream that lasted until his muscles contracted to close it. The locations of his wounds were pure coincidence, but those who believed in fate may have seen some meaning in the fact that they mirrored those of Kornelias Lutz.

Incredibly, von Reuentahl pushed the commander's chair off himself and, despite his massive blood loss, got calmly to his feet. Not a hint of pain showed, at least in his face or his movements. He was resolute to an almost impudent degree. Von Reckendorf screamed for a medic, and one came running to hastily begin first aid.

"Your Excellency," von Reckendorf said, cheeks shaking with rage, "we must teach the traitor Grillparzer a lesson. I will muster the fire of the apocalypse to send him to hell, where cowards belong!"

"Leave him."

"But—"

"Survival will be the greater misfortune for him in the end. Do you think the kaiser or Mittermeier will ever forgive what he has done?— Well, how does it look?"

His final question was directed at the medic, still tending his wounds. The medic wiped the sweat from his brow with the back of a hand now stained red with von Reuentahl's blood.

"There is damage to the blood vessels connecting your heart and lungs. I will freeze it to stop the bleeding, and seal the wound for now, but you will need proper surgery as soon as possible."

"I don't much like surgery, I'm afraid."

"It isn't a question of like or dislike, Your Excellency. Your life depends on it."

"On the contrary, doctor, it's about far more than like or dislike. Surely you can agree that it wouldn't suit me to die in my pajamas on a hospital bed?"

Von Reuentahl's pale but almost insolently calm smile forestalled all counterargument from the medic as the rolls of the dead swam into view in von Reuentahl's mind.

Siegfried Kircheis. Kempf. Lennenkamp. Fahrenheit. Steinmetz. Lutz. Even his enemies, Bucock and Yang Wen-li. It seemed to him that, in the end, all of their deaths had been appropriate to their lives. In what manner would he, Oskar von Reuentahl, take his place alongside them? He had not thought too deeply on this before, but at Valhalla they might have begun sweeping the path to the gate for him.

Once the cryotreatment stopped his internal bleeding, his wounds were covered in bandages and jelly palm and he was injected with antibiotics.

After thanking the medic and instructing him to see to the rest of the injured, von Reuentahl righted the commander's chair and lowered himself into it. He was far from the only one to have been injured. The bridge had become a ghastly exposition of blood and flesh. In one corner, a soldier still in his teens cried for his mother as he groped about for a missing arm; another man wept tears of agony and terror as he used both hands to stuff his innards back into the abdominal wound they had spilled from.

He had a student orderly wipe his soiled desk. The orderly did so, hazel hair still in disarray, but then turned his face to von Reuentahl, revealing that he was on the verge of tears.

"Your Excellency, you will aggravate your injuries. Please do not overexert yourself."

"No need to worry," von Reuentahl said. "But you can go and get me a change of clothes. Shirt and uniform. Smell your own blood for five minutes and it starts to get tiresome."

The fires on *Tristan's* bridge were finally extinguished, but its offensive and defensive capabilities were both severely degraded, and it was forced to withdraw from the battlefield at forty minutes past midnight on December 8. Von Reuentahl's fleet was on the brink of defeat, but his calm, measured control ensured that at least part of it was able to withdraw in an orderly fashion along with his flagship.

"With no further treatment beyond periodic injections of painkillers and hematinics, Marshal von Reuentahl remained upright in the commander's chair overseeing the entire fleet. He changed his uniform, fastening every button correctly, with an utterly impassive expression. I cannot imagine the agony that must have assailed him, and yet his judgment and command remained flawless. As I watched this demonstration of true fortitude played out before my eyes, I felt proud to be among his subordinates. I entirely forgot, if only for a moment, the awesome truth: that we had placed ourselves in opposition to the great Kaiser Reinhard himself…"

The source of this testimony was Lieutenant Commander von Reckendorf, but even he could not deny that the blood was draining from von Reuentahl's face. At one point he passed out from cerebral anemia, but when his subordinates tried to carry him from the chair to the medical ward, he regained consciousness, rebuked them, and ordered them to return him to his chair. They felt as if they beheld a man who challenged the very lord of death, and their awe and respect for him grew even stronger. They also realized that this fortitude was only made possible by the sacrifice of his physical form, meaning that the commander's remaining life was rapidly dwindling.

Grillparzer would disgrace himself five times in the end. The first time was his initial support, however feigned, for von Reuentahl's revolt against the kaiser. The second was his betrayal of von Reuentahl after having sworn fealty to him. The third was his choice of the worst possible time to enact that betrayal. The fourth was the failure of the betrayal itself, which saw him defeated by von Reuentahl's forces. And the fifth came when, having achieved nothing, he asked permission to surrender to a man who thought such acts despicable. Given that Mittermeier was von Reuentahl's friend, it was natural for Grillparzer to choose Wahlen instead, but it only exacerbated the already unfavorable impression he gave of low cunning.

Mittermeier did not even meet this dishonorably surrendered deserter. He was not sure he could control his tongue if he did.

III

In the thirteen years since von Reuentahl's graduation from officer's school, he had taken part in more than two hundred battles of all sizes, as well as thirty private duels. As a warrior, he was far more aggressive than he was as a tactician, and seemed to enjoy putting himself in danger. Of course, it may be that his heterochromatic eyes made such an impression that those who saw his noble, even features were especially inclined to search for two sides to his personality. Whatever the case, in all of his public and private battles, von Reuentahl had never been seriously injured before. Even in brawls outside the contexts of war and dueling, the only person who had successfully landed a punch on his face was Wolfgang Mittermeier.

For von Reuentahl, his injury at Rantemario may have seemed the vesper bell of his life. And, at the realization that Grillparzer, of all people, had struck at him from behind, he perhaps felt more scorn for himself than loathing for the youthful turncoat.

The Mittermeier fleet were not aware that von Reuentahl had been wounded, but they had seen the damage to his flagship *Tristan*. The withdrawal that followed settled the matter completely.

Grillparzer was not the only one to surrender. Many ships' crews, wounded or tired of fighting, shut down their engines and abandoned all resistance. Had their enemy been the Coalition of Lords or the Free Planets Alliance, they might have fought more doggedly, but not against former brothers-in-arms who rallied around the Goldenlöwe too.

"We are not abandoning von Reuentahl. We only seek to return to the kaiser and the correct way for imperial soldiers…"

In response to this claim from one surrendered officer, Senior Admiral Wittenfeld snorted and replied, "Sophistry, all sophistry. You fear for your lives, and nothing more."

The soldiers of lower rank spoke more candidly, feeling less need to justify themselves. One teenage soldier, wounded and picked up by a hospital ship, responded to questioning as follows:

"We risked our lives in battle against the Gale Wolf and the Black Lancers. I think our responsibilities to Marshal von Reuentahl have been fulfilled. When I leave hospital, I hope to resume military duty under the kaiser—unless you think that enlisted men will be court-martialed too?"

When he received that report, Mittermeier struck his subordinates as less angered than deeply shocked.

"I see," he said eventually. "His responsibilities have been fulfilled, have they? I see."

This was when Mittermeier knew the Reuentahl fleet was no more. The soldier's words perfectly encapsulated the thinking of those who had served in this pointless civil war. In their minds, at least, the war was over. Only von Reuentahl could have led them even this far, but even von Reuentahl had limits, and it seemed that he had reached them. His troops were pledged to Kaiser Reinhard, not to him, and they recognized no duty to share von Reuentahl's fate as he went from defeat to final downfall.

"It's over…"

Mittermeier's shoulders slumped as he muttered the words, as if he had lost the conflict himself.

His insight proved correct. The Neue Land Security Force, once

5.5 million troops strong, continued its rapid disintegration from surrender and desertion.

So many ships sought to surrender that they hampered the Mittermeier
fleet's advance. Authority to process them was delegated to Admiral Büro.
Many of the troops surrendering were injured; conversely, some ships
that were half destroyed continued to resist. Bringing the situation under
control would be a surprisingly time-consuming task.

Mittermeier chose one wounded captured officer for questioning.

"What happened to your commander, von Reuentahl?"

"He is escaping toward the planet Heinessen in the Baalat system, Your
Excellency."

Mittermeier frowned. The word "escaping" seemed to have touched a
nerve, but he did not pursue it.

"He may seek to restart the conflict in the Baalat system. Prepare for
immediate pursuit."

Death seemed likely for von Reuentahl. It was not the first time Mittermeier had made this inference. At the Second Battle of Rantemario—even
before, in fact—von Reuentahl had surely viewed defeat as certain death,
and fought with no intention of surviving it. This was not merely Mittermeier's interpretation, but a gloomy understanding shared by all of his
staff officers who had fought von Reuentahl.

"Whatever page we turn to in the chronicles of our lives, we find it
written in blood," said a rather morose Wittenfeld to Wahlen. "We can
dress it up with humanism, but the red stain can never be erased. Even
so, there are some things I'd rather not experience. Like fighting to the
death with a comrade…If the kaiser ordered you to take me down, would
you obey?"

"Ja," Wahlen replied, after so brief a pause that Wittenfeld was somewhat put out.

"You might at least pretend to be torn on a question like that."

"It's a bad question. I urge whoever asked it to reconsider their behavior."

Wahlen was not in the mood for hypotheticals. Von Reuentahl was one
of the Twin Ramparts of the Imperial Navy, an admiral among admirals,
and look at the tragic fate he had called down on himself. Wahlen could

not help feeling uneasy when he imagined how Reinhard's faith in his admirals might change as a result. Who could say that Wittenfeld's question would remain hypothetical forever?

December 11. The fleet Mecklinger had brought through Iserlohn Corridor rendezvoused with Mittermeier's main forces on the outskirts of the Gandharva system, which was home to the fateful planet Urvashi.

Mecklinger had not participated directly in any combat, but after passing through the corridor he had maneuvered as if to cut off the Reuentahl fleet's rear. By increasing the pressure on von Reuentahl to retreat, he had contributed to his side's strategic victory.

It was decided that Mittermeier, Wittenfeld, and Wahlen would push on to Heinessen without landing at the imperial base on Urvashi, but Mecklinger and his fleet would stay to ensure that order was reestablished and upheld. Grillparzer had stayed on Urvashi only briefly, and now that von Reuentahl's fleet had been put to rout the base had once more become a small iron boat floating on a sea of uncertainty and unrest. Mecklinger's ability and name, combined with the military might of his fleet, would be more than enough to bring stability. After a hurried but precise consultation on these matters, Mecklinger expressed to Mittermeier his wish to investigate the original plot against the kaiser immediately. "In my opinion," he said, "it is unlikely that the attempt on His Majesty's life here was directed by Marshal von Reuentahl."

(Strictly speaking, von Reuentahl had already been stripped of his title, but even the admirals who had been forced to fight against him seemed unwilling to refer to him without a title at all. The only exception was Mittermeier, who had long been accustomed to doing so and had never been reprimanded by the kaiser for it.)

"Why do you think so, Admiral Mecklinger?"

"First, it does not comport with his personality. Second, it is not commensurate with his ability."

"Hmm." Mittermeier frowned. A troubled shadow descended on his youthful features.

Mecklinger's arguments were undeniably correct. Had von Reuentahl decided to raise the flag of revolt in order to surpass the kaiser, he would have advanced his forces directly and openly for a stand-up fight. To do otherwise would be inconsistent with his motive for rebelling in the first place. On the other hand, if his sole aim was to seize power by any means necessary, he could have simply waited for the kaiser to reach Heinessen before imprisoning or murdering him. Risking an attack while Reinhard was on Urvashi made no sense. Furthermore, after Reinhard's flagship *Brünhild* had lifted off, von Reuentahl had simply sat on his hands and allowed it to leave. Had he been serious, he would surely have stationed ships in orbit to prevent the kaiser and his retinue from escaping.

The sense of wrongness that Mittermeier had felt regarding this "revolt" from its earliest stages may have been rooted in these inconsistencies and disparities. However, at this point, his position required him to focus on the situation's outcome rather than its causes. Given his position, he had to pay more attention to the result of the situation than its causes. Leaving Mecklinger to seek the truth on Urvashi, he pushed on toward Heinessen.

After Mecklinger stationed his troops at key locations on Urvashi's surface, he began his investigation even as he set about retaking the base, with Vice Admiral Wünsche as his lieutenant. Wünsche had the look of a simple farmer, but he was the staff officer Mecklinger trusted most.

"If Marshal von Reuentahl was not behind the attack on the kaiser, why did he not loudly protest his innocence?" he asked.

"As you know, Marshal von Reuentahl is a man of great pride. To admit that unknown conspirators had placed him atop a sacrificial altar would be quite impossible for him."

In all likelihood, Mecklinger thought, von Reuentahl *wanted* them to believe that his revolt was driven by his own will and ambition. By nature, he would rather stand and fight than protest that he had been wrongly accused and beg for the kaiser's mercy.

"It seems that the galaxy is too small for two people of ambition to share the same age…"

Despite this lament, what Mecklinger found difficult to accept was von Reuentahl's apparent failure to identify and hold to account those who had been behind the Urvashi Incident.

"Even if he was not behind the disturbance, why did he make no attempt to punish those who were?" Mecklinger said. "This is what baffles me. Your thoughts?"

"The situation developed at a rapid pace, after all. Perhaps the marshal simply had no time for a close investigation."

This seemed possible to Mecklinger, too, but he was not completely convinced. He continued to seek answers from captured officers from von Reuentahl's fleet and when interrogating soldiers stationed at Urvashi base. Eventually, he learned that Grillparzer had come to Urvashi on von Reuentahl's orders to suppress the disturbance and investigate its cause, but had not delivered a full and accurate report of his findings. He had intentionally concealed several pieces of evidence that suggested the involvement of Church of Terra die-hards, instead claiming that the responsible parties remained unclear. This discovery revealed to Mecklinger the common thread that ran through all of Grillparzer's thoughts and deeds.

When Grillparzer was summoned to appear before Mecklinger, his expression was equal parts unease, disgruntlement, and expectation. The unease and disgruntlement were because he had received no praise from senior officers for his services as a turncoat, and the anticipation was because he believed that Mecklinger recognized that he was more than just a warrior.

However, Mecklinger had nothing but the sharpest criticism for him, denouncing him as a criminal who had used the Terraist intrigue to goad von Reuentahl into rebellion with the aim of profiting from it personally.

"Grillparzer, great things were expected of you, both as a military man and a scholar. Betrayal and deception were unnecessary; you would surely have attained high position and great authority in the fullness of time. Regrettably, you were so infatuated with your own ingenuity that you brought shame on the last phase of your life."

At this ominous intimation, Grillparzer's body temperature dropped. Cold sweat dampened his shirt from the inside.

"You have committed a double sin," Mecklinger continued. "The first was turning away from the kaiser's friendship. The second was betraying

Marshal von Reuentahl's trust. Had you reported the true findings of your investigation on Urvashi to him, this revolt would have ended before it began. But, driven by your own petty calculations, you drove your superior officer to dishonor his name with rebellion."

The young admiral attempted a defense. He had only done what he thought best for the kaiser, he said. Marshal von Reuentahl had, in fact, risen in revolt—and had not he, Grillparzer, contributed to the marshal's defeat?

"Do you believe that victory through betrayal pleases the kaiser?" Mecklinger asked, his voice growing even calmer. "Yes, I suppose you do, which is exactly why you betrayed Marshal von Reuentahl. A mouse's intellect cannot comprehend a lion's heart. In the end, you simply were not fit to be that lion's friend."

Grillparzer opened his mouth, but his lips only trembled and twitched, and not a word came out. His shoulders fell; he hung his head. He had realized, it seemed, that he had lost both past and future. After he was taken away, soldiers guarding him on both sides, Mecklinger sighed wearily. He felt no small regret over the waste of Grillparzer's talent and potential. Beyond that, he was not sure how he could explain the truth to Kaiser Reinhard and Marshal Mittermeier—that the Reuentahl Revolt had been set in motion by the remnants of the Church of Terra, and then pushed beyond the point of turning back by Grillparzer's ambition.

IV

The Reuentahl fleet returned to Heinessen just over one-tenth the size it had been when it set out: 4,580 ships and 658,900 soldiers. Roughly half of those who did not return had died in battle, while the other half had surrendered or been captured. There also appeared to be a small number who simply went missing.

It was a devastating defeat. Nevertheless, the order and discipline of the returning units and their maneuvering was testament to von Reuentahl's powers of command—even if it was like the last rays of the setting sun, when only enough light remained to set the edges of the cliffs agleam.

Tristan was still heavily damaged, and shook so violently when it entered warp that the wound in von Reuentahl's chest was torn back open. Once more the hemorrhaging was severe, and he even lost consciousness for a moment. But after an emergency transfusion, he came to and smoothly reassumed command of the defeated fleet. Bergengrün urged him to transfer to a hospital ship, or at least a vessel flying without damage, but von Reuentahl laughed.

"Müller won praise even after abandoning his flagship, but only because he remained in the chaos of battle to lead his forces. If I abandoned ship while fleeing in abject defeat, the name 'Oskar von Reuentahl' would become a byword for cowardice." He remained in the commander's seat until the end.

An ordinary man would already be sliding down the slopes of coma toward the abyss of death, but von Reuentahl's mind remained clear. He appears to have retained his coolheaded reason and steely self-control even in his final hours. On one point, all the direct testimony agrees: Marshal von Reuentahl remained Marshal von Reuentahl until the moment of his death.

When he stepped out of the landcar before the front entrance of the governorate's offices, he was still impeccably dressed. Only his pallor gave any indication of death's embrace.

Of von Reuentahl's senior staff officers, Bergengrün and Sonnenfels were still with him. Barthauser and Schüler had died in battle, and Dittersdorf had been wounded and surrendered. At the governorate, more than four thousand officers and enlisted men had gathered, fully armed, determined to do their duty right up until the governor-general's death.

"I see," von Reuentahl said. "There are more fools in the world than I thought."

And you are the greatest among them, said the coldly sneering face looking back at him from the mirror. Even as he sneered, his deep, wide-ranging reason, one of the two wheels that supported the chariot of his psyche, understood that he could not martyr these loyal subordinates to his own idiocy. Once he had dragged himself behind the desk in his office, his first act was to call in Julius Elsheimer, Lutz's protégé and the director-general of civil affairs, who was still under house arrest.

When he arrived, Elsheimer was visibly rattled by von Reuentahl's cadaverous appearance. Von Reuentahl smiled wanly. "Nothing you need to worry about," he said. "I know I have no right to show my face here again, but, well, here I am."

"Fortune was against Your Excellency, I gather."

"No, I think the result would be the same if I tried it again. It appears that this is the limit of my abilities."

If there were no Kaiser Reinhard... But von Reuentahl knew more than anyone how meaningless this hypothetical was.

"Director-general, I have a request to make of you."

"By all means."

"I want you to take control of all governmental and administrative affairs for the governorate. It pains me to force on you the task of cleaning up the mess I made, but, whoever the work falls to, the responsibility is not one to be taken lightly."

Once Elsheimer had solemnly agreed and left the office, von Reuentahl called to his aide, Lieutenant Commander von Reckendorf.

"Call in Trünicht. It's always unpleasant to see him, but it'll be good practice for the unpleasantness of death."

Von Reckendorf appeared to have objections to this astonishing order, but, presumably thinking it wrong to argue with a superior officer on the verge of death, obeyed at once and went to fetch Job Trünicht.

The high counselor made a startling contrast to the man who had summoned him. Von Reuentahl was near death, black and blue eyes glittering in an unnaturally pale face with a light that was as sharp as ever, if not as powerful. Trünicht was unapologetically vigorous, healthy of complexion, and overflowing with the ambition and potential of a political animal in his prime. He was more than ten years older than von Reuentahl, but in terms of proximity to death their positions were clearly reversed.

"A pleasure to see you in such fine health, high counselor," said von Reuentahl.

"I owe it all to Your Excellency's favor."

This venomous exchange was followed by a short silence. Trünicht's voice had been far stronger than von Reuentahl's, both in volume and in intonation.

"Well, you can see what has become of me," von Reuentahl said. "I fell into the pitfall of autocracy, launched a fruitless revolt, and am on the verge of a death that will be lauded by no one. I suppose democracy, the system you served, is immune to tragicomedies like this?"

Von Reuentahl's point was far from clear, but Trünicht apparently concluded that this was due to the confusion of approaching death. A faint smile flickered across his lips.

"Oh, democracy is not so grand either," he said. "Just look at me, marshal. Imagine—a man like me, seizing the reins of power, deciding who lives and who dies as he pleases. If this is not a flaw in the democratic republican system, what is?"

His words were flowing freely by the end of this speech. The stink of self-intoxication rose, overpowering his cologne.

"Odd," said von Reuentahl. "It sounds as though you despise democracy. Isn't that the system you exploited to the utmost to attain the power you craved? Doesn't that make democracy itself your benefactor? Surely there's no call to be so disrespectful of it."

"If autocracy will grant me power, then let my next benefactor be autocracy. I will serve it even more sincerely than I have praised democracy in the past, I assure you."

"Am I to gather that you intend to seize control within the Lohengramm Dynasty, too, as chancellor?"

"If the kaiser so desires."

"And, just as you drained the Free Planets Alliance dry, you will do the same to the empire."

He is a monster, thought von Reuentahl, between pulses of pain. Not in the way von Oberstein was a monster—Trünicht was a monster of egoism. He had only fed on democracy because he happened to be attached to its camp. Had he been born in the empire, he would have used a different approach to feed on autocracy instead. Around its egoistic core, Trünicht's psyche was amorphous as an amoeba, greedily devouring anything within reach.

"Which is why you continue to knowingly allow the Church of Terra to use you."

"No. *I* am the one using *them*. I use anything and everything. Religion, politics, even the kaiser. Yes, even the kaiser you rebelled against—the one who, for all his gifts, is far from a perfect human being—is, indeed, an immature little boy. I am sure that Your Excellency, too, saw something ludicrous in the golden-haired little fellow playing the arrogant genius."

In this flowing eloquence, Job Trünicht signed his death warrant with his own tongue. Strangely, he does not appear to have even considered the possibility of being killed by von Reuentahl. After all, von Reuentahl had no reason to kill him; more to the point, he had nothing to gain by doing so.

When von Reuentahl, with an almost majestic grace that actually required every scrap of strength he had left, pointed his blaster at Trünicht, the former head of the Free Planets Alliance's smile did not falter. He was still smiling when the hole opened in his chest. It was only when the agony seized control of his entire nervous system and the blood that gushed forth discolored his tailored suit that his expression changed. Not to a look of fear, or pain. Rather, it was more a look of rebuke, as if to criticize the man who had been irrational enough to harm him in defiance of his judgment and calculations. Trünicht opened his mouth, but instead of the usual golden-tongued rhetoric, blood from his lungs spilled out.

"Insult democracy, loot the state, deceive the people—none of that is my concern. However…"

The blazing light in von Reuentahl's mismatched eyes lashed Trünicht across the face, making the former head of the alliance reel.

"However, I will not permit you to befoul the kaiser's dignity with your filthy tongue. I neither served nor rebelled against a man who deserved to be insulted by someone like you."

By the end of this speech, Trünicht had already lost the strength to stand and collapsed to the floor. He gazed into space with eyes brimming with disappointment and despair. This rare man, who had attempted to manipulate two different systems with a single inborn nature, still held vast potential within him, but his future had been stolen from him by his dying heterochromiac interlocutor. Freed from all concern for the justness of his cause or even the law, von Reuentahl had shot him dead from atop a torrent of private feeling. Trünicht, a genius of self-preservation who had preserved both life and status flawlessly in dealings with Kaiser Reinhard and Yang Wen-li alike, was being forced out of space-time by an "outrage" committed by a failed imperial rebel. In the end, this was the only type of act that proved effective against Trünicht's sort of immortality.

What lay on the floor was no longer Job Trünicht. Not because it was dead, but because it could no longer speak. A Trünicht that could not make use of tongue and lips and vocal cords was already no Trünicht at all. It was nothing but an assemblage of cells, not even human any longer. Von Reuentahl let go of his blaster—or, more accurately, his blaster left his hand and violently kissed the floor before spinning away.

"He really was an unbearable man, right to the end. To think that the last person I killed wouldn't even be armed… What a dishonorable thing he made me do."

In this way, just before his own death, von Reuentahl made a slight correction to the history that would unfold afterwards. His act was not discovered until after he was dead, and even then it would be some time before the full picture of Trünicht's unceremoniously interrupted ambition and vision was uncovered.

V

After von Reuentahl had Trünicht's body removed, it seemed that the invisible hand of accumulated fatigue pushed him into death's abyss. When an unexpected visitor was announced, he begrudged even the effort of showing his puzzlement.

"Leave me alone," he said. There was something like a rueful chuckle in his voice, and even perhaps a kind of relief at knowing his debts were paid in full. "I'm not just dying, I'm in the process of dying. And I'm actually finding it quite enjoyable. Don't interrupt my last moments of pleasure."

His skin was pale and waxy, beaded with cold sweat. It was a strange feeling to slowly die from a wound over the course of a week. The pain that spread from core to extremities had become an inseparable part of his sensorium; when he lost it, he would be hollowed out inside, and collapse on himself.

Trünicht's murder had taxed von Reuentahl's strength greatly. He was as exhausted as a knight that had slain a venomous dragon; he was entirely consumed, and longed for sleep leading directly to death. What held him back, like a drop of water falling from a stalactite, was a cold female voice.

"It's been a while. And you're a traitor now—high treason. Of course."

Von Reuentahl raised his eyes. When they came into focus, he clearly saw the woman's outline. But it took another five seconds for the vision to materialize in the domain of his reason. The door of memory felt as if it were made of heavy stone, but he finally heaved it open and recognized her.

"The last of the Lichtenlade clan," he muttered. Her position must have left a greater impression on him than the name she went by: Elfriede von Kohlrausch.

"Now that your own ambition has hurled you into total defeat, I'm just here to watch your miserable death," she said. Her voice was guarded, just as he remembered, but today it seemed to tremble strangely, even unstably.

"So kind of you to make the effort." His bland, passionless response may have betrayed Elfriede's expectations. "Wait just a little longer. You'll get your wish. I'd like to make at least one woman happy, since I have the opportunity."

Venom, it seemed, could not be sent out without the power to do so. He felt the desire to observe her face in detail—it was glowing with hate, no doubt—but lacked the energy. From the starting point of his life to that very day, negative emotions toward woman had been cultivated within him, but now they seemed to be evaporating along with the rest of his vitality.

"Who brought you here, anyway?" he asked.

"Someone kind."

"And their name?"

"None of your business."

"No, I suppose it isn't…"

Von Reuentahl wanted to say more, but was held back by what invaded his hearing at that moment. He hesitated—doubted his ears. Why, at a time like this, in a place like this, should he be hearing a baby's cry?

He poured his last dregs of life force into his vision and realized for the first time that Elfriede was not alone. What she held in her arms was unmistakably an infant of perhaps six months.

The baby had pink skin and brown hair. It opened its eyes as wide as it could, stared at the man who had unwittingly become a father. Its left eye was the color of the sky in the atmosphere's uppermost layers. Its right was—the same color.

Von Reuentahl heard himself breathing, long and deep. He did not know what emotion this represented. Still not knowing, he asked, "Is it mine?"

Elfriede had surely expected this question, but she nevertheless seemed unsure how to answer. In two moments, she replied, adding another piece of information she had not been asked for. "He's your son."

"Is that why you came? To show him to me?"

There was no reply. Whether the question itself had been spoken aloud was itself hazy. Von Reuentahl's vision filled with the sky blue of his son's eyes, as if the infant beheld his father's entire life. In the deepest recesses of his heart, von Reuentahl heard a voice speak to the child.

Your grandfather and your father were more alike than they seemed. Both devoted their entire lives to searching for what would never been theirs. Your father may have done so on a greater scale, but what made up his core was no different. What kind of life will you lead? Will you vainly water a barren field, as befits the third generation of the von Reuentahl line? Or…or will you be able to create for yourself a wiser, more fruitful life than your father or your grandfather?

"What do you plan to do with him?"

Von Reuentahl's pain spiked, shoving him out of his reverie and back to reality. Dying was a rare opportunity, in its way. You no longer needed to concern yourself with your own future. But the living would have to come to terms with that future eventually.

Again, Elfriede did not reply. Had von Reuentahl been possessed of his usual keenness and perspicacity, he would doubtless have noticed that her expression was one he had never seen before. He was on the verge of losing himself, and she of losing him. It was a loss beyond her previous experience, and it was unclear whether she could endure the realization of what it meant. Crushing his final fragments of vital energy between his molars, von Reuentahl struggled to verbalize his feelings.

"There's an ancient legend about some pompous ass and his pompous pronouncements. According to him, if you have a friend you can entrust your child to when you die, that's life's greatest happiness…"

A single drop of cold sweat fell onto his desk. Another drop of life leaving his body.

"Meet with Wolfgang Mittermeier. Put the child's future in his hands. That will guarantee the best life possible for him."

There was a couple far more qualified to be parents than he and this woman were. Nevertheless, that couple was childless, while he and Elfriede had a child. The birth of life was clearly under the control of a being either grossly incompetent or bitterly sardonic.

The curtain fell on von Reuentahl's vision, and his view of reality receded along with his consciousness.

"If you're going to kill me, better kill me now. You'll lose your chance forever, otherwise. Use my blaster if you need to…"

When his faded vision grew brighter again, perhaps five hundred seconds had passed. Death, it seemed, had refused to accept him, but he knew both rationally and emotionally that his reprieve was temporary. On his desk lay a woman's handkerchief, damp and heavy with his perspiration. Self-mocking thoughts became a new stream of cold sweat that ran down the nape of his neck. *The definition of a downfall. I'm not even worth killing anymore.*

As von Reuentahl closed one hand lightly around the handkerchief, a young orderly came fearfully into the room. His golden-brown hair was in disarray and confusion was in his face, and he cradled the baby from earlier in his arms.

"The lady has left. She…she said to give this child to Marshal Mittermeier. What should I do, Your Excellency?"

The boy's expression and voice made von Reuentahl smile. *Well, well—the mother leaves, but the child remains. Like father, like son, it seems. Perhaps too alike for your own good…*

"Sorry to do this to you, but please hold him until Mittermeier gets here. Oh, and one more thing. Could you take down that whiskey from the shelf, and get two glasses out?"

Von Reuentahl's voice was weak, beginning to fall below even the lowest levels of audibility. The orderly could not have known this, but at that moment, von Reuentahl was turning the final sneer of his life on himself. This was because, with the last powers of intellect remaining to him, he had recognized that, with the approach of death, he was beginning to lose even his flaws. Would he, Oskar von Reuentahl, die in a way that even moralizers would praise as virtuous at the last? A ridiculous concept, but perhaps not so bad. Everyone's life was their own, and so was their death. Still, at the very least, he hoped for a more beautiful death to come to the very few people he loved and respected.

Still cradling the infant with one arm, the orderly placed two glasses on the governor-general's desk and poured the amber liquid into them, like melted fragments of sunset. His lungs and heart were leaping within his breast, but somehow he carried out his orders and retreated to the sofa against the wall.

Von Reuentahl placed both arms on the desk. Facing the pair of glasses—no, facing the friend who should have sat beyond them—he spoke without raising his voice.

"You're late, Mittermeier…"

The smell of good liquor gently intruded into his vision, in which colors were already losing their clarity.

"I meant to hold on until you got here, but I'm not going to make it. Some Gale Wolf you turned out to be…"

Seeing the former marshal's head fall forward, the boy on the sofa leapt to his feet with a silent gasp. After a moment's hesitation over what to do with the baby sleeping in his arms, he placed him on the sofa and ran to the desk, where he brought his ear close to von Reuentahl's still-moving mouth.

The boy hastily, desperately, scribbled down the handful of words that weakly tickled his tympanic membrane. Pen in hand, he gazed at von Reuentahl's pale, even features. Death spread its wings soundlessly and settled over him.

"Marshal! Your Excellency! Marshal von Reuentahl…"

It was 1651 on December 16 Oskar von Reuentahl, who had been born in the same year as Yang Wen-li and spent his entire life on the side opposing him, died. He was thirty-three years old.

CHAPTER NINE:

I

WHICH OF THE TWIN RAMPARTS of the Galactic Imperial Navy was victorious at the Second Battle of Rantemario? The chronological tables are clear: "December, 2 NIC: Reuentahl defeated, mortally wounded at Second Battle of Rantemario." But the other party to the battle took a different view.

"On the surface, von Reuentahl and I may have seemed equally matched. But I had Wahlen and Wittenfeld, while he had no one. On the question of who deserves the title of victor, there is no room for debate."

This was the correction Mittermeier offered whenever he was described as the victor of the battle. Nevertheless, it was an objective fact that he had survived the encounter, and von Reuentahl had certainly been first to withdraw his forces.

When Mittermeier arrived with Wittenfeld, Wahlen, and Bayerlein at the spaceport on Heinessen, they were met by two men representing the civil and military bureaucracy respectively: Julius Elsheimer, director of civil affairs, and Vice Admiral Ritschel, the deputy inspector general. This was when Mittermeier learned of his friend's death. His face remained motionless as he took in the news. When he heard that Job Trünicht had died too, he did not wait for them to explain the cause of death before letting out a sigh.

"Let me guess," he said. "Von Reuentahl did some spring cleaning of the Neue Land as a parting gift to the kaiser."

Waiting for him at the governorate were Admiral Bergengrün, Vice Admiral Sonnenfels, Lieutenant Commander von Reckendorf, and a few others. When he arrived, the soldiers stationed there trained their weapons on him, but Sonnenfels rebuked them sternly, despite the bloody bandage still around his head. "This is a friend of the governor-general and a representative of His Majesty the kaiser! Have some respect!" At this, the soldiers presented arms and allowed the new arrivals through. It was two hours since von Reuentahl's death. In his office were three bodies, one dead and two still very much alive.

"Marshal von Reuentahl was waiting for Your Excellency. But, in the end…"

Von Reuentahl's young orderly burst into tears before he could finish, and the baby in his arms began to wail as if in response. He was so loud that the youngest of Mittermeier's companions, Bayerlein, took him to an adjoining room, awkwardly comforting the infant as best he could.

Without a word, Mittermeier removed the cape of his uniform and draped it around his friend's shoulders.

Von Reuentahl's last words were recorded, but not without certain inconsistencies.

According to the record of his student orderly—whose name, incidentally, was Heinrich Lambertz—those words were:

Mein Kaiser
Mittermeier
Sieg
Sterben

The meaning of the word "Sieg" is disputed. Some argue that it has its usual meaning "victory"; others, that it is part of a sentence that also includes "sterben," "to die": "Sieg Kaiser, even in death." Still others hold that von Reuentahl meant to say "Since Siegfried Kircheis's death…" but expired before finishing the thought.

Lambertz, who was fourteen years old at the time, said: "I only recorded the meaningful words. There were other, indistinct sounds that I did not write down. I cannot take responsibility for how others may interpret the whole." He never participated in any further discussion.

Von Reuentahl had left the theater made up of space-time and humanity. The question now was how to deal with those he had left behind.

Mittermeier wanted to save von Reuentahl's staff officers from punishment, and this feeling was shared by all the admirals of the Galactic Navy. This was partly because Grillparzer had made such an intensely negative impression that all of their hatred and loathing had concentrated on him alone. For those who had been loyal to von Reuentahl, Mittermeier's men felt more sympathy than anger.

And so Mittermeier issued a proclamation, declaring that he would request clemency from the kaiser on their behalf, and urging them to do nothing hasty. Most of von Reuentahl's forces obeyed, but there was one exception. Senior Admiral Hans Eduard Bergengrün, inspector general of the military, committed suicide.

"Marshal Kircheis is dead. Marshal von Reuentahl, too. Meeting them in Valhalla is all I have to look forward to."

So Bergengrün said to his longtime friend Senior Admiral Büro, who was trying desperately to reason with him via visiphone from outside his firmly locked door.

"Give His Majesty the kaiser a message for me," Bergengrün continued. "Tell him he must be lonely, losing one loyal general after another. Ask him if Marshal Mittermeier is next. Tell him that if he thinks rewarding service with punishment will help his dynasty flourish, then by all means he should continue to do so."

No one had ever criticized Reinhard so sharply before. After ending the visiphone call, Bergengrün tore the badges of insignia from his uniform and threw them to the floor, then pressed the muzzle of his blaster against his right temple and pulled the trigger.

On December 16, year 2 of the New Imperial Calendar, or 800 SE, the

Reuentahl Revolt, also known as the Neue Land Conflict, came to an end. Wolfgang Mittermeier's resolution to "end it within the year" was fulfilled.

Mittermeier had already received approval for the postwar arrangements from the kaiser. Wahlen remained on Heinessen with responsibility for the necessary funeral arrangements. Mecklinger was posted temporarily on Urvashi to keep the peace in the Neue Land. Wittenfeld stayed with Mittermeier himself, who departed Heinessen the very next day to report the conclusion of the campaign to the kaiser on Phezzan.

Von Reuentahl's "treason" did not resonate with what remained of the alliance's military, and ended so swiftly that it did not rouse any other anti-imperial forces or further rebellion. A long-term occupation by an excessive force would not win the hearts and minds of the Neue Land; the best way to restore normalcy and order was for the imperial military to depart and let the people forget.

Mittermeier also had personal reasons for putting Heinessen behind him. He went straight from the governorate's offices to the spaceport, where he bid Wahlen farewell and ordered *Beowulf*'s crew to prepare for immediate departure. By all appearances, he wanted only to leave this cursed land which had craved the blood of his friend as quickly as possible. Heinrich Lambertz came with him, cradling the infant.

In a softly lit corner of *Beowulf*'s bridge, away from the bustling preparations for launch, Mittermeier stood with his back turned to his staff officers. Unwilling to address him, they maintained a respectful distance and watched over him from behind. The incomparable young marshal was now the sole remaining Rampart of the Imperial Navy, and its greatest treasure. The shoulders of his splendid black and silver uniform trembled slightly, and his head with its honey-colored hair drooped. Faintly, very faintly, a sob borne on the air-conditioned breeze grazed the ears of his officers.

In the breast of the young and loyal Admiral Karl Eduard Bayerlein, sensitivity turned to emotion and whispered, "Do you see that? I won't forget it for the rest of my life. The Gale Wolf is crying..."

II

When the news of Oskar von Reuentahl's death reached Kaiser Reinhard, the golden-haired conqueror was already halfway from Schattenberg to Phezzan, having foreseen the conflict's end.

He received the report in his private chambers aboard the fleet flagship *Brünhild*. The death of Job Trünicht was mentioned in the same report. This was a highly unexpected development, but, compared to the sadly predictable death of von Reuentahl, the sense of loss it engendered in Reinhard's spirit was negligible. In the end, that spirit had never once crossed paths with Trünicht's, nor had their association ever borne fruit of any kind for him. A very different case from that of Yang Wen-li—and, of course, von Reuentahl. His spiritual path had indeed crossed Reinhard's, and together they had shared a journey through blood and flame to the depths of the galaxy and the limits of human society.

Could Reinhard have given von Reuentahl the satisfaction he craved by meeting him in combat? Even as he contemplated the question, Reinhard failed to notice the self-deception underlying it. Was it not Reinhard himself who had wanted to fight? Had not von Reuentahl's tactical genius been worthy of a response led by the kaiser personally? When Mittermeier had agreed to put down von Reuentahl instead, had not the warlike griffin deep in the kaiser's heart felt a secret disappointment? Having devoured all of his enemies, was not that griffin now hungry for the blood of his allies instead? And was it not the very roar of that griffin that had roused von Reuentahl to rebellion?

All must remain within the realm of speculation. Questions of the heart do not have solutions that can be derived through equations in the manner of elementary mathematics.

Reinhard's bodyguard Emil von Selle entered the room with hot milk on a tray. "How is Your Majesty today?" he asked.

Reinhard, half-sitting up in bed, nodded to reassure the boy. "Fair, I suppose. I am more concerned about your burns—how are they?"

During the incident on Urvashi, Emil von Selle's left hand had been burned in the forest of flame. "A wound of honor for a small hero," Reinhard had said as he applied ointment to it himself. This, in fact, was the true honor, one that no one had received since Reinhard had tended to Kircheis's injuries when they were boys.

"Fair, Your Majesty."

Reinhard nodded once more, then allowed a smile to appear on his feverish cheeks. It was as if the goddess of beauty had pressed the tips of her little fingers into them.

These bouts of fever, which would be known to later ages as "the Kaiser's Malady," continued to afflict him periodically. The cause appeared to be some kind of collagen disease, with fever as the superficial indication of a slow erosion of his youthful vitality. Outwardly, however, his beauty was unharmed. His skin grew even fairer, and when the fever rose within him it was like watching the sun shine through virgin snow on a rose petal. At times, it must be confessed, the impression was somewhat inorganic, but mysteriously he never struck others as drawn or haggard.

The very day Reinhard received word that von Reuentahl had died, he posthumously restored him to the rank of imperial marshal. It may have been an error to install von Reuentahl as governor-general, but not, at least in Reinhard's view, to appoint him a marshal. Nor did Reinhard demote those like Bergengrün—subordinates of von Reuentahl who had stood loyally by him, neither defecting nor dying in battle or by their own hand. However, feeling only disgust for Grillparzer's double betrayal, Reinhard stripped him of the rank of admiral and ordered him to end his life. As for von Knapfstein, who had died unwillingly at the Second Battle of Rantemario, his posthumous rank was left untouched, but none among the living knew what a bitter outcome of fate this difference was.

If there was room for criticism of these measures, it was on the grounds that they were products not of law or rationality but of emotion. However, the overwhelming majority of those involved were emotionally satisfied, so no particular problems arose.

The Reuentahl Revolt was all but over. It only remained to await the return of the punitive fleet.

Reinhard had already offered the fiancée of the deceased Kornelias Lutz a yearly pension of 100,000 reichsmark, but she had declined. She had been a nurse for ten years, she explained with quiet dignity; she could support herself. What was more, as she and Lutz had not actually married, she could not possibly accept such treatment.

An autocratic ruler whose attempt at kindness is rebuffed cannot but feel disgruntled, and that tendency was present even for Reinhard. It was Hilda, still on Phezzan, who eased his irritation. She pointed out to him that the independence of Lutz's fiancée was presumably what had captured his heart in the first place, and suggested that Reinhard instead establish a foundation in Lutz's name and use that yearly 100,000 reichsmark to cover training fees and benefits for army nurses. Lutz's fiancée would later agree to join the foundation's managing committee.

Reinhard was delighted by this demonstration that Hilda's sense for politics was as sharp as ever.

"I hope Fräulein Mariendorf has been well during my absence. Without her, all work at headquarters grinds to a halt."

If not a lie, neither did this represent perfect honesty on Reinhard's part, since some of the truth remained concealed. He was aware by now of his need for her, but still tended to see her as a counselor of rare intellect rather than the only woman for him.

.· ·   ●
·.   .   .

Hilda was already nearing her fourth month of pregnancy. Her expected delivery date was June 10 the following year, and her father Count von Mariendorf had been informed.

"I'm going to be a grandfather?"

His smile was somewhat hesitant and bashful, but two days later he made an announcement to his daughter.

"Hilda, early next year I intend to resign my position as minister of domestic affairs."

"But father, why?"

In the past, it had always been Hilda who surprised her father. But, since that night at the end of August, his accurate discernment of her limits and efforts to provide the support she needed had often surprised her instead.

"You are serving the empire wonderfully as minister," she continued, "You have not incurred the kaiser's displeasure. Why would you say such a thing?"

Even a daughter as wise as Hilda had blind spots when matters concerned her personally.

"It is a simple matter, Hilda," said her father, "Regardless of your response to the kaiser's proposal of marriage, in a few short months you will be the mother of his heir. As your father, I will be grandfather to that heir. No good has ever come of someone in that position holding a ministerial post as well."

Hilda recognized that her father was right, but worried over who was qualified to be his successor. Here, once again, her father surprised her.

"If it were up to me," he said, "I would recommend Marshal Mittermeier."

"Marshal Mittermeier? But he's a military man through and through. He isn't a politician."

"If the job was within my power, it's certainly within his. Joking aside, Hilda, I think that, rather than becoming minister of military affairs, he would be better suited to lead the cabinet as minister of domestic affairs. What is your opinion?"

Perhaps, Hilda thought, her father was right in his quiet asseveration. The minister of domestic affairs did not need to be skilled in conspiracy or intrigue; conversely, few were as insightful, trustworthy, or just as Marshal Mittermeier. But would the kaiser accept such a proposal? That, she felt, remained to be seen.

III

Osmayer, Reinhard's secretary of the interior, often had difficulty deciding if his luck was good or bad.

Earlier in his career, when he had been sent from sector to sector on the frontier, handling planetary development and establishing regional police forces, he had felt that his talents were not properly valued. When the great Kaiser Reinhard had chosen him for his current position, his rejoicing had been cut short by the threat of Heidrich Lang, and anxiety over when he would be pushed out for good had frayed his nerves to their limit. Now Lang had been hoist with his own petard of intrigue, and his imprisonment had finally permitted Osmayer the mental ease he had long craved.

Lang was interrogated daily at military police headquarters, frequently by Senior Admiral Kessler himself in his role as police commissioner. As yet, however, no satisfactory testimony had been obtained. Wearing a frankly insolent expression on his baby face, Lang even had the gall to threaten retribution when he eventually recovered his position.

"Think back on how you treated criminal suspects in the past," Kessler said. "This will surely help you understand why you should not be so stubborn. I am more than happy to try out any of the investigative methods you have claimed for yourself in the past."

Even Lang could not hide his unease at this threat, but he still refused to talk. He knew that confession would be the end, with only execution waiting in store, and this made the formless doors that barred his mouth sturdier than ever.

In the last weeks of December, news of Marshal von Reuentahl's death reached the prison. After a moment's wide-eyed shock, Lang began to laugh madly and did not stop for an hour, angering and unsettling his captors.

After this, Lang began to cooperate, confessions coming forth in a torrent—although they were really less confessions than bizarre compounds of self-justification and blame shifting, and the entire flow fed the lake of his victim complex. According to Lang's testimony, he was a loyal vassal of the kaiser, without even a milligram of selfish motives. He had simply been misunderstood as a result of being caught up in the wicked intrigues of Adrian Rubinsky, former landesherr of Phezzan. (Had Rubinsky been listening, he would likely have bragged that this much, at least, was correct.)

Therefore, Lang insisted, it was only right for the dastardly Rubinsky to be punished before him. He also brought the minister of military affairs into the discussion. How, he asked, could he have taken any action without

Marshal von Oberstein's consent? He urged a probe into the marshal's role in affairs, as if directing the investigation himself.

Putting aside, at least on the surface, Lang's claims regarding the minister, Kessler ordered a military police raid on Rubinsky's hideout. But Rubinsky, the Black Fox of Phezzan, had already fled his bolt-hole. He had presumably sensed the danger when Lang was arrested and made good his escape. Lang, through his own silence, had bought Rubinsky the time he needed to slip away.

At around this time, Lang's wife visited military police headquarters to plead for clemency on her husband's behalf. She met with Kessler, explaining through tears that her husband was a kind and decent man to his family.

"Mrs. Lang, your husband was not accused because he is a good husband or a loving father," Kessler said. "It is not for private wrongdoing that he has been imprisoned. Let us be clear on that."

He did, however, permit Mrs. Lang to visit her husband. As he watched her leave in tears once the visit was over, Kessler could not help but contemplate how vast the gulf could be between a person's public and private faces. As a family man, after all, Lang was undoubtedly far superior to Reinhard or von Reuentahl.

At that time, the Galactic Imperial Navy had two marshals and six senior admirals. Since Reinhard's coronation, Lennenkamp, Fahrenheit, Steinmetz, Lutz, and von Reuentahl had left the mortal plane one by one, leaving a powerful mood of desolation among the others who had fought alongside Reinhard to found the new dynasty.

One of the two surviving marshals, minister of military affairs Paul von Oberstein, had been shut out of the Reuentahl Revolt entirely, offered no chance to exercise his gifts. It appears that he had prepared several proposals for putting down the rebellion, but, ultimately, disapproving historians of later ages would coldly describe him as having "buried his counterpart without even needing to bloody his hands." Of course, von Oberstein had little interest in what others thought of him—certainly in life, and most probably in death as well.

"Do you understand why Marshal Mittermeier chose to lead the expedition against his friend?" von Oberstein asked his staff officer, Commodore Anton Ferner.

It was late in the year, one day before Mittermeier's return. Under von Oberstein's strict, coolheaded, and impartial leadership, the ministry's operations had not paused for a moment, a fact that historians would later support with testimony from Ferner.

"I fear it entirely surpasses my understanding," said Ferner. "May I inquire as to Your Excellency's thoughts?"

"If the kaiser had been the one to subjugate von Reuentahl, Mittermeier could not have avoided some resentment. Cracks would have appeared between lord and vassal, and if they had grown too large, their relationship might have been damaged beyond repair."

"I see," Ferner said, glancing sideways at the minister's sharp features.

"By leading the expedition himself, Mittermeier made himself the murderer, with no reason to bear a grudge against the kaiser. That was his reasoning, and the kind of man he is."

"Is there any evidence that he reasoned this way, Your Excellency?"

Von Oberstein's half-white hair swayed slightly. "It is my private interpretation of events," he said. "Its truth or falsity is beyond me... But listen to me," he added, with a wry smile that astonished Ferner, "How talkative I have become."

After that, not a single word about the Reuentahl Revolt escaped the minister's thin lips again.

IV

Just before the new year, on December 30, commander in chief of the Imperial Space Armada Marshal Wolfgang Mittermeier arrived at the imperial capital of Phezzan. It was too heavy, too bitter a return to deserve the term "triumphant," nor was the look in the young marshal's gray eyes that of a feted hero.

"Marshal Mittermeier, we are fortunate to have you, at least, home safely," said Neidhart Müller. "Allow me to express my joy at your return."

Mittermeier shook the hand Müller offered—healed at last—without a word. Wittenfeld followed a few steps behind him, the same wintry despair weighing on his shoulders.

The two of them presented themselves at Imperial Headquarters and officially reported the conclusion of the disturbance to Kaiser Reinhard. They then excused themselves, but Reinhard called Mittermeier back. The young kaiser stood apart from his desk, golden hair shining in the pale sunlight that came through the window. When Mittermeier offered a reverent salute, he offered a fleeting smile and broached an unexpected topic.

"Mittermeier, do you remember the time you and von Reuentahl came to visit Kircheis and I, when we lived on Limbergstraße?"

The memory almost stopped Mittermeier's breath. "Yes, Your Majesty," he said. "I remember it well."

Reinhard brushed his hair back from his forehead. "Of the four of us who gathered on that day, only you and I remain alive.

After a pause, Mittermeier said, "Your Majesty…"

"Do not die, Mittermeier," Reinhard said. "Without you, there would be no one to teach the entire Imperial Navy what tactics are. I would also lose a valued brother-in-arms. This is an order: do not die."

It was a self-centered demand, perhaps. But, at that moment, Mittermeier shared the emotions that gripped the greatest conqueror in history—no, of the youthful brother-in-arms by whose side he had led armies that toppled the Goldenbaum Dynasty and brought the Free Planets to heel.

Five years ago, on May 10, IC 486, it had been a fine day. The color of the wind was just beginning to change from late spring to early summer. Mittermeier and von Reuentahl had visited Reinhard's rented apartment to discuss how they might eliminate the tendrils of court intrigue that threatened the Gräfin von Grünewald, his sister Annerose. The four youths sitting around the table that day had gone on to conquer the galaxy, and half of them had departed for Valhalla. The survivors bore a responsibility to live on. To preserve the memory of the dead forever. To make sure that generations to come knew who they had been…

As he left the kaiser's presence, Mittermeier felt heat sting his eyelids.

And, although the kaiser stood motionless at the window, looking out, he was sure that the same was true of Reinhard.

•

After leaving Imperial Headquarters, but before returning home, Mittermeier visited the von Mariendorf residence. Heinrich accompanied him, still carrying the infant that von Reuentahl had left behind. Mittermeier asked to see Hilda. After explaining the situation to her, spoke of the purpose of his visit.

"As you know, my wife and I have no children of our own. Accordingly, I would like to raise this child as ours. I would be grateful, fräulein, if you would lend me your assistance in obtaining His Majesty's permission."

"The child of Marshal von Reuentahl…"

"Yes. In legal terms, the child of a monstrous traitor, whose sins may be passed down the family line—but I will accept responsibility for that."

"I do not think you need worry on that score, marshal," Hilda said. "Since the child was not born in legal wedlock, the sins of his father should not be held against him. And this is the child of Marshal von Reuentahl, raised by Marshal Mittermeier—what a marvelous general he may grow up to be!"

Hilda looked down at the infant and smiled.

"You will hear no objections from me," she said. "It will be my pleasure to speak to His Majesty on your behalf. But there is one thing that worries me."

"And what is that?"

Seeing Mittermeier's face stiffen, muscles tensing like slow-motion footage, Hilda could not suppress an inward smile.

"What Mrs. Mittermeier will think, marshal. Will she agree with you on all this?"

The pride of the Imperial Navy blushed a deep crimson.

"Thoughtlessly," he said, "I had not discussed it with her. Do you think she will grant her consent?"

"Knowing her, I am sure she will do so with pleasure."

"I believe so too—so strongly that I forgot to ask her." Of course, Mittermeier did not intend to brag.

He further explained to Hilda that the boy serving as his orderly had recently lost both parents, and that he planned to discuss taking him into the Mittermeier household as well, if possible.

As he was about to leave, Hilda called out to him.

"Marshal Mittermeier."

"Yes, fräulein?"

"You are the Imperial Navy's greatest treasure. His Majesty has lost many companions, but I hope you will continue to stand by him as always."

Mittermeier returned a salute that combined resolve and warmth in perfect harmony.

"I am a man of meager talents, far below the lofty heights scaled by Siegfried Kircheis or Oskar von Reuentahl. It pains me to receive praise I do not deserve simply because I happen to have survived—but I promise to do what you ask. I will serve the kaiser not just for myself but for them too. Whatever designs His Majesty may conceive, my loyalty to him will remain unwavering."

He bowed his honey-haired head. Then the slightly built martial, resplendent in his black and silver uniform, turned and left the presence of the woman who would soon become empress of the Galactic Empire.

Evangeline Mittermeier's delight to see her husband home safe was quickly followed by surprise. No sooner had her husband kissed her than he somewhat awkwardly said, "Eva, I brought something for you—or rather, someone."

He had not felt so nervous speaking to her since the day he proposed. This time, instead of a bouquet of yellow roses, what he held out to her was an infant, still less than eight months old. His wife accepted it from his unskilled hands and soothed it tenderly. She turned her shining violet eyes to him.

"And what cabbage patch is this from, Wolf?"

"Well, I…that is…"

"I know. You found it in the von Reuentahl gardens, didn't you?"

Mittermeier was speechless. His wife explained that she had received a visiphone call before he arrived from the Countess von Mariendorf, who had given her all the details.

"I think you did the right thing bringing the child here. I would be delighted to be its mother. But please let me decide one thing: his name. Will you grant me that, darling?"

"Yes. Of course. And what name will you give him?"

"Felix. His name is Felix. I hope you like it."

"Felix…"

In an old, old language, Mittermeier knew, the word meant "lucky." His wife must have known that too, and carried the name in her breast for years. For a child yet unborn. For a child that might be born one day. And finally for a child that might never be born at all…

"Felix. A fine name. So be it. Form this day on, he is Felix Mittermeier."

And one day, when he reached adulthood and developed his own powers of judgment and values, he might go by his biological father's name if he wished. For Mittermeier would make sure he knew who that biological father was—a man of pride, a man who would bend the knee to only one other in all the galaxy…

Suddenly, Mittermeier remembered his other news, and hastily opened the living room door. His student orderly stood in the entrance hall, still holding the baby's bag of supplies. He sneezed once, then, despite his evident cold, smiled at Mittermeier.

ᴠ

At almost exactly the moment Wolfgang Mittermeier became a father, another man was informed of his own fatherhood. That man's name was Reinhard von Lohengramm, and he was the twenty-four-year-old ruler of the entire Galactic Empire.

The Countess von Mariendorf's visit to the kaiser's private chambers in Imperial Headquarters that day was in a private capacity. Reinhard invited her to sit at the round table in his combined living room and study, and had his bodyguard Emil von Selle bring them coffee with cream. As they gazed out the window at the winter sky, its blue seemingly blocked by cryolite, he said, "It's a chilly day, isn't it, fräulein? I hope you haven't caught a cold."

Despite Reinhard's outward magnificence, this was as close as he could get to solicitude. Knowing this, Hilda smiled. Casually, but decisively, she allowed the fateful words to slip through her firm lips:

"I hope so too, Your Majesty. A cold might be bad for the baby I carry."

Reinhard's eyes flew wide open, reflecting the winter sky. He gazed at Hilda's form, and his porcelain cheeks flushed red. Blood raced through his body, bearing a torrent of thought and emotion, and it took several dozen seconds before these exploded into his mind.

When he had finally gotten his breathing and heartbeat under control, he parted his pink lips and said, voice melodious with rich emotion, "I beg you once more: Fräulein von Mariendorf, will you marry me?"

That he did not ask a foolish question like "Whose is it?" is, perhaps, evidence that there was hope for his psychological makeup yet. He continued.

"I have finally come to understand how much you mean to me. These past months have opened my eyes. Your counsel has never led me astray. If I am honest, you are a far better woman than I deserve…"

Reinhard's features were the pinnacle of aesthetic refinement, but this proposal was light-years away from such grace. Moreover, he spoke only of his own feelings, making no allowances for hers. But Hilda knew that this did not reflect poorly on his youthful sincerity. It was simply the kind of person he was: a martial genius, a political prodigy, but no master of love or romance. His dazzling inventiveness and expressive power lit up the battlefield, but did not make the bedroom sweet. This was the man who had chosen her, as she had hoped he would. She knew his flaws well—but, as her wise father perceived, she thought those flaws invaluable too.

"Yes, Your Majesty. I will. If you will have me…"

Hilda had intended to first go directly to Odin and meet with Reinhard's older sister, the archduchess Annerose von Grünewald, but the discovery of her pregnancy made interstellar travel an impossibility. She had not the slightest intention of allowing harm to come to the child in her womb. In the end, she had sent an FTL transmission to Odin's Freuden Mountains in mid-November, establishing a direct circuit to Annerose's estate.

"Fräulein von Mariendorf—no, Hilda—thank you for falling in love with my brother."

Thus said Annerose when she heard the news. Her voice was warm, and seemed almost to tremble with feeling. It made Hilda think of a gently falling shower of spring sunlight.

"My brother is lucky to have someone like you by his side. Please take good care of him."

Take good care of him—Hilda was the second person to whom Annerose had spoken those words. The first, of course, had been Siegfried Kircheis.

"Reinhard never had a father of his own," Annerose continued. Hilda understood, of course, that she was speaking metaphorically. By "father," Annerose meant a paternal element during his formative years. A father that a boy, and later a young man, could resist, rebel against, and finally overcome—a presence that would tear him from the maternal element and bring to him psychological independence. Reinhard's true father had not been up to this task.

For Reinhard, the concrete manifestation of the maternal element was, of course, his sister Annerose. And what had torn him from her in his youth was not his true father, as things should have been, but Emperor Friedrich IV and the tyrannical might of the Goldenbaum Dynasty—the worst aspects of the paternal principle, amplified to a scale encompassing all humanity.

The uniqueness of Reinhard's personality had been conceived here. Though he himself did not realize it, toppling the Goldenbaum Dynasty was, for him, the equivalent of overcoming his father in his formative years. With that father figure eliminated, to battle and defeat powerful foes became the meaning of life itself for him. Reinhard knew war, but not love, and so Annerose feared for him, placing distance between them that so he would have to do more than chase her shadow. But she had never been able to express this clearly, and, with matters partly complicated by her own peculiar connection to Siegfried Kircheis, Reinhard may have been hurt by her parting words. The gratitude that Annerose felt toward Hilda was both factual and truthful.

It is interesting to note that virtually all the historians who have criticized Annerose for not loving Reinhard enough were female. For this reason, male historians voiced sometimes severe criticism of their female colleagues:

> In the end, we cannot avoid the conclusion that they [female historians] view Archduchess von Grünewald's actions solely through the lens of motherhood and its abandonment. Would they be satisfied if the archduchess had continued to cling to her brother's side into his twenties, indulge and spoil him, meddle in politics, and undermine his psychological independence? Of course, the same authors would doubtless claim that to be robbed of one's virginity by a tyrant at the age of fifteen, and then imprisoned for the next ten years, is not enough to make Annerose herself a sacrificial victim.

Of course, neither can it be said that the judgments of male historians were perfect. In the end, only the balance of probabilities can be compared—but whoever has the better of the argument, Annerose's influence on Reinhard was undeniable. Had she objected to his marriage to Hilda, Reinhard might have suffered some distress, but ultimately he would have put his sister's will first. But Annerose did not do this; instead, she offered Hilda nothing but encouragement, granting her blessing and rejoicing that she could entrust her brother's future to the wise young countess. And nobody could deny the fact that this decision helped move history in a constructive direction.

VI

Life and death, light and dark—the galaxy contained all these things and more. But in one corner of the stars lurked a group of people who had nurtured the same hatred, the same obsession for eight hundred years. With religious unity as one weapon and humid conspiracy as another, they had interfered in countless ways with the workings of history—all to restore the glory of Mother Earth. In recent years, as they approached what seemed to be a long-awaited consummation, the leader of a new generation was emerging from among them.

They were the Church of Terra, and he was Archbishop de Villiers.

At this time, the glow of ambition on his still-youthful face was covered by a shadow of startling severity.

When he had added first Yang Wen-li and then Oskar von Reuentahl to the rolls of the dead, it appeared that all his intrigues had been successful. The future of the universe, it seemed, would be his to command from atop his dark throne. However, immediately after the death of von Reuentahl, it was discovered that they had lost a crucial pawn in the form of Job Trünicht. Now he sensed a faint stirring, a certain distrust in the eyes the church leaders turned on him. One of his fellow archbishops, long unhappy with how rapidly de Villiers had risen in the church hierarchy and how far his power had expanded, expressed the group's unease in a frankly stated challenge.

"We have lost more than just Trünicht. The kaiser plans to marry. What is more, rumor has it that his fiancée, Count von Mariendorf's daughter, is already with child…"

Venomous foam sprayed from the corners of the speaker's mouth with every word. De Villiers shifted his gaze slightly, but bore up under the unpleasant pressure. The speaker continued, voice growing even louder. He had favored a plan to assassinate Kaiser Reinhard directly, and could not be dispassionate in pursuing de Villiers's responsibility for choosing a different course.

"If an heir is born to the kaiser, will that not become the core around which the Lohengramm system continues? In bringing about the death of von Reuentahl—as well as Yang Wen-li—we will have accomplished nothing but eliminating any of the golden brat's potential challengers and clearing his path."

The man fell silent, out of breath.

A moment later, the miasmic quiet was broken by a low laugh.

"What need is there for this unseemly urgency?" asked de Villiers. "The kaiser's heir is not born yet. And even once it is, then there is no guarantee it will strengthen his position."

De Villiers laughed again. There was a certain exaggeration in the confidence he sought to convey by this, but it was not entirely hollow. The galaxy was vast; a million, a billion more conspiracies could be woven within it with room to spare.

・ ・   ●
 ・
          ・   ・

Yang Wen-li's successor Julian Mintz had received high praise for not taking Iserlohn to war that year. If war broke out in the coming year, would he be praised even more?

Julian did not know. But to join the military had been his original ambition, and he believed that some fights must be fought. Ironically, though, after the death of Yang, his ambitions had shifted slightly, and the desire to tread a non-martial path was slowly accumulating in the reservoir of his heart.

When receiving the news of von Reuentahl's death the previous day, Julian had seemed to hear Yang's mild voice in his mind.

"Millions went to their death under my command. Not because they wanted to. Every one of them would have preferred to live out a peaceful, fulfilling life. And I'm no different. If it didn't mean the death of those we loved, war might not be so bad, but..."

Julian let out a long, deep sigh. He had never been on the same side as von Reuentahl. The heterochromatic admiral had always been an enemy to Yang and Julian. But Julian could not help taking his death as the implosion of a giant star. Was their age coming to an end with such startling rapidity? With whose death, or perhaps birth, would it finally end? Overcome by a regular but suffocating sensation, as if time itself whirled within his body, Julian rose from the park bench and began to walk through the trees at a somewhat brisk pace. He did not know at this time that Job Trünicht had died.

Leaving the park, Julian was met by bustling activity. A hubbub, but one born of peace. The whole of Iserlohn Base had come together to prepare for the New Year's party to bid farewell to SE 800 and ring in SE 801. Some had protested that it was inappropriate to celebrate the end of the year in which Marshal Yang had died, but Frederica had rejected those arguments. "He never objected to a festival mood among his friends. Rather than holding back, for his sake, please make it a lively event."

Julian saw Dusty Attenborough and Olivier Poplin approaching, trading their usual insults. When they saw the youthful commander of the revolutionary forces, they called out to him cheerfully.

"Hey, Julian, I hope we're not going to sit out all the fun next year too."

"We're counting on you, commander."

"Talk to the kaiser, not me," said Julian. "That would be a more certain thing."

In Julian's mind, the calendar pages turned backward, and a scene from four years ago reappeared before him—the first New Year's party on Iserlohn Base. Some of those who were by his side then were still there today: Frederica, the Caselnes family, von Schönkopf, Poplin, Attenborough. Also with him today were Merkatz, von Schneider, Soon Soul, Boris Konev, Machungo, and of course Katerose "Karin" von Kreutzer.

Yang Wen-li had been there. Murai had been there, Patrichev had been there, Fischer had been there, Ivan Konev had been there. Apart from Murai, who had departed for the planet Heinessen, Julian would never meet any of the departed again—at least not while he lived. But he had inherited their thinking, and it fell to him to ensure its flowering. The tiny shoots of democratic republicanism: self-determination, self-governance, self-control, and self-respect. Until these took root across the galaxy, he would have to prepare for the coming spring.

"Julian, the party's about to start. Shall we go together? Frederica and the Caselnes are waiting."

The voice was Karin's. She had taken a momentous step: she had called him by his first name.

Julian nodded. "Let's go, Karin," he said, somewhat self-consciously. As the two of them walked off side by side, Karin's father watched from afar, with *Well, here we go* written on his face. Drifting across the expression was a thin mist of alcohol from the glasses he had raised in von Reuentahl's memory. Leaning against his broad shoulder was a young woman whose name he did not know.

⁘

In due course, SE 801 would dawn—year 3 of the New Imperial Calendar, the third year of the Lohengramm Dynasty. In its first month, Kaiser Reinhard was to formally take the Countess Hildegard von Mariendorf as his empress. Some welcomed the prospect. Others did not. Could the new galactic order, established just one year previously, endure forever? Or would it prove a momentary bubble on the river of history, soon to vanish forever? The year in which this would be decided was about to begin…

ABOUT THE AUTHOR

Yoshiki Tanaka was born in 1952 in Kumamoto Prefecture and completed a doctorate in literature at Gakushuin University. Tanaka won the Gen'eijo (a mystery magazine) New Writer Award with his debut story "Midori no Sogen ni..." (On the green field...) in 1978, then started his career as a science fiction and fantasy writer. Legend of the Galactic Heroes, which translates the European wars of the nineteenth century to an interstellar setting, won the Seiun Award for best science fiction novel in 1987. Tanaka's other works include the fantasy series The Heroic Legend of Arslan and many other science fiction, fantasy, historical, and mystery novels and stories.

HAIKASORU
THE FUTURE IS JAPANESE

TRAVEL SPACE AND TIME WITH HAIKASORU!

USURPER OF THE SUN—HOUSUKE NOJIRI

Aki Shiraishi is a high school student working in the astronomy club and one of the few witnesses to an amazing event—someone is building a tower on the planet Mercury. Soon, the Builders have constructed a ring around the sun, threatening the ecology of Earth with an immense shadow. Aki is inspired to pursue a career in science, and the truth. She must determine the purpose of the ring and the plans of its creators, as the survival of both species—humanity and the alien Builders—hangs in the balance.

THE OUROBOROS WAVE—JYOUJI HAYASHI

Ninety years from now, a satellite detects a nearby black hole scientists dub Kali for the Hindu goddess of destruction. Humanity embarks on a generations-long project to tap the energy of the black hole and establish colonies on planets across the solar system. Earth and Mars and the moons Europa (Jupiter) and Titania (Uranus) develop radically different societies, with only Kali, that swirling vortex of destruction and creation, and the hated but crucial Artificial Accretion Disk Development association (AADD) in common.

TEN BILLION DAYS AND ONE HUNDRED BILLION NIGHTS—RYU MITSUSE

Ten billion days—that is how long it will take the philosopher Plato to determine the true systems of the world. One hundred billion nights—that is how far into the future Jesus of Nazareth, Siddhartha, and the demigod Asura will travel to witness the end of all worlds. Named the greatest Japanese science fiction novel of all time, *Ten Billion Days and One Hundred Billion Nights* is an epic eons in the making. Originally published in 1967, the novel was revised by the author in later years and republished in 1973.

WWW.HAIKASORU.COM